THE BETA MUM
ADVENTURES IN ALPHA LAND

THE BETA MUM

Adventures in Alpha Land

ISABELLA
DAVIDSON

SilverWood

Published in 2017 by SilverWood Books

SilverWood Books Ltd
14 Small Street, Bristol, BS1 1DE, United Kingdom
www.silverwoodbooks.co.uk

ISBN 978-1-78132-652-7 (paperback)
ISBN 978-1-78132-653-4 (ebook)

British Library Cataloguing in Publication Data
A CIP catalogue record for this book is available from the British Library

Page design and typesetting by SilverWood Books
Printed by Imprint Digital on responsibly sourced paper

To my father

The Beta Mum
Welcome to Alpha-Land

Alpha-Land is inhabited by creatures called Alpha Mums and Alpha Dads (with a few Betas around), who are closely related to the macaque monkey.

Like macaque monkeys, Alphas follow a social-dominance hierarchy, where they dominate the social structure and there is little space for the poor or the weak. Alphas use similar agonist methods of aggressiveness, grooming and threatening behaviours to ensure their dominance, just like the despotic macaque monkeys.

Here, it is a Darwinian survival of the fittest, where natural selection weeds out the weakest based on the Alpha's ability to compete, survive and reproduce. In Alpha-Land, there is aggressive, competitive, capitalistic individualism.

The Alpha Women are beautiful, strong, resilient creatures that have attracted their Alpha counterparts with intelligence, beauty and charm. The Alpha Men are rich, intelligent, successful and powerful. There is a conscious, self-selecting mating process based on superior physical and mental qualities.

Their progeny, the Alpha Children, are bright, beautiful and photo shoot-ready. Alpha Mums make them believe they are "special" and the "best" at running/singing/reading/writing, until they believe it themselves.

It is war of who has the cleverest children, the biggest house, who is the slimmest, most successful and has the most picture-perfect life. I live in the shadows of the Alphas and I wonder how long I can last. Do you think you could handle it?

Chapter One

Learning Your ABCs

'London, Ontario?' I looked at him, perplexed, not yet fully aware that this was a moment that was irrevocably going to change my life and how I saw the world.

'No. London, England,' he replied.

'London, England. As in, London-England-where-it-rains-every-single-day-London-England?'

'Not quite. But yes, London, England.'

'You're telling me that *you* want to move to London, England, and leave everything we've built here in Oakville?'

We were sitting in our living room on the burgundy couch we had bought together eleven years ago after graduating from university, and had just finished a *Breaking Bad* box-set marathon. I was in my favourite dark-blue fleece sweatpants and sweater, so soft and warm that I could happily stay in them all day and all night. (If it were my choice, I would have a set of them in every colour.) These days, with a toddler, Saturday night with our TV was the highlight of our week and we had grown accustomed to a comfortable weekly routine that involved takeout, TV and a little teasing. And now he had to ruin it all.

'I said I've been offered a job in London and I think we should seriously consider it. They chose me out of two hundred candidates to run their RailLink Project. It's huge. And it would only be for three years.' He frowned at me as if I was the one being unreasonable.

We had only moved to Oakville a few years ago when Michael had been offered a job at Siemens and I knew he was hoping for a promotion this year. I just hadn't expected it to be halfway across the world.

'What about our house and mortgage?' I looked around our house, which we had stretched ourselves to buy, taking on a mortgage we could barely keep up with. We had fallen in love with it and its quiet, tree-lined street. There was the brown-orange stain in the carpet from the time Kaya dropped her strawberry-jam yogurt on the floor…the walnut coffee table we had spent at least six weekends looking for in the antique shops on Lakeshore Road…the TV we had argued over: he'd wanted the bigger size; I'd wanted the smaller one. Obviously. I looked at the spot where Kaya had taken her first steps, until she crashed into the coffee table and hit her head, causing a bump that swelled up to the size of a small clementine. It had made us cry with pride – not the bump-the-size-of-a-clementine part, but witnessing her first steps, like they were an astronaut's first steps on the moon.

'We'd put the house up for rent, and I would get a significant increase in my salary that I could never get here in Canada. We could pay the mortgage off even faster,' he said.

'We would still have to pay for rent and London just happens to be one of the most expensive places in the world to live in. It costs twenty dollars just to sneeze over there, you know,' I proclaimed authoritatively.

'Ha ha. I know and I told them that, but they came up with an amazing expat package for us, which these days is unheard of.' He seemed to have an answer to everything. He was winning this battle, but I still had hope of winning the war. This wasn't over.

'You've already had these conversations without discussing any of this with me first?' It was my turn to frown, and to use the wounded-bird routine.

'Sophie-Bee, I didn't want to even mention it to you until I was sure about it and thought it was worth talking about,' he implored. Michael only called me Sophie-Bee when he was very serious or wanted something from me.

'You've got a point.' My frown softened. Michael knew me too well; he had come prepared and ready to fight on all fronts.

'They'll provide housing and a relocation agent. Pay for nursery fees and school fees. England has some of the best schools in the world. Look at it as an opportunity for us as a family. They even threw in a nursery consultant.'

'What's a nursery consultant?' I looked at him, bewildered. 'We don't need to decorate a nursery. Kaya's too old for one and as far as I'm aware, I'm not expecting a present from the stork any time soon.'

'A nursery consultant helps you find the right nursery for your child,' he said.

'Can't we just Google the nurseries?'

'I don't think it works like that over there…I was talking to Robert Curtis, who's going to be my new boss, and he said that there are waiting lists but the nursery consultant will help us get into one, since we're coming quite late in the game.'

'Late in the game? Kaya is three. And it's just nursery. Don't they just learn to finger paint and not to stick their fingers up their nose?'

'It sounds a bit more complicated than that…' He drifted off.

'You're right, it all sounds very complicated. Even more reason to stay,' I said, steadfast.

'Sophie-Bee…'

'This is the second time we're moving for *your* job. What about my job? I've only gone back to work a few months ago at PerformArts. It's going to look terrible on my CV if I quit right now.' I already had a hole in my CV from the move to Oakville and I had only recently found a job that had fit; it was part-time, flexible, and fit around Kaya's childcare. This would be the final nail in my CV-coffin.

'I know that, Sophie. Which is why I resisted. But the guys here in Canada really pulled a lot of strings to get me this job, and I don't think I have much choice.' He sighed; leaned back into the sofa, looking away into the distance before turning to me. 'It could really change my career. In a good way. Please think about it. And with my new salary, you wouldn't even need to work.' He started stroking my hand, as if this was going to be enough to sway me.

'But I enjoy what I do and I want to work. And that's not the point. I'm not going to know anyone. You would be uprooting not only me, but Kaya too. All of our family and support networks are here. Emma is here and you know how hard I find it to make new friends,' I said, blabbering on nervously, feeling my pulse race just thinking about having to meet new people. Emma was my best friend, whom I shared everything with. I was generally on the shy side and making new friends had never been easy for me.

'I get it. But I'll be there. And I'm sure you'll meet people through Kaya,' he said.

'Easier said than done,' I said. A memory of me sitting alone during lunchtime on my first day of high school flashed through my mind and I squirmed. I had felt so alone and shy that day. 'We're just starting to feel really comfortable here. It's our home.'

'I know it won't be easy at first but I'm sure you'll love it.' He paused. 'We'll love it.'

'I don't know…' I said, as I pushed back the strand of hair that had fallen over my face. 'Kaya is happy here…*we're* happy here. I don't want to risk it.'

'Sophie. Please?' He looked at me with pleading eyes. 'It would mean so much to me. I don't think I'll get another opportunity like this in a really long time…if ever.'

'OK, OK! Let me think about it. And only for three years. You know I don't like change,' I said, looking into his eyes. I then curled up against his chest, pulling the thick, red and green tartan blanket over us, letting the shock of the announcement sink in. Moving to Oakville and meeting people here had been hard enough. Now I couldn't imagine any other life but this one.

Wasn't I too old to start over? I wanted to ask Michael. But when I turned around to ask him, I looked at his lit-up face and his twinkling eyes, like he was the first boy to be picked on the varsity baseball team, and saw how much it meant to him. He had worked so hard to prove himself at Siemens and this was the acknowledgement he was looking for. It was only for a few years, I thought to myself. I was now a grown woman after all. And then, although I wasn't pleased about it, I slowly came to the realisation that there was a very high probability that I was on my way to London.

'Nursery choice in London is of the utmost importance and must not be underestimated. The most selective nurseries have waiting lists and are very competitive to get into because they are feeders to the best schools in London. Generally, with private nurseries, one has to register the day the child is born and the application should be followed up with telephone calls, visits and a recommendation, but not to worry – this is what I am here for.' Edward Calthorpe-Huntington beamed at us with a crisp, almost constipated smile.

A few weeks later in early May, we were sitting across from Edward Calthorpe-Huntington, the London nursery consultant that Robert Curtis had recommended. He was a fifty-something, well-spoken, slightly camp gentleman wearing a green, red and yellow tweed suit that looked like it was at least as old as me. He had a long, sharp nose, a thin moustache over a droopy smile and a thinning scalp. I couldn't stop thinking that he reminded me of a combination of John Cleese and Mr Bean's droopy face.

His office was in Battersea, just south of the River Thames, with far-reaching views over the north side of the city. There was a low fog hovering over the surface of the river and a hazy sun hiding behind the clouds. The building was glass-fronted and felt very impersonal, far from what a nursery should be like, but I trusted that Michael and his boss knew what they were doing.

We had left Kaya in Canada with my parents and we were in London for a reconnaissance mission to: a) choose a flat, b) look at nurseries, c) meet Michael's new boss, and d) for me to give the final approval stamp on our move to London.

Ahead of the trip, Edward Calthorpe-Huntington had sent

us an entire questionnaire to fill out about Kaya: her personality type, her likes, dislikes, her favourite foods, toys, books and nursery rhymes, her medical history and her imaginary friends. There was enough information to write an entire *My Life at Three* biography.

'So, tell me what your dream nursery would look like?' he asked, looking at me with beady little eyes.

'Um...somewhere Kaya will be happy?' I replied after a pause, having not put much thought into my "dream" nursery ever before. 'That's the most important. I want her to be happy. Apart from that, close to where we live. Oh, and with lots of green, outdoor space preferably.'

He stiffened. 'This is London,' he explained curtly. 'There's not much outdoor space in most nurseries, let alone green spaces. And what part of London were you thinking of relocating to?' He was jotting down notes furiously while slowly speaking, as if he were a doctor taking down my medical history. It was all very serious.

'We were thinking of somewhere in Kensington or Notting Hill.' I looked at Michael, who looked at me in agreement. 'They're not too far from Michael's work and close to Hyde Park.' We knew that many expats lived in those neighbourhoods, and that there were lots of parks close by and plenty of accessible garden squares around. It seemed like the obvious choice for us.

That morning we had visited six flats with a relocation agent and had found a three-bedroom, lower-ground-floor flat leading onto a thirty-square-foot garden that we had both liked. We were planning on making an offer on it the next day.

'There are about ten nurseries in the vicinity of Notting Hill and Kensington that are excellent, but I have the perfect nursery in mind. It is a very happy place. The only problem is that it is very, very difficult to get in. Like I said, most places are given away at birth. But like very exclusive restaurants, there are always a few places kept for walk-ins. I'm very close to Mrs Jones, the headmistress, and I am sure I can secure you a place.' He looked at me proudly, as though he was negotiating an international diplomacy deal rather than entry into a nursery. 'It's called Cherry Blossoms and it is one of the best nurseries in London – if not *the* best – and feeds into the top London schools. It better prepares the children for school than any other nursery, and it is very international. A global nursery. For future global citizens.' Edward Calthorpe-Huntington smugly went on. 'Lots of Americans.'

'But we're Canadian,' I said, looking at him, wondering whether he'd actually listened to anything I'd said.

'Oh yes, of course. North Americans, I meant.' He cleared his throat and corrected himself, though clearly he felt no distinction between the two. 'They have infused a wonderful community spirit at the nursery,' he continued. 'They organise a few fundraisers for various local charities throughout the year. It's a very socially conscious place. And there is a lovely social aspect to it. Parents who meet at this nursery make friends for life.'

'That sounds good.' Michael glanced at me, his eyes looking encouraging. 'Social is good, right, Sophie? It'll help you meet new people. This nursery sounds like a great option.'

'The children are very happy there, and it also has direct access into one of the biggest and most beautiful private gardens in London. I will make an appointment for you to visit it tomorrow. You will absolutely adore it,' Edward said.

Chapter Two

Twinkle, Twinkle, Little Star

3rd September
Dear parents,
To all the new families joining us at Cherry Blossoms this year:
welcome! We are so very excited to meet all your little ones and
hope that they will love the nursery as much as we do. Cherry
Blossoms is vibrant, dynamic and a very tight-knit community.
We look forward to fostering close relationships with both the
children and parents of the Cherry Blossoms community.

If you have any concerns, please don't hesitate to pop into
my office or to discuss them with your child's teacher. Don't
forget term fees are due this week! We are honoured that you
have chosen Cherry Blossoms as the first step in your child's
lifelong education. We hope that everyone has a magical year
ahead!
Mrs Jones, Headmistress, Cherry Blossoms Nursery

'Twinkle, twinkle, chocolate star, I drive my daddy's purple car!'

It was Kaya's first day of nursery on an early September day and I was pushing her stroller down Great Western Road against a blustery, stubborn wind that was trying to push us over. Of course,

I was late. In typical fashion, I hadn't set the alarm properly and it hadn't gone off. Then, Kaya had decided that porridge was meant for hairstyling rather than eating and there had been no hot water. It was one of those mornings when I felt that perhaps I should reconsider homeschooling, purely for timekeeping purposes, as long as Kaya didn't become a friendless, socially awkward outcast.

We had arrived in London three and half weeks ago, and the flat we had originally seen and loved when we visited during our reconnaissance mission three months before had disappeared, leaving behind its damaged, ugly twin with a leak drip-dropping from the yellowing ceiling, damp marks creeping and bubbling up the walls and a broken hot water tank that looked like it hadn't been changed since 1975. It probably hadn't. I had resorted to a cocktail of perfume, hair gel and dry shampoo to make myself look and smell somewhat like a human rather than a humanoid version of Chewbacca.

Instead of our house, full of memories and worn-in furniture, the flat we had rented looked like a showroom for rental furniture: made to look beautiful on the outside, but uncomfortable and impractical, full of cold, sharp surfaces and edges. When we had visited, the tenants' decorations and memorabilia had made it feel homey, but now without them, it felt so sterile, coloured with variations of taupe, grey and brown, as if all the colours had been sucked out of them.

When I turned the corner from Great Western Road, I could make out the gates of the nursery, which were surrounded by a crowd of glamorous women huddled together around them. I stopped, and couldn't keep myself from staring. These women looked like their private jets took a wrong tailwind and they were queuing for Milan/Paris/New York Fashion Week instead of waiting in line for a nursery. I had heard about these "yummy mummy" types – just as I had Odysseus' mermaids – but I hadn't expected an army of them.

The women were all standing tall, ready for battle, carrying very expensive handbags with big, bold logos as shields, high heels as horses and a strong stare as strategy, preparing themselves to conquer the world (I knew I would lose a stare-off with them within seconds). Their luscious, glossy, thick manes were out of a "Because I'm worth it" L'Oréal commercial and their clothes and accessories straight out of the first twenty pages of *Vogue* magazine, which I loved to flip through when I occasionally needed a form of escapism or a break from Kaya's tantrums.

Not only were all the moms – or, as I should now say, mums – beautiful and stylish (no slummy mummies here), they were slim and fit; there were no women above a size ten in this lot. This was a Pilates-yoga-personal-trainer-barrecore-Zumba-dancing group I was up against. Not so great for my wibbly-wobbly, above-size-ten body. And the women exuded wealth, with an obligatory diamond solitaire and diamonds dripping from their ears, which were so big they looked fake.

As I took my place in the crowd, I thought that they all looked like supermodels. Wait, they were supermodels! I recognised Alice Denham, who had been on endless magazine covers and had started an empire of health, fitness and ethical clothes. She was rumoured to be the next Gisele Bündchen. On top of that, she had a foundation, the Alice Denham Foundation, aimed at eradicating poverty and malnutrition in Africa. Could she make me feel any less adequate? I mean, she was saving the world, carrying a tousled blond little boy on her hip, wearing hemp clothes, all the while looking like a Greek goddess.

On second thought, it seemed like I was the one who taken the wrong tailwind and found myself in an alternate reality where everyone was beautiful, stylish and rich, and I was the frog at the princess ball. How had I ended up here, and why did they let me in? I looked down at my beat-up and frayed Converse and realised why I was shorter than all these glamazons: I was missing the prerequisite four-inch heels. I was starting to feel like I had drunk the "Drink Me" potion in *Alice in Wonderland* and was shrinking, smaller and smaller every second, and turning into a miniature version of myself.

I caught another woman in mid-stare, sizing me up and down,

which caught me off guard. Of course, just as I was observing them, they were observing me. She was certainly not noticing me for my fashion sense, but probably for my lack thereof. My jeans-T-shirt-and-sweatshirt combo did not quite make the trendy/hip/fashionable cut in this crowd.

In the street in front of the nursery, swarms of black SUVs, Rolls-Royces, Bentleys and Mini Coopers were swerving in and out of parking spaces, like ants on a piece of apple pie. This wasn't a battle of who had the Rolls-Royce of strollers; these children actually *rolled* in Rolls-Royces. Behind a cream Rolls-Royce, a large, black nine-seater Mercedes van stopped right in front of the school with two men in the front and three shadows in the back. Out came a child with a young woman who was probably her nanny. Behind them appeared a tall, dark-haired, intimidatingly attractive woman wearing black leather trousers and a coat that looked like it was made out of the leftovers of a stuffed toy decapitation.

It was Irina Dimitrov, the wife one of London's richest oligarchs, Vladimir Dimitrov, who even I had heard of. Not that I knew much about Russian oligarchs, but they were so unashamedly blingtastic that it was impossible to avoid seeing pictures of them on their yacht off of Saint-Tropez in any *Hello!/OK!* type of glossy magazine. As she stepped out of the van, one of the men in the front seats followed suit and stood next to her. He was wearing a black parka and black jeans, with an ominous look in his eyes, like a bad guy in one of those action movies with Bruce Willis. Very intimidating. I wouldn't want to step on any of his toes. Without a word, he lurked protectively over Irina, the young woman and the child.

I couldn't just stand there staring dumbstruck at supermodels, I told myself, as I took Kaya out of the stroller and held her hand tightly.

I remembered what Michael had said about meeting new people. You can do this, Sophie, I said to myself. These are just normal women like you. Just with expensive handbags. You can do this for Kaya.

'Hi,' I said, turning to the woman behind me with the biggest, friendliest smile possible on my face. Holy crap, she was gorgeous.

Thin, blonde, American (you could tell from those Hollywood-white teeth, the blow-dried hair and those gravity-defying breasts). Her daughter was standing next to her and looked around Kaya's age. She was wearing an embroidered pink smock dress with a Peter Pan collar, and her long, blonde curls spilling down her back were fastened with a pastel-pink bow. Her face glowed like a doll's, with small, perfect features.

My voice faltered, but I held out my hand. 'I'm Kaya's mum. We just relocated from Canada.'

The tall blonde barely looked at me, as if she hadn't heard me, and I felt my smile grow rictus on my face, my hand still held out.

She blinked and then walked past me, calling, 'Becky, darling! It's so good to see you.' I turned as she sidestepped me in favour of a shorter and plumper version of herself, who looked thrilled to have been spoken to.

Becky, the mousy friend, beamed as the blonde air-kissed her on both cheeks.

'Hi, Kelly!' Becky said. 'It's been so long! You're *so* tanned – you look great. Where have you been all summer?'

Did she just completely ignore me, I wondered? I realised I was still holding my hand out, and I had my mouth open in shock. I stepped away, embarrassed. Perhaps it was an accident and she hadn't seen me or heard me.

The tall blonde, Kelly, was talking to Becky, but more women gathered around her, eager to be part of her conversation. She spoke for all of them to hear. 'We were in the Hamptons this year, staying at our friend Joshua Lieberman's house. You know Joshua Lieberman, don't you?'

'No, err, I don't think so,' replied Becky, fiddling with her Hermès handbag and laughing nervously. 'Well, not personally, anyway.'

'What a shame. It was *fabulous*.' Kelly gave a dismissive flick of her manicure. 'He just built a synagogue on his estate in East Hampton so that he would never have to step a foot out of it the whole summer! He's already got a helipad, so now all that's missing is a runway for his private jet.' She laughed, her blonde hair bouncing up and down. 'Where did *you* summer?'

Kaya tugged at the hem of my sweatshirt. 'Mama, who's that? She looks just like my Barbie.'

Kelly did indeed have a tiny waist that you could wrap both hands around. She was wearing a fur-lined gilet and skinny jeans stuck to her skinny legs that were so tight you probably had to pry them off with special pliers.

'That's Kelly,' said another tall, striking woman next to me. 'She lives on Ledbury Square Gardens. She has the most *amazing* house. You haven't been? She throws the most *amazing* parties. It has ten bedrooms, a spa and a sauna. They just had it valued at twenty million pounds.' Wow. Twenty million pounds? I couldn't even begin to imagine having that much money, or even a tenth of it. Or spending it on a house. Surely there would be better ways to spend that kind of money.

'I heard they're having a double-storey sub-basement put in for another four million,' another woman said, joining in. 'I think she wants to build a swimming pool for Olivia's private swimming lessons.'

I thought of our leaking, decrepit flat and clutched Kaya's hand a bit tighter. The landlord had already sent someone to fix it once, but a few days later, the leak reappeared and it still hadn't been fixed.

'She's amazing,' the first said. 'She runs the winter fair like Steven Spielberg runs a film set. Genius.'

I tried to nod, but they were no longer paying any attention to me. They had gone to join the others congregating around Kelly. Other groups of mothers had also formed and were chatting away in various languages. I looked around. It was a modern-day "Nursery of Babel".

'*Ola! Que tal? Come te fue las vacaciones?*'

'*Muy bien, gracias! Fui en Ibiza para dos meses.*'

'How was Delhi? Too hot again?'

'*Coucou! Ça va? Vous avez passé un bon été? Où est-ce que vous étiez?*'

'*On était a l'Île de Ré. Mes parents ont une maison la bas. Et vous?*'

'*On était à St Trop, comme d'hab. Mais il y avait trop de circulation – c'était épouvantable!*'

'*Wie gehts,* Christina?'

'*Sehr gut, danke.*'

'*Ciao,* Mia!'

'*Ciao,* Alessandra! *Ciao, bellissima ragazza!*'

'Sorry for the delay.' A voice interrupted all the chattering. Mrs Jones, the headmistress, stood at the top of the steps in front of the nursery next to the wrought iron gates, guarding the entrance of the nursery. 'We've been working so hard to make today the perfect day for your children, which is why we are opening a few minutes late. I know you will be delighted with what we've done with the nursery over the holidays. Please come in.'

When the gates opened, there was a sudden rush of bodies, as if they were the last people on board the *Titanic* trying to fit in the remaining lifeboats, or the last animals on Noah's Ark.

Kelly, who had been standing a few feet away from me, forged ahead with her daughter, not realising that Kaya was standing in front of me, and with the force of a seven-foot wrestler knocked her over. I was stunned. She hadn't even noticed that she had hit her, and there was no apology or look over the shoulder to see if she was OK. This was a proper child hit-and-run. I quickly grabbed Kaya into my arms to protect her from getting trampled again.

There were about ten supermums who had evidently been sharpening their elbows instead of their children's pencils for this first day of school, pushing their way to the front of the line, while the rest of the mums politely and respectfully stood behind them, waiting to get in. Even Irina had waited until everyone was through the front door before getting in line.

Once inside, I found the Lion Cubs class already buzzing with activity, with children pushing babies and prams around, playing with building blocks and cars and sitting down to read books. Kaya quickly separated from me and picked up *The Very Hungry Caterpillar* and sat reading quietly by herself, babbling away while I stood over her, looking proudly.

Kaya was on the shy side, which I was sure stemmed genetically from my side of the genealogical tree. I had been cripplingly shy as a child and my shyness had followed me around like a shadow; no matter how hard I tried to run away from it, it always caught up with me. But over the years I had managed to cope with it, using humour as a detractor, and was finally able to conceal it in adulthood. I was no longer the girl who hid behind her parents whenever she met someone new, but I hoped that Kaya wouldn't have to endure the same childhood. I had always secretly hoped that she would take on her father's traits, but instead, it appeared that her shyness was sticking around like a piece of Bubble Yum chewing gum under her shoe.

Over in another corner, I noticed Kelly with her daughter, chatting away to that other woman, Becky, and internally I groaned to myself. Really? Did I really have to have the sharpened-elbowed mum and her Robin-like sidekick in Kaya's class?

In the rest of the room, I saw other mothers milling around. One was in a black-skirt-and-blazer-combo power suit, glancing at her watch and her phone every ten to fifteen seconds, as if she were late for a meeting. I mustered all my courage and started walking towards her to try to start a conversation, but before I could reach her, she rapidly exited the classroom, not acknowledging me, leaving her child behind without even a look over her shoulder to see that he was OK. When her son finally caught on that she had left, he started wailing. Another mum, also dressed in a power suit, followed the first mum's lead.

Out of the corner of my eye, I could see Irina dropping off her child with a woman who appeared to be her Russian nanny, and Alice Denham floating in with her cherubic son at her hip. They also quickly left as soon as their children were settled.

Three other mothers had formed a small group and were talking in French to each other, and another group of mothers were starting to form around the teacher, bombarding her with questions about the class:

'How often do they go outside to the garden?'

'You only serve organic food, right?'

'When do they start learning to write?'

'When is the best time to start teaching them phonics?'

I inched towards them, hoping to speak to the teacher or to one of them, but there was no way I was ever going to get a word in, so I walked back towards Kaya. The more I stood there, the more I felt out of place and wanted to be back in Ontario on a silent lake somewhere, far away from this madness.

'Hello, are you Kaya's mother? I'm Miss Sarah, the teaching assistant,' said a pretty young woman who had been observing Kaya. 'You can leave any time you want. She seems very settled.'

'Are you sure?' I said, being that overprotective, overanxious mother I promised myself I would never be.

'Don't worry, she's in good hands,' she reassured me.

I left Kaya, who appeared happy and settled, and who hadn't even noticed that I was leaving. As I walked out the nursery, I could see the other mums engrossed in conversation outside the gates. They smiled at me as I walked by, but then quickly went back to their conversations. There was no chance of meeting anyone today, I thought resignedly. I was hoping that I could strike up a conversation with one of the mums, but it hadn't happened. Edward had been right that the mums were social at Cherry Blossoms. Just not with me.

'How was Kaya's first day of nursery?' Michael kissed my cheek softly as he entered the flat. His familiar aftershave instantly lifted me up when he arrived home that night. He started pouring himself a glass of red wine and sat down on our couch. It was 9.30pm and he had only now gotten home, yet again arriving too late for dinner. I had resorted to a microwave chicken curry dinner by myself, feeling overwhelmed and exhausted by our move to London.

Michael had been working late every night and at first I hadn't minded; it was a new job, new boss, new responsibilities. But now, eating alone at night in our damp, leaky flat was getting tiresome. Michael had promised that he would come to Kaya's first day of nursery, but he had cancelled at the last minute. He had rambled on about "an important meeting on-site I can't miss". I knew he was working really hard to integrate into the UK team and had an enormous amount of pressure from his bosses, but it was hard not to feel disappointed.

'Surprisingly, there was no crying. I was expecting tears and tantrums but I was able to leave her early on and she seemed very happy, engrossed in her books without as much as a look back at me when I left,' I said.

'And what about you? How was it for you? Any tears from you?' he said.

'Apart from the motorcade of bulletproof cars, bodyguards, and the army of Alpha Mums running down innocent children, it was absolutely fine,' I said, sighing.

He looked at me quizzically. 'Bulletproof cars and bodyguards?'

'Oh yes. There were bulletproof cars and bodyguards. Irina Dimitrov's daughter is in Kaya's class. And it seems that she needs her personal bodyguard outside the nursery at all times. We can feel safe and secure that Kaya will be in the most protected nursery in London. Until, of course, she gets mowed down by the Alpha Mums.'

He looked puzzled. 'What happened?'

'We were all standing outside the gates of the nursery, waiting for them to open, and I had a tall, glamazon, blonde American standing next to me with her gorgeous little girl. When the gates open, it was almost like a wildebeest stampede and she rushed in, not looking down, and pushed Kaya down to the ground. I don't know how she couldn't have noticed – but she didn't even look back or apologise.'

'I'm sure it was an accident. I can't imagine someone running over a child and not looking back.'

'Maybe, but some of the mums were in it to win it, even if there wasn't anything to win. It was strange – they wanted to be first in the nursery, as if that would give them a special pass with the teachers.'

'What about the other parents?'

'I didn't get to meet any of the other mums. Most of them rushed out after dropping their kids off. And then some of the mums were really intimidating, like Alice Denham, the supermodel-cum-eco-ethical-warrior-cum-philanthropist who was swanning around like a live sculpture. She is so beautiful.' I paused. 'And then you had the trilingual kids who spoke French, Spanish and English better than I do. I'm not sure what planet I've landed on, but if I landed on Mars, I'm from Venus.'

'Relax, Sophie, it's just the first day of nursery.'

'You're right,' I said, and thought about the day we had visited the nursery for the first time, and how much I had loved it. 'But Kaya is going to have to take up tae kwon do if the children are anything like that mum.'

Chapter Three

Charlie and the Chocolate Factory

Cherry Blossoms had seemed so different when we had first visited it with Edward back in May. The day after meeting him he had magically orchestrated ten nursery visits. But he had been right. I had instantly fallen in love with Cherry Blossoms. It was in Kensington, not far from Kensington Palace, and was housed in the ground floor and lower ground floor of a beautiful, white-wedding-cake corniced mansion that actually felt old, unlike the "pretend-old" buildings I was used to in North America. It was a beautiful, stand-alone building where I imagined grand balls like something out of *Pride and Prejudice* had taken place.

Inside, we walked by colourful, vibrant, geometrical Rothko-like paintings hung up on the walls of the nursery's corridors. Each room was colourfully and intricately decorated in a theme: "the plains of Africa", "farm animals", "fairy tales" and "under the sea". I could hear the uneven tunes of children singing "Frère Jacques" filtering out of the classrooms.

We had reached a bright office space where we met Mrs Jones, the headmistress. Mrs Jones was a soft-spoken, warm, enthusiastic, grandmother-like figure who had opened the nursery thirty years ago and was dedicated to making the nursery a place where children would "thrive, be happy and fulfil their potential".

She had led us downstairs through two French windows and showed us to the garden. It was a sunny, early May day, and wafts of freshly cut grass mixed with sweet floral smells filled the air and my lungs. The air was crisp, fresh and breezy, but warmed by the sun's rays, which fell on my bare skin. There was a magical aura to the garden that reminded me of the book *The Secret Garden*, which I'd often read as a child. I was charmed. It was true what they said: the English knew how to take care of their gardens. No, it wasn't Algonquin Park, but it was one of the most beautiful gardens I had ever seen.

I never imagined that there could be a garden this big in the middle of London. It consisted of three hectares of green, lush, outdoor space with two age-appropriate playgrounds, two grass tennis courts, and a fountain with a fish-like stone sculpture spitting water out of its spout. There were four main lawns separated by paths leading to the fountain, and around them were blooming hydrangeas, magnolia stellatas, camellias, agapanthus and belladonnas, producing multicoloured flowerbeds. Around the perimeter of the garden were cherry trees, which had just bloomed and snowed down white and pale-pink petals with each gust of wind, laying down a layer of petal-snow on the grass.

'This is how I named the nursery Cherry Blossoms,' Mrs Jones explained as we walked past the cherry trees. 'The sight of the cherry blossoms in springtime is one of the most wonderful sights to see. It is so very special,' she gushed, holding her hands together as if she were about to say a prayer. Mrs Jones was warm, soft-spoken, calming and seemed very caring. I immediately felt like I could trust her with Kaya.

After the garden visit, we walked past the classrooms, where I noticed that the children were polite, cooperative, well dressed and well behaved, eager to please their teachers. Some children were learning how to count on the two class computers, others sat reading books with the teaching assistant, while others were practising writing their names on coloured paper at their miniature tables.

There was something magical about the nursery and the children looked so happy playing, as if they had won a golden ticket to *Charlie and the Chocolate Factory*'s Happyland. It was toddler heaven. Forget life coaches and therapists, I wanted to open up a place like this for grown-ups.

I smiled while Mrs Jones explained the Early Years Foundation curriculum to us. I noticed Michael glancing at me with a mischievous smile, as if to say, See, this isn't too bad, is it? I couldn't argue that these were perfectly behaved toddlers. After the visit came the "interview" with Mrs Jones. Edward had briefed us that morning before the visit about the interview process and primed us with dos and don'ts.

'So, you're both from Canada?' Mrs Jones asked us, as we were sitting in her office, which had floor-to-ceiling windows with views onto the garden.

'Yes, we live in Oakville. It's about forty-five minutes outside Toronto,' Michael said, turning on the charm, sitting tall and handsome in a brand-new suit he had splashed out on to celebrate his new job. 'It is a really difficult decision for us to move to London. We're very happy in Oakville and Sophie's job is there too, but I've been offered a great position at Siemens to run their new RailLink Project. You may have heard of it?'

'Oh, of course,' she replied, smiling at him. 'I've seen it in the news. It's a very exciting project and should make the lives of so many commuters much better.'

'I think you know my new boss, Robert Curtis? His children went to Cherry Blossoms. He loved it here and raved about it.'

'Little Belle and Zack Curtis? Of course! The Curtis family is wonderful!' Mrs Jones enthused, as if there couldn't be a better family than theirs in the entire world, though I suspected she said this about every family.

'It's a beautiful nursery,' Michael said. 'And I think this nursery may be the only thing that is going to convince Sophie to move to London.' We all laughed politely in unison.

'The children look so happy,' I said, 'and your garden is amazing. It's huge. I would never have guessed that there was a hidden garden like this in the middle of the city.'

'The children love running in the garden, rain or shine,' she said in a sing-song voice I could imagine her using often with the children. 'We want our children to be happy and the garden brings them a lot of joy. Of course, we also prepare them for big school with literacy and numeracy skills from very early on.'

It was difficult not to be impressed. 'How did you decide to open this nursery?' I asked.

'I opened Cherry Blossoms when I was looking for a nursery for my own children. I searched everywhere for a warm, safe, caring environment for them, but when I couldn't find what I was looking for, I opened it.' She beamed.

'That's a great story. How old are your children now?' Michael asked.

'One is thirty and the other is thirty-three. My youngest is a singer and actor in the West End and my eldest is a lawyer.'

'They've obviously done well. I'm sure it's all down to your teaching and your nursery,' Michael said, flattering her, laying on the compliments, making her feel as important as the queen.

Of the two of us, Michael was the extrovert, the one everyone gravitated towards when he was in a room. Just as I had at the campus party, the night we met during our first year of university. I had been dressed in a duck costume for a themed party and was drunk on vodka orange juice and Rolling Rock beer, and courageous enough to tell him that he was the most delicious man in the room and that he smelled as sweet as strawberry shortcake. Drinking alcohol was the only thing that allowed me to talk like nobody's business, and he laughed at my self-deprecating jokes all night.

The next day I had been mortified when he'd showed up at my dorm room with strawberry shortcake. He had managed to track me down by asking the host of the party who the drunken duck was. Luckily, the host happened to be my roommate's cousin and sent him to our dorm. It was quite the modern Cinderella story.

He was one of those people who was born with an innate confidence that I admired and wished I had. After years of not believing in myself and going through terrible teenage years which involved a) too many hormones, b) not enough waxing and c) being shyer than a hibernating Canadian brown bear, I had come out of my teenage years quite scarred. But Michael made me believe that I was this funny, kind-hearted and generous person that I didn't see myself. He not only made me a better person, but he'd made me believe in myself.

By the end of the "interview", I could tell he had charmed Mrs Jones as she purred at him. I recited my line that Edward C-H had coached me on, word for word: 'We have looked at many nurseries, and we really feel that Cherry Blossoms is the best fit for us and Kaya.' I felt like I was reading a teleprompter at an awards ceremony, but as he had said, there were rules to this game and one had to play by the rules in order to win it.

I had to admit that I had been really impressed by the nursery and knew that this was where I wanted Kaya to go. The children had seemed so well behaved and happy and the curriculum seemed so creative, helping the children learn through play. The next day while we were still in London, I sent in a handwritten letter, as prompted by Edward, thanking Mrs Jones and emphasising how much we had enjoyed meeting her and visiting the nursery.

A few days after we returned to Canada, I received an email from Mary Studnick, the administrative assistant of Cherry Blossoms:

To: Sophie Bennett
From: Cherry Blossoms
Sent: May 16 2016, 10:00
Subject: Offer

Dear Mr and Mrs Bennett,
It was a pleasure to meet you the other day. We are delighted to offer your daughter Kaya Bennett a place at Cherry Blossoms Nursery this September.
Yours sincerely,
Mrs Jones, Cherry Blossoms Nursery School

I called Michael immediately. It was midday and I knew he would be on his lunch break and would have some time to talk.

'Michael! We got a place for Kaya at Cherry Blossoms!' I said.

'That's great news, Sophie-Bee,' he said enthusiastically. 'I know how much you wanted her to go there.'

'Yes, it's great,' I told him. 'I feel that Kaya will be well looked after there. Now, I'll just need to find a few nice mums and all will be fine,' I said nervously.

'You should try to meet other mothers at the nursery,' he had said, 'and you should try getting involved, just like Edward and Mrs Jones said. There's the fundraiser and the parent-teacher association. If you put in a little bit of effort, I'm sure you'll quickly meet other mothers.'

'I'll just have to push myself a bit,' I said, thinking that I would have to push myself a lot more than a little bit.

'You can do this. Keep an open mind. Look, in the first three months, you should say yes to any invitation you get. It'll give you a chance to meet a lot of people and then you'll figure out who you fit with.' He was officially giving me a full-on pep talk.

'That's if I get any invites and if I meet anyone that I fit with,' I replied.

'Come on, it'll be fine, all you have to do is talk about potty training and learning the alphabet and I'm sure you'll make friends,' he teased, trying to lift the weight that I had started feeling by making light of the situation.

After that phone conversation with Michael, I promised myself that I would make friends with the mums at the nursery. I still found it hard making new friends, probably due to being shy as a child, and also having a habit of saying the wrong thing at the wrong time, but this would be different. I would make it happen. How hard could it be?

Chapter Four

The Body Beautiful Cult

A few weeks on and I still hadn't met any mums at Cherry Blossoms, despite my efforts. Many of the polished and manicured mums had been replaced by their Filipina/Eastern European/Continental European nannies. I hadn't seen the power-suited mothers again, who were likely back at work after the summer holidays. The other mums I had tried to engage with had quickly said "hello" and "goodbye", but had never stopped to have a proper conversation. Everyone seemed so busy and in a rush, their expressions mimicking the I'm-so-busy-I've-got-somewhere-important-to-go looks on their faces. Unfortunately for me, I had a hard time mimicking the important I've-got-to-run-home-to-see-the-BT-guy look on my face. It was a far cry from the friendly, "Hello, how are you?" from anyone you met on the street, which often happened in Canada. I still wasn't used to London life and knew that it would take some time to feel comfortable here.

Even the nannies were an entirely different breed than I was used to. Here, the nannies at Cherry Blossoms were either part of the Filipina tribe, who all huddled together at pick-ups and drop-offs, speaking Tagalog, or they were part of the "language immersion programmes", speaking French, German, Italian or Russian to the children. Some of the nannies wore branded shoes, handbags emblazoned with logos, and sported sunglasses branded with Prada, Gucci or Michael Kors. One nanny wore knee-high boots and a short skirt and looked like she was ready to go clubbing rather than picking up a toddler.

Kaya went to nursery five days a week from 9am to 1pm, which left me a few hours of the day to myself to take care of all the admin of moving to a new country: getting a mobile phone, setting up a bank account and our Internet, calling our landlord about the leak and buying decorations for our flat to make it more of a home, which took twice as much time as it should because I knew nothing about London.

I had started job-searching and had sent ten CVs out, but so far had not had one response. I was hoping to find a part-time job at a non-profit but knew that my CV didn't look good. I had a gap after our move to Oakville and had only been back at work for less than a year before moving to London.

I had been working part-time at PerformArts, a performance arts non-profit, as a grant writer. It wasn't as grand and exciting as when I worked at GreenSpace in Toronto, an environmental charity lobbying to increase green spaces, save the environment and fight climate change, but that's what happened when kids and a husband interfered with the "perfect job". Although my new job had been a step down for me, it kept me engaged and kept one of my feet in the working world. I was planning on increasing Kaya's hours at the nursery once I found a job, but so far, I hadn't had much luck.

After picking Kaya up from nursery, I would bring her home for a nap and an afternoon snack. I had tried bringing her to a playgroup and a music class in the afternoon, since she had loved them back in Canada, but each time she screamed, 'Nooooo!' so loudly I worried that one of the neighbours was going to call the police to check for a potential domestic abuse case. I soon realised that she was so tired from nursery that she preferred staying home to play quietly with her toys and spend time with me.

I had also tried taking her to a playground for her to meet other children and for me to perhaps meet another mum, but the one time we made it to the playground, a four-year-old boy pushed her down the slide by accident and she sprained her ankle and scraped her knee. She had then sobbed uncontrollably for two hours. Since then, every time I asked her if she wanted to go to the playground was as if I was asking her if she wanted to go to a war-torn country on holiday.

When Kaya was in nursery, I sometimes wandered the streets and looked slightly enviously at the mums "lunching" together in one of the quaint, awning-covered cafés or restaurants lining the trendy streets full of fashionable French stores, and it made me feel homesick. I missed Emma and my family.

Emma was my closest friend in Oakville and she had a daughter the same age as Kaya. We had met at a baby music class and had bonded immediately over developmental milestones reached and favourite films, and laughed at the same jokes. Our daughters had also become great friends and our husbands liked each other as well. I knew how rare it was to find a friendship like that.

I also thought about my mother and father, who were always willing to help out, from the time I was in bed with shakes and chills from the flu to the time I had twisted my ankle on the Juan de Fuca trail on Vancouver Island. My family was far from perfect, but they were great grandparents to Kaya and one of them could always be counted on for emergency babysitting.

I missed Michael too. He was home very little and even when he was home, he wasn't really there. He was so preoccupied with work that his thoughts were always somewhere else. He rarely saw Kaya during the week and often had to go into work on the weekends. And when he was home, he was exhausted and went straight to bed, which didn't leave much time for the both of us. I knew he was doing this for us, but I hoped that it was temporary.

As Kaya and I sat together for yet another tea party in our flat, I remembered the promise I made to myself that I was going to meet mums through the nursery. There had to be at least one or two nice mums there, I was convinced. I wasn't going to give up at the first hurdle. I was determined to persevere.

*

One morning, I saw Kelly after drop-off one day. She looked like she was on her way to a gym class wearing a skintight, Catwoman-like, neon yellow and green gym outfit, showing off her perfect curves and her pert bust and bum. She was sipping a green juice that looked as tempting as swamp water. It was clear that she seemed very serious about her workouts. The mothers had all cleared out and there was no one but us outside the school gates.

I should give her another chance for Kaya's sake, I thought. Maybe it had all been an accident. It took all my courage to stop her casually. Keep it cool, I said to myself.

'Hi, I'm Sophie. I think your daughter Olivia is in my daughter Kaya's class?' I ventured, putting out my hand to shake hers.

She glanced at me, upping-and-downing me in a flash, and then a bored stare glazed her face.

'Maybe. There are a lot of Olivias in this school,' she answered lamely, taking my hand and shaking it limply. 'Sorry, darling, I'm late. I've got to rush to Body Beautiful. I have my Pilates class in five minutes,' she added with a forced smile.

She didn't look the least bit rushed, but at least this time she had acknowledged me and spoken to me. It was definitely better than being ignored. It was a start.

'What's Body Beautiful? Is it a gym? I've just moved here and I'm looking for a place to work out,' I asked, knowing I sounded slightly desperate but hoping this would get the conversation started.

'Body Beautiful? You haven't heard of Body Beautiful?' She looked at me in complete wonder. 'It's *more* than a gym. It's a lifestyle. It's the best. That's how Elle Macpherson became "The Body".' She sauntered off, her bum swishing past me as if to say, "There's a reason you'll never get a sexy bum like mine. It's because you stand around trying to make small talk with the mums outside your child's nursery. Get yourself to a gym, woman!"

Taking Kelly's bum's advice, I looked up Body Beautiful that afternoon and found a website that offered books, nutritional advice and plenty of photos of the owners, Elena and Ben, a gorgeous-looking couple who were photographed sprawled on various beaches around the world, looking toned, tanned and taut. They were the perfect advert for their gym – I mean, lifestyle. Reviews I found in the *Telegraph*, the *Guardian* and the *Times* declared that Body Beautiful had reached "cult status", with all the supermodels and celebrities addicted to it.

I decided to book an introductory meeting and trial class, thinking that exercising would probably do me some good. 'Keep an open mind,' I remembered Michael telling me. In Canada, we would often go to the lakes to hike, kayak or cycle on the weekends. Joining Kelly's gym seemed like it would be a perfect way to exercise and possibly meet other people.

'Body Beautiful is so much more than a gym. It's a lifestyle, a movement and a philosophy,' Elena, the owner of Body Beautiful, was explaining to me as she was showing me around their "temple". 'It transforms. It empowers. It's about realising your full physical and mental potential.' Her eyes lit up as she continued explaining how the gym worked. 'It's about thriving and transforming. I guarantee that after four weeks you will feel like a new person.'

'That sounds good to me,' I said, beaming. 'I definitely need to feel like a new person. I used to go hiking and kayaking in Canada, but it's a little hard to do that here,' I joked. 'Many of the mothers at my nursery come here, so I thought that I could try it out.'

'You've come to the right place!' She smiled so much that I hoped it would rub off on me if I joined. 'At Body Beautiful we will look after you holistically, both body and mind. It isn't only about exercising – it's about nutrition, evolving and meditating. Body Beautiful will give you that sense of peace, of tranquillity, of vitality that I am sure you are missing, right?' she said as if she had known me for ten years.

'Uhm, yes, that's right.' Perhaps she was onto something, I thought to myself.

'We also carefully monitor what goes in and out of your body.'

I was imagining her serenely carrying a plastic bag, ready to pick up whatever came out of my body as if I were a dog, ready to analyse it. But then she interrupted my thoughts and yelled, 'Cut the CRAP!'

'Sorry, what? Did I say something wrong?' I asked, confused.

'Cut the CRAP!'

'What crap?'

'CRAP! Caffeine, Refined sugars, Alcohol and Processed food.'

'Oh, right.'

'Our bodies are overindulged on a daily basis, so instead of three meals a day, we have two shakes per day and one meal consisting of a paleo, macrobiotic, organic, plant-based food.' She spoke so confidently and convincingly that I pushed away thoughts that made me think that this daily menu sounded dreadful. 'And on alternate weeks, we juice. Do you want to try a juice? The Green Power has kelp, spirulina, spinach and kale. It's a cleanser and a retoxer. Or try one of our shakes. Here, have a Body Beautiful shake. Cassandra, can you make one for her please?' She nodded over to me while Cassandra – another gorgeous-looking woman – took a glass from the juice-and-shake bar and started preparing the mixture.

'The Body Beautiful drink is my favourite!' Cassandra gushed enthusiastically. 'It tastes just like a milkshake! It's the best!'

'Absolutely,' another staff member echoed. 'It's also my favourite!'

Everyone was so cheery and excited that I couldn't help but get excited along with them.

'Here's your drink!'

I took a sip of the cold, thick liquid and as soon as it hit the back of my throat I started coughing, trying my best to stop myself from throwing it up. It did not taste like a milkshake; it tasted like I had just swallowed a cup of sand laced with bitter cocoa powder and something that tasted worse than almond milk. I looked at the staff, who still looked convinced that this shake was the best-tasting milkshake in the world. Was this a case of the emperor's new clothes, and was I the only one who had clothes on?

'How much does it cost to be a member here?' I asked curiously, given that I had noticed that the Body Beautiful "milkshake" cost seven pounds, and since I hadn't found the gym membership rates anywhere on the website.

'Memberships start at thirty thousand pounds a year,' Elena answered. I coughed again, bringing up the vile drink into my throat. Thirty thousand pounds? That was more than my annual salary! What were they doing in there? Giving massages every day and all day long like a Wagyu cow? I couldn't imagine any gym being worth that kind of money, even if you were a millionaire. Nothing seemed to make sense to me these days.

This was my cue to leave, but she continued talking. 'But of course, private training sessions are on top of that, and classes as well. Don't forget, here it's not about detoxing – it's about retoxing.'

'Retoxing?' I asked.

'Retoxing is about staying detoxed all of the time. It won't work to just detox once a year. It's about being on a constant detox mission.'

'But doesn't retoxing mean the opposite of detoxing?'

'No, Sophie. You've got to put your preconceptions aside. You have to open your mind. Just stop and just be. Stop questioning.' She stopped me and put her hands on my upper chest and closed her eyes, as if she were taking a ten-second meditation break from our conversation.

'Oh, OK, right.' I stumbled backwards, feeling more and more alienated by the Body Beautiful lifestyle.

'Now why don't you start with one of our Body Beautiful strengthening classes?'

'Maybe another time,' I said, taking a few steps backwards, wanting to get out of there as fast as possible.

But Elena cornered me and led me into one of the studios, where I saw a trainer screaming at his client, 'Quicker! Faster! Stronger!' It looked more like army training than anything else.

'You can try the class today. Right now, actually. Hans will be happy to take you on. Right, Hans?' Elena looked at me as if she had had a brilliant light bulb moment.

'Of course!' Hans – a six-foot-three personal trainer who looked like he should be working at Abercrombie & Fitch – answered (yelled) back.

'Oh, I don't think I can do a class today, I don't have much time…' I said as I started slowly walking away again.

'There is no time like the present.' She spoke breathily, grabbing both of my hands. 'It's only thirty minutes and I can tell that you need to relax. This will take you on a journey of self-discovery and self-relaxation.'

'I'm not sure…' I tried to inch away, but she held on to my hands firmly.

'Come on! Your destiny is in your hands!' She pulled me by the hands and led me to the studio floor.

Half an hour later, I hobbled out of the class with every fibre of my body aching in pain. The strengthening class was Guantánamo Bay torture disguised as a gym class. Not only that, but you had to pay thirty thousand to be tortured, starved, given colonics, force-fed sandy cocoa drinks and brainwashed. Body Beautiful hadn't just reached cult status; I was beginning to believe that it was an actual cult. Clearly, Body Beautiful wasn't right for me after all.

Chapter Five

Mother's Guilt-and-Failure Voice

'Kaya is settling in well, Mrs Bennett, but she is rather on the quiet side. Some days, I don't hear her speak at all. She seems very independent and happy to play on her own, but she hasn't really been interacting with the other children much.' Miss Katie, Kaya's blonde, twenty-something, pretty-as-a-princess nursery teacher, as they called them here, paused as she told me how Kaya was getting on at Cherry Blossoms.

I had asked for a meeting with her teacher because Kaya had so far given me verbal and non-verbal cues, through stomping, tantrums and tears, that: a) it was all a bit overwhelming for her too, b) she missed her home and her friends, and c) she was having a hard time integrating into her new nursery. Which were basically exactly the same feelings I was having, but I wasn't allowed to have a full-blown tantrum, throwing myself on the floor in the middle of a supermarket and screaming, 'I miss home!' I'd quickly be locked up in a mental institution if I did that. Children have all the fun.

Of course, at the nursery, her feelings were manifested in shyness, not playing with other children, and not speaking for entire days, to the point that some parents had probably started thinking she was mute.

'Has she been in a nursery setting before?' We were standing in the classroom at 8.55am, a few minutes before class was starting. Kaya had seemed more and more introverted recently, and I was beginning to worry that she was becoming a socially awkward, friendless, fringe-of-society outcast, despite not being homeschooled. I could see her turning inwards, like a clam, shutting up tight. There was only room for one of those in our family – me, and I didn't wish it on my daughter.

'Yes, we dropped her off at day care in Canada, but nothing like this was ever raised,' I replied. I scanned back to the days when Kaya was happily paddling, giggling and frolicking in the play pool with my friend Emma's daughter in our backyard. Another memory of them popped up in my mind, when I had left Kaya at day care and came back to find them in a giant, inseparable bear hug; we had to bribe them with chocolate-chip cookies to pry them apart. A stab of pain and homesickness struck me in the middle of my chest at the memory, and I struggled to hold back my tears. If they started to fall, it would be like opening a dam to Niagara Falls, and then it wouldn't be the children that Miss Katie would be worried about.

'Perhaps it has to do with your move. It's a big transition and different children react differently. Some adapt immediately, some take longer. Even though they are still young, I would hope to at least see some parallel play, but it's early days. I wouldn't worry too much. I'll keep an eye on her.'

'She is on the shy side,' I explained, then pictured her grey-haired at sixty, still living at home, with only hairballs, cats and her imaginary friends keeping her company. It was my duty to stop this at all costs.

'Perhaps you should consider organising play dates with some of the children. The other children have already started going on play dates, and that could make her transition into nursery easier. This way she could feel comfortable with the other children in a more intimate or comfortable home setting.'

'Play dates? Oh. Right. Of course, that's a good idea. But she doesn't mention anyone in class. Is there anyone I should ask?'

Already, I had started feeling the "play-date pressure" from the second week of nursery, when I heard snippets of conversation between mothers: 'Have your nanny bring so-and-so over to ours,' or 'They were so cute, chasing and hugging each other all over our garden,' or 'The bath overflowed. It was a mess! Luckily I had Anna to clean up.'

No one so far had asked Kaya for a play date. It was only the third week, after all, and yet I couldn't stop hearing my "mother's guilt-and-failure voice" as it visited me and taunted me: You haven't organised a play date! Your child is missing out and it is *all your fault*.

'How about Olivia, Chloe or Anastasia? They seem to have similar temperaments to Kaya's. They are quieter and softer than some of the other high-energy children, who may overwhelm Kaya.'

'Thanks. That's helpful, I'll get right on it.'

I sighed internally as I left the classroom and headed home. Olivia was Kelly's daughter, and I remembered a quiet girl standing wordlessly next to Kelly on the first day of nursery. She had looked shy and quiet against her mother's aggressive, get-out-of-my-way Alpha behaviour.

Later that day, by coincidence, I received an email from Kelly.

To: Group (Lion Cubs Mums)
From: Kelly Miller
Sent: September 20 2016, 10:00
Subject: Important Dates

Hello ladies,
I wanted to welcome you to Cherry Blossoms Nursery and to introduce myself; I am your class representative for the year. We have a busy few weeks ahead of us and I wanted to let you know of some important dates for your calendar.

September 30th @ 9:30am: welcome coffee morning for mums at Pain et Chocolat. This will be a chance to meet other mums in the class, so please come along.

October 10th @ 8pm: parents' evening; Serafina's members' club at 45 Jermyn Street, W1 4JF.

October 12th @ 12pm: class lunch and intro winter fair meeting.

November 1st @ 10am: winter fair planning meeting. Discuss new fundraising ideas and start winter fair planning. All ideas welcome.

November 10th @ 8–9am: parent-teacher conferences, Lion Cubs class.

November 15th: winter fair final meeting.

November 28th–30th: final preparation days for winter fair.

December 1st: winter fair.

December 8th: nativity play & Christmas party.

December 15th: last day of school.

Please sign up for the winter fair committee as soon as possible; it is the charity highlight of the year and it is our way to give back to our community. We are donating the proceeds towards building a new community centre for underprivileged children in North Kensington. Each and every parent's help is invaluable.

I look forward to meeting you at the coffee morning.

Best wishes,

Kelly

Reading the email sent my heart running on a treadmill. The list of activities and events that I was expected to attend felt like a long list of chores I had to do. It was overwhelming. I would actually have to speak to strangers, small talk, one word after another, while looking them in the eye. I was already tired even before I'd started. Did I really need to attend all of these events?

But then I remembered that I was completely friendless, and so far I hadn't met anyone in London. Michael had told me that I should accept every invitation that came my way, whether I wanted to or not. 'You never know who you'll meet,' he had said to me.

This was my chance to meet mums at the nursery, although it was completely contradictory to my nature to socialise with fifteen people I didn't know. I wasn't outgoing as a child, and I wasn't going to start in my mid thirties. But I would have to make the effort for Kaya. Despite the warning bells going off right, left and centre in my head, I calmed myself down and sat down in front of my computer to compose an email response.

To: Kelly Miller
From: Sophie Bennett
Sent: September 20 2016, 10:15
Subject: Re: Important Dates

Hi Kelly,
Thanks for your email! I really look forward to the coffee morning and I will be there!
See you soon,
Sophie Bennett xx

My email was probably too eager, like a Labrador puppy, but lately I had started feeling a slither of tenacious loneliness that was slowly spreading over me like a slow-growing epidemic. I was going to give Kelly another chance. Whether or not I wanted her to, Kelly was going to be in my life. She was the class rep, so wasn't she meant to look after the class? I hoped the coffee morning would be a safe and secure environment to meet a few mums and to scavenge for a few play dates for Kaya.

Chapter Six

Coffees and Play Dates

'Good morning, ladies, thank you for coming. I'm Kelly Miller, and I'm very honoured to be your class representative this year. I would like to start with apologies and introductions before moving on to more informal conversations.'

We were sitting in Pain et Chocolat, an organic café around the corner from Cherry Blossoms which served gluten-free, nut-free, dairy-free pastries, soups and salads. Its chalkboard menu had words like "superfoods", "green juices" and "raw food" sprawled across it. It had originally started in the '90s as one of the only places in Notting Hill to serve decent coffee and pastries, but eventually had to change with the neighbourhood gentrification, replacing the chips with sweet potato, cupcakes with quinoa, and croissants with kale salads. In the back of the café were oversized, brown leather couches with small, distressed, rustic shabby-chic wooden tables and chairs.

Kelly was at the head of one of the larger tables, with ten mothers sitting around her. Her bottle-blonde mane was perfectly coiffed, sitting softly on her shoulders, and her bright-blue eyes were serious but engaging. She sat confidently with a ballerina's straight, tall back, wearing an asymmetrical, bejewelled top with ultra-skinny jeans. It was difficult to tell her age, or whether she had had any work done to her face or nose, or whether it was Botox that kept her wrinkle-free, but she was definitely defying age remarkably. Perhaps it was that green juice she seemed to drink every day.

'I have received apologies from many of the working mums: Christina Richter had an important meeting in Munich she couldn't miss, Mary Wright is in San Francisco for the week for her company's annual general assembly meeting, Alice Denham is busy with Fashion Week and Irina Dimitrov's PA wrote to say she was unavailable. Finally, Poppy Sevigny-Bruce had an emergency at her country house so had to leave early this morning, something to do with her house being flooded.' She was looking down at a neat pile of papers, the top sheet of which looked like an Excel spreadsheet filled with class names, addresses and emails. Instead of feeling like a casual coffee morning, it was like a Monday morning boardroom meeting, going over the day's agenda.

'Why don't we start off by introducing ourselves?' Kelly's direct, no-nonsense, to-the-point voice projected loudly. 'Tell us your name, where you're from, a little about you, and something interesting about yourself that we may not know. I'm Kelly,' she repeated, as if we hadn't heard her the first time. 'I'm from Iowa and I studied economics at Dartmouth before I moved to New York and started working for Coleman Lazaar, where I met my husband Chris. But then we had to move to London when he was asked to head the European office for his hedge fund, Aquarian Asset Management. You may have heard of it? It's one of the biggest hedge funds in London.' She looked around smugly, ensuring that everyone had heard her.

'I stopped working when we moved and I had my son Max,' she continued. 'Then I had Olivia three years ago. I couldn't imagine going back to work, especially when I didn't have to. I really want to be involved in my children's education.' She was telling us her entire biography, and seemed to really enjoy listening to her own voice. 'If you're going to have children, it's important to actually look after them.' Dig number one to the defenceless, absent working mums. Her lips smiled tightly, while her eyes looked out at us, feigning innocence.

'So…something interesting…' she continued. 'We're renovating our house on Ledbury Square Gardens. It's a *huge* undertaking.' Kelly's manicured hand reached for her green juice and she brought it to her lips, sipping it slowly. She then exhaled as if she had finished an important presentation that required the utmost attention and involvement. Kelly was not afraid to let her thoughts and opinions be known, and her tone of voice ensured that everyone knew she was the head of the table. 'Becky, why don't you go ahead?'

Becky was sitting next to her. She had short, brown hair, a slightly oversized jaw and pretty brown eyes.

'I'm Rebecca Goldberg, but you can call me Becky. I am also American, from Georgia. I went to Duke and studied at Georgetown Law and worked in corporate law after university. I went back to work after my first child, but after I had Caroline I had to stop when the hours became too long. It's just not possible to work part-time in the type of job I had.' She looked a smidgen regretful as she said the last part, but quickly erased that regret, perhaps fearing that she would displease Kelly. 'Something interesting… I once won the under-twelve gymnastics competition in Georgia, but then puberty hit, and I grew too fast in the wrong places.'

Everyone laughed forcefully and smiled, probably hoping to make the right impression for Kelly at our first social event.

The introductions continued, many of them also reeling off perfect résumés of Ivy League schools or Oxford or Cambridge educations, and working at illustrious companies. They were an impressive array of women who had all stopped working or switched to working part-time when their children were born. These were not brain-dead, *Desperate Housewives*-of-London types; they were overeducated, overachieving, stay-at-home mums who had chosen the easy or hard route, depending on how you looked at it. And despite female CEO Lean In encouragements, they had opted out of the workforce, especially since their bank accounts allowed them to, which seemed to be the case for many of these women.

Then it was the turn of the French woman sitting next to me, dressed in a conservative pantsuit, who looked as comfortable as someone who had just fallen in a bush of poison ivy, which comforted me, although I knew it shouldn't. She played with her cappuccino cup as she talked in a heavy French accent, twisting and turning the cup in circular motions. Her hair was tied back in a neat bun, and she must have been in her mid thirties like me. She cut her introduction short, not wanting to partake in divulging anything interesting, furtively looking up and down at her coffee cup.

'Hello, I am Laetitia. I am from Paris and I work for my family's fashion company, Corrine, but I am taking some time off to raise Chloe, my daughter.'

I realised Chloe was one of the girls Miss Katie had mentioned to me, and Laetitia looked as uncomfortable as I was in this random, circumstantial grouping of women. I made a note to chat with her afterwards.

When it was finally my turn, the anticipation had slowly been building and my anxiety had reached Mount Kilimanjaro levels. For me, speaking in front of a group of intimidating women was as pleasurable as meeting the norovirus over a toilet bowl. I quickly summed myself up in three sentences.

'Hi, I'm Sophie Bennett. I'm from Canada and I studied environmental sciences in university. Something interesting: I moved to London six weeks ago and I still have trouble understanding the taxi drivers.' Judging by the blank faces staring back at me, I knew I was being particularly unexciting, but at least I wasn't attracting any attention to myself, which was a relief.

The last person to introduce herself was Francesca, a gorgeous Italian ex-model who took the image of the glam stay-at-home mum to another level; she was an ex-Victoria's Secret model with Elle Macpherson's body, Angelina Jolie's lips and JLo's defining posterior. She was a sculptor's masterpiece. Some women seemed to have it all – the boobs, the bum and the bankroller. She was certainly used to attention, and seemed to relish it.

'Hello, I am Francesca, I am twenty-eight years old and my

son is Luca. He is the crazy one already trying to kiss all the little girls.' She laughed, throwing her long locks of brown hair back with a confidence that only drop-dead-gorgeous Victoria's Secret models had. 'I am Alice's best friend – she's sorry she isn't here but she is at Fashion Week at the Vivienne Westwood show. I will need to run off very soon too. Alice told me about Cherry Blossoms, and it is so cute. Am very happy here.' She smiled a dazzling white smile with teeth that had probably never had braces, or bits of food stuck in said braces.

After the introductions were over, small group conversations started up around the table regarding which schools everyone was applying to and how they had gotten into Cherry Blossoms.

'Cherry Blossoms is *the* best nursery in London, hence the world. Did you read the article in the *Times*, "All You Need to Be Successful is Cherry Blossoms and Oxford"?'

'You haven't sent in your school applications? You needed to send the application the day they're born!'

'My best friend, Shelley Sanders, the CEO of croprock.com, vouched for me.'

The conversation then moved to their common acquaintances and friends.

'You went to Dartmouth? I went to Brown. Did you know Joe Moss?'

'Your husband works in derivatives trading at Coleman Lazaar? He must know my cousin, Andy Pearson, who works in derivative sales.'

I tried to participate but it was like yelling into a sound vacuum. No matter how loud I was, no one seemed to be listening. Even if I was heard, I knew I didn't have anything in common with these women because: a) I didn't work in or know anyone in finance/tech/law/fashion, b) I didn't know anything about the British schooling system, nor about house renovations, and c) I didn't have a loudspeaker voice that could go decibels over everyone else's.

The loud voices pounded in my brain until I had a headache, though it was Kelly's dominating voice that kept talking over the meeker ones and constantly brought the attention back to her. It was overwhelming, and I felt invisible and alone. I didn't fit in at all and felt myself shrinking again, like Alice, looking at these women with wonder.

I missed Oakville and Emma and my family so acutely that I felt my chest constricting. All I wanted was to be back in Canada, smelling the fresh mountain air and coniferous trees or canoeing on a silent, tranquil lake, listening to the sounds of the whistling birds and trees.

Instead, all I heard was Kelly's new monologue about her daughter Olivia's intensive scheduling.

'Olivia has swimming on Mondays, ballet on Tuesdays, French on Wednesdays, gymnastics in Mandarin on Thursdays and she has Fridays off so we can spend some time together. I don't want her to get too exhausted...'

I wanted to tell her, "Stop speaking!" But I couldn't move or talk, and there was nothing I could do but put a smile on my face and continue listening to her.

'Then on Sundays she has tennis and music classes. I thought about stopping some of her classes but her gymnastics coach and her tennis coach have told me she really has a natural talent. They were the ones who really *insisted* we continue them. And swimming is a life skill to have. She's already swimming by herself without armbands. It's a life-saving skill!' Kelly uttered those words with such conviction and certainty, as if she believed she was actually, physically saving her daughter's life at that precise moment.

'Music needs to be learned at such a young age,' she rambled on, 'and ballet gives poise, discipline and works on her balance, which will be invaluable as she grows older.' She spoke about Olivia as if she were a science project rather than a living, breathing child who had her own needs and limitations.

'Isn't it a bit much for a three—' I timidly began to ask her, but she cut me off before I had a chance to finish my sentence, more interested in listening to herself speak as she listed her justifications as to why learning gymnastics in Mandarin from an ex-Chinese

Olympic gymnast was a perfect way to kill two birds with one stone. Kelly elevated intense mothering to a whole new level of competitiveness, setting the bar so high that it was almost impossible to keep up, even if you wanted to.

It was useless trying to speak to her, so I turned to Laetitia, who looked as deer-caught-in-headlights as I felt, and struck up a conversation.

'Where are you from in Paris, Laetitia?'

'The sixteenth arrondissement. Not very far from the Eiffel Tower.'

'I really want to visit Paris. I've never been there.'

'Oh, Paris is so beautiful. You must go. Do you speak French, since you are from Canada?'

'It's so embarrassing, but I don't. I studied it for ten years and sadly all I can say is *Voulez-vous coucher avec moi?* and *Où sont les toilettes?*'

She laughed, and I let myself relax a little.

'You're Chloe's mum?' I said.

'Yes. Do you have a boy or a girl?'

'A girl. Kaya.' So far, so good. We had exchanged three or four sentences politely and she had laughed appropriately at my very poorly butchered kindergarten-level French. These days, it wasn't about getting butterflies in your stomach from dating any more; it was about assessing the body language and gestures of the mum facing you to determine if she was someone you could potentially have a friendship with and make a connection. This was my chance to make my move.

'Maybe we can organise a play date with the girls sometime?' I suggested politely.

Laetitia looked a little shocked and offended, recoiling at my question. 'Er, *non*. I don't think so. No, thank you.' She turned away and joined the other conversation at the other side of her, while my cheeks flushed and a wave of anxious sweat filled my armpits and surged up my neck. She was like the mouse in Alice's Wonderland who was bristling all over and really offended after

Alice spoke to him in French. What had I said to offend her?

This play date expedition was not proving successful. Chloe's mum had looked at me like I was from Mars, Anastasia's mum was "unavailable" today, as dictated by her PA, and it didn't seem like Kelly's daughter had any time for play dates.

After the coffee morning came to an end, I was surprised to see Kelly walking towards me.

'Hi. Sophie, right?' She gave me a small smile, taking my hand and shaking it in a manner that a professional handshake analyser would describe as "firm but not fully engaged". She looked at me intently, like she was discovering a new species of bird.

'Yes, I'm Sophie. We met once before outside the nursery gates.'

'Oh yes, that's right. Welcome to Cherry Blossoms. I've been meaning to speak to you since you're one of the new mums but the beginning of the school year is *so* hectic. Feel free to ask me any questions.' Kelly seemed professional rather than friendly but it gave me enough of a boost to ask her about a play date, even though I was preparing myself for a negative answer.

'You also have a daughter, Olivia? I think she's the same age as Kaya. I was wondering whether you wanted to try to organise a play date sometime? Miss Katie suggested it. We've just moved here and Kaya is rather shy and it would be really nice for her to meet other children in a setting outside the nursery.'

'Sophie, darling, I'm sorry but Olivia is really too busy.' Her forehead wrinkled ever so slightly. 'And anyway, she only wants play dates with Caroline.' Kelly's pretty face kept smiling, but her eyes were emotionless and hard. I was stunned, trying to process what she had just told me. Did she really tell me that her three-year-old daughter already discriminated against her play dates? Or did Kelly just not want to do a play date with me and Kaya? I couldn't actually believe that Olivia already had play date preferences, and even if she did, wasn't it up to her mother to try to teach her to be inclusive and kind rather than exclusive and rejecting? That "mother's guilt-and-failure voice" in my head came back and told me, "See, you are

53

a failure – you can't even organise a simple play date!"

'Oh. OK. Bye.' I was officially tongue-tied and didn't really know what to say, and quickly hurried off in the opposite direction, embarrassed, my cheeks burning and tears stinging my eyes.

'I'm sure you're imagining things, Sophie,' Michael said that night when I told him about the coffee morning. We were sitting over a soggy dinner of overcooked, salty broccoli, carrots and steak that I had made in a hurry when I heard Michael was going to make it home for dinner that night. It was so rare that he came home for dinner these days that I had rushed to slip out of my sweatshirt and sweatpants and put on a nice dress shirt and jeans for him. By the time I got back to the kitchen, the vegetables had boiled over and the steak was as thick and chewy as a leather shoe sole.

'I couldn't even get a single play date, Michael! I was actually rejected by two mums. This is like in middle school when I tried to become friends with the popular girls and they told me I looked more like the beast than the beauty in *Beauty and the Beast* because of my crazy hair, except now it's happening to me at Kaya's nursery! It's like a popularity contest that I am losing. In fact, I'm coming in last place right now.'

'You can't let two women make you feel this way. You don't even know them, and they don't know you.' He shrugged his shoulders, fully engrossed in his food, politely pretending that he was actually enjoying it.

'And the other ones barely spoke to me. They were too busy looking up to Kelly or talking about their children's over-scheduled lives.' I fidgeted with my jeans, which felt too tight. I wished I could get back into my sweatpants and sweatshirt. 'It feels like instead of the scarlet letter, I've got "loser mum" tattooed on my forehead. They all stay away from me like I'm a leper.'

'So don't pay attention to any of them. You can't put so much value on what these mums think. Kaya will be fine.' He continued chewing his steak, slowly and deliberately, not really concerned with what I had just told him.

'But she's becoming more and more introverted by the day, and I'm worried about her. I've tried playgroups but she won't go, and she screams bloody murder when I suggest the playground. And you know what Miss Katie, her teacher, said: she told me to organise play dates for her to settle into the nursery.'

'OK. Then try organising some more play dates,' he said, seemingly uninterested, as if he was hearing what I was saying but wasn't really listening.

'Michael! Have you listened to anything I've just said? No one seems to want to do any play dates with us and I've had enough self-esteem bashing for a while.'

'What am I supposed to do? I'm trying to help but you keep putting down everything I say.' He put his hand through his long, ruffled brown hair, which he did when he was stressed. Like all men, he saw a problem and found a solution, but he was missing the female gene that close female friends had of listening and empathising.

'I just want you to listen. Sometimes there are no right solutions. So please just be supportive.'

'I am supportive.'

'But you're never home. We've moved halfway across the world for you, and you come home late at night while I'm left alone all day to take care of Kaya. I have no friends, no one to talk to and you're not even there. I'm lonely, and I feel like a complete outsider here.' I shook my head and spoke more softly. 'I've tried looking for a job and I haven't received a single response. I sent out over fifteen CVs and I didn't even get one interview! We keep moving for your job and each time I have to leave a job I love!' I started to spill my tears into my overcooked brown, leathery meat and my sorry-looking vegetables, adding more salt and water to them that they didn't need. This dinner was officially over for me.

'But you don't even need to work any more. Why are you stressing over job applications?'

'I've already told you that I want to work,' I said, feeling like he wasn't taking my job search seriously at all. 'I can't stay at home and wait for you all day.'

'Sophie-Bee.' He came around to my chair and hugged me. His strong muscles held me tight, in an envelope of love and comfort, which just made the crying worse. 'I love you and we will get through this. I promise,' he said.

'And that mum, Kelly, is just so awful,' I continued through my tears. 'I don't even know what to do about her. She makes me feel so small, so insignificant. I might as well not be alive to her.'

After ten minutes of intense sobbing, the sniffles started to subside, leaving me with puffy, red eyes and a nose brighter than Rudolph's.

'Are you sure you still love me?' I looked into his chocolate-brown eyes, feeling more insecure than I had felt in a long time, needing his reassurance.

'You're the most beautiful woman in the world to me, big nose and all.' He kissed my swollen nose and took my hand, stroking it soothingly.

'Wait until you see Francesca, the ex-model in our class, I think she will change your mind. She could turn a gay man straight. As a matter of fact, I'd rather you never did a pick-up or drop-off at our class. You are officially banned from Cherry Blossoms.' I made a cross sign with my two index fingers, and Michael laughed while I broke into a very slight smile.

'The only woman I care about is right here in front of me. I know it hasn't been easy with my late hours. But the project is going full speed and I have hundreds of people depending on me. It's a big responsibility.'

I knew he was right and that I sounded silly, worrying about a few mothers at nursery, but the emotions had all caught up to me. I knew I was being irrational but being alone all day was doing that to me. I had to get myself together and get a grip. I breathed in deeply and wiped my remaining tears away.

'I know. I'm sorry, Michael. It's not your fault. It's just that I feel homesick and everything seems to be against me.'

'Look, it's only been a few weeks since Kaya started nursery. Give it time. I am sure things will get better.'

*

The next day the gloom returned when I remembered the shocked look on Laetitia's face and Kelly's rejection. In a panic, I called Edward as soon as I had dropped Kaya at nursery and had a few hours to myself in the flat. I started cleaning the flat vigorously, something I did when I felt tense, while talking to him on the phone. It was one skill I had learned as a mother: phone multitasking. I wasn't one to do nothing while on the phone; it was always possible to be doing something useful while holding your phone at the perfect angle between your ear and your shoulder.

'Edward, it's Sophie Bennett.'

'Oh, hello, Mrs Bennett, it's lovely to hear from you. How is Cherry Blossoms treating you?'

'Cherry Blossoms isn't for me.' I scrubbed the dining room table with Pledge, on the same spot, over and over again.

'Mrs Bennett, now what's wrong with Cherry Blossoms?'

'It's just…' I didn't know how to articulate how I felt, feeling like a complete idiot telling him that I couldn't find anyone to have a play date with Kaya, and how I felt like a complete outsider, but I had no choice. 'The mums don't seem that friendly to me. I just don't feel like I have that much in common with them.' I moved to another spot and scrubbed some more, over and over again.

'But you're American – there are lots of Americans at Cherry Blossoms.'

'Edward, I'm Canadian! I like trees, forests, lakes and a bit of maple syrup on my pancakes. I wear sweatpants and sweatshirts at home instead of Ralph Lauren or Chanel, and I don't look like Claudia Schiffer. I don't own a labelled bag or a multi-carat diamond ring! I'm the *opposite* of a Cherry Blossoms mum!' I spoke louder than I wanted to, and that's when it all came out, my tears spilling out in unglorified dignity. Even though Edward frustrated and irritated me mostly, I also felt strangely dependent on him, like a harmless father figure one went to for advice.

'Oh, I'm so sorry, Mrs Bennett. When you came into the office, you were articulate and looked very polished, and I thought it would suit you wonderfully. And then you really wanted to have outside space. Cherry Blossoms is the only place with this kind of outside space.'

I tried to remember that day, and recalled that we had gone to a Michelin-starred restaurant to meet Michael's boss after the nursery visits, and I had dressed appropriately in the black dress I used for interviews and a string of pearls my grandmother had left me after her death. I had felt overdressed for the nursery meeting but it finally made sense that Edward had thought we were looking for a fancy, gleaming nursery like the pearls I had been wearing.

'I'm sure it is a wonderful nursery, Edward. I just don't know if we – I – really fit in.'

'I would suggest that you give it some time – there are plenty of different mothers at the nursery who come from varied backgrounds. Perhaps a little tolerance and open-mindedness would be advisable. And perhaps adjusting yourself and your expectations may be wise?'

All the cryptic wording was just making my head spin. What was he trying to say? That I wasn't open-minded or tolerant enough? I wanted to tell him that it was the other mothers who needed to be more open-minded and tolerant, but I didn't think he would understand.

'Do you have any problems with the nursery itself?' he continued, changing subjects adroitly.

'No.' I tried to think of any problems I had with the actual nursery, but couldn't find any. He was making me realise a good point: I loved the nursery, just not its mums. 'Kaya's teacher, Miss Katie, seems really good, and Kaya seems to really like Cherry Blossoms even though she's shy. But I can't seem to find anyone to have a play date with her.'

'Have you tried asking around?'

'The three girls Miss Katie suggested were unavailable. The first one has a French mum who looked at me like I was a two-headed monster when I asked her. The next was an American who told me her daughter only does play dates with one girl in the class, and the third Russian mum I never see and only communicates through her personal assistant.' I tried to restrain my frustration, but it came pouring out. This was turning into a therapy session with Dr Edward Calthorpe-Huntington. All I needed was a couch to lie on, and for him to sit behind me cross-legged with a far-off stare, asking me, 'What do *you* think went wrong?'

'Oh, Mrs Bennett, I wouldn't worry too much about it. Firstly, French mums don't do play dates. It's not really part of their culture. The American one sounds like you are better off without her anyway, so she is doing you a favour. And why don't you email the personal assistant and then you might get an answer, but don't take it personally if you don't hear from her. I am sure there are other lovely girls in the class for your daughter.'

'I don't know if I can handle any more rejection,' I told him honestly.

'You've only been there for four weeks. It would be very, very hard to find a new nursery at this point in the term and you may be surprised…it could be that you change your mind soon enough. Cherry Blossoms is one of the finest nurseries and it would be a shame for you to walk away from it because of two unfortunate incidents. I highly encourage you to stick with it. If after this term you are still not happy, then we can look into other nurseries.'

He was right. I needed to give it more time. I wasn't going to let a few negative experiences with a few mums bring me down.

'OK, let's give it until Christmas,' I agreed. He was the "nursery guru", after all.

Chapter Seven

Castles, Queens and Housekeepers

The following day, I began an email to Irina Dimitrov's personal assistant, whose address was provided on the class list. The Dimitrovs were so private that one had to go through a first gate of privacy to communicate with them: the personal assistant.

The PA to the super-rich was "one of those positions created to benefit the super-rich and provide jobs for well-to-do posh girls out of so-and-so school," I had overheard one mother gossiping to another at the school gates. This was beyond the realm of my reality and when I wrote to the PA, I wasn't sure whether I was meant to be chummy, friendly or professional with her. I had never met Irina or the PA, but Miss Katie and Edward had encouraged me to initiate communication, so it was worth a try. At this point, I had nothing to lose.

To: Emily Stone
From: Sophie Bennett
Sent: October 03 2016, 15:30
Subject: Play date

Dear Emily,
This is Kaya Bennett's mother from the Lion Cubs class at Cherry

Blossoms Nursery. I was wondering whether Anastasia would like to do a play date with my daughter Kaya some day? Happy to have Anastasia over here or to bring Kaya to her house.
Best wishes,
Sophie Bennett

After three days of "will-they-won't-they-reply?", I received a warm and apologetic email from Emily:

To: Sophie Bennett
From: Emily Stone
Sent: October 06 2016, 18:30
Subject: Re: Play date

Dear Mrs Bennett,
Sorry for the late reply and thank you for the email. Yes, of course Anastasia would love a play date. Why don't you bring Kaya to Anastasia's house, 115 Kensington Palace Gardens, on Saturday at 10am?
Best wishes,
Emily Stone, PA to Irina Dimitrov

My heart skipped a beat when I opened the email and read those welcome words. I had finally arranged a play date! I was beaming from ear to ear. And not just with anybody – with Irina Dimitrov's daughter! Here I am, a capable and effective mother, actually able to arrange a play date! I was thinking to myself, and then stopped my thoughts in their tracks. If anyone were in my head, they would think I was absolutely loony tunes getting this excited over a play date. It was ridiculous. Sometimes I felt as if London was turning me into a completely crazy person. Still, I quickly wrote Edward a text to tell him:

Got a play date with Anastasia's personal assistant. Well, with Anastasia, rather. Looking forward to it. Thanks for your advice.
Sophie.

This was what I was reduced to, two play date rejections later, feeling isolated and lonely in a new country, with new rules, game plans and customs that were harder to decipher than the rules of cricket, turning me into an absolute nutcase.

Of course, there was the mother's guilt that loomed over me every day because Kaya's behaviour hadn't improved much. She often had bouts of uncontrollable crying for no reason on top of other extreme three-year-old behaviour, Jackson Pollocking our kitchen with apple sauce, bolognese sauce and yogurt, murderous screams that kept our neighbours up all night, and demolishing anything that was remotely breakable that she could get her hands on: computers, telephones, tablets and remotes. We had to build a locked storage cupboard especially for (or against) her, with a sign that read, "Breakables: Beware of Small Children".

Despite her behaviour, Kaya, in my mind, could do no (real) wrong; she was absolutely the most gorgeous, beautiful, inspiring baby I had ever seen when she was born, and I was completely in love and smitten the moment I saw her. I was convinced that there was a baby hormone that was only released once you laid eyes on that innocent, helpless, strange creature lying in the crook of your arm, which produced an intense, overwhelming, all-encompassing love that caught hold of you and never let you go.

This hormone could also turn you from a rational, sane human being into an irrational, insane being, full of anxiety, always on the lookout for any imminent danger. The early days of motherhood were a strange state of being, where you were full of paranoia and anxiety, always in a state of fear that something could happen to your most prized possession, like Leonardo DiCaprio's Howard Hughes in *The Aviator*, when he is tormented by paralysing phobias.

During pregnancy, I had felt my body changing and moving in ways that I didn't think were possible, and with these changes came questions of identity and mortality. What if something happened to me? What if something happened to the baby? Who was I now that I was a mother? And how could I handle the overwhelming weight of responsibility that made me so fearful? There were moments when I didn't know who I was any more.

At the same time, when Kaya had first babbled the word, "Mama" at ten months, I thought she was the cleverest little baby in the world, as if it were as momentous as the discovery of the first Egyptian mummy. When she took her first steps back in our house in Oakville, I had been the proudest mother in the world and wanted to shout about it to the whole neighbourhood, but thankfully restrained myself, knowing that I would be called the Scary Mummy if I did.

It was there and then that I knew that I couldn't go back to work full-time; no one would care as much as I did when she built that three-block tower, or finished the wooden animal puzzle by herself, or spoke her first full sentence that didn't begin with 'No!' It was hardwired and programmed in my motherhood DNA that I needed to be there for my floppy, bouncy baby. Nothing else really mattered to me, apart from this crying little creature and our family.

But after the talk with Miss Katie, I was getting worried that Kaya wasn't quite adapting the way I had hoped and imagined. I'd hoped she would be so popular and instant best friends with all the girls in her nursery; that she would be so funny and entertaining, the other parents would laugh, point and say, 'Kaya is so funny and cute, we have to have to her over for a play date,' and that she would come in the classroom singing and dancing to *Mary Poppins* to show the others how happy and well adapted she was. But no, we don't choose our children, and we certainly can't force them to be happy-go-lucky or show ponies all the time. Kaya was who she was and I loved her all the same. I just didn't want everyone thinking that she was the odd one who didn't speak and was never invited to anything.

When I received the email from Irina Dimitrov's PA with the play date acceptance, I felt like I was on cloud nine. It was better than an actual date. It was a play date!

Saturday rolled around and I wore my black interview dress and the black handbag and black stilettos I had in my closet that I kept for job interviews and important work dinners, but that were dusted about once a year these days. Edward had said that I should try to be open-minded and adapt to their ways. I didn't know what Irina was going to be like, but I wanted to make a good impression, grateful that she was the first to accept my play date invitation. Or rather that Emily, her PA, had.

What I knew about Irina from the papers and the Internet was that she was the third (and youngest) wife of Vladimir Dimitrov, a Russian oligarch who had made his money during the privatisation of Russia in the '90s. He had made millions from selling everything from rubber duck toys to tyres and showerheads, when Russians were looking to buy anything and everything they could get their hands on. He then moved to natural gases and oil, eventually becoming politically involved until he was forced into exile in the UK by President Putin, who had felt that he had grown too big for his own good.

In London, Vladimir Dimitrov bought a fifty-million-pound mansion on Kensington Palace Gardens, renovated it – twice, because once wasn't enough – and kitted it out fully with all the mod cons you could think of (does anyone really need an elevator for their cars?). He had bought a collection of private jets, yachts, owned a car-racing team to keep him occupied, and was living the life of exile on a fifteen-billion-dollar fortune, as reported by Wikipedia.

There were rumours of attempted assassinations, which was why he moved with an entourage of bodyguards that made the American president's security detail look like a beauty-queen contest. It was thought that Putin still wanted to get rid of him, since Dimitrov had become one of his biggest critics and still held an enormous amount of power amongst the other Russian oligarchs. He was wealthy, but also very clever. Not that I actually knew any of this, but it was what the newspapers had written about him. It was as captivating reading about him as reading a Russian spy novel involving politics, arms dealers and billionaires.

Irina was his statuesque, ice-queen wife, who many thought controlled a lot of his power. She was involved in many foundations in Russia – feeding, clothing and educating the poorest provinces that weren't getting enough financial support from the government. On the other hand, she was also a glamorous wife who was seen bejewelled with hundreds of carats at any one time. She was private, but at the same time a very public figure with a lot of power.

There wasn't going to be very much we had in common, but I was willing to meet her halfway. I wasn't going to go all reverse-snobbery on her, was I? Her foundation seemed to be exemplary and well regarded by the media and the Russians. I didn't know how involved she was with her children, as it was mostly the nannies who brought Anastasia to nursery and I had only seen Irina on the first day of school, but I was as prepared as I could be for our first play date.

That Saturday, as Kaya and I arrived by taxi at Kensington Palace Gardens, we were let through a security barrage, headed by two security guards in black-and-white uniforms who let us through a red and white crash barrier gate, which opened onto a tree-lined avenue. Inside, the taxi drove to a wrought iron gated entrance, which was helmed by another two security guards. It was better protected than the White House.

One of the guards stopped and leaned over as we rolled down the window.

'Hello. We're here to see Anastasia Dimitrov,' I told him as he nodded, smile-less, and then let us through. He opened the gates and we saw Anastasia's home looming above us. It was a large house, more like a stately mansion than a city home, with a front staircase leading to its grand main door, flanked by four Doric columns, which were at least ten feet high. The mansion stood at least five storeys high and was protected by four towers at each of its corners.

'Mummy, does Anastasia live in a castle?' Kaya asked me as she looked at the mansion with wonder. She was right. It did look like a castle.

'Uhm. Kind of,' I answered, not quite sure how to answer. It was the biggest house I had ever seen, and I tried to hide how awestruck I was.

'She's like Princess Sofia!' Kaya said to me, clearly impressed.

We got out of the taxi and climbed up the stairs, and before I even rang the doorbell, a butler who seemed to have stepped out of an episode of *Downton Abbey* opened the door. He ushered us inside the house, which opened onto a large inner lobby, more than twice the size of our flat, with shiny, smooth marble floors, a Versailles-style hall of mirrors, and a giant chandelier overhead with at least a million dangling crystals, which reflected rainbow-coloured light rays through their prisms. It felt like I was visiting a museum rather than entering someone's home. I was blown away by how grandiose it was.

The butler walked us through a hall on the right and past four or five doors until we reached the end of the hallway, and led us into a sitting room, next to a sweeping staircase. One of Anastasia's nannies, Katrina, whom I had met at the nursery, appeared with Anastasia. Anastasia seemed thrilled to see a friendly child's face amidst this austere, adult environment.

'Hello, Mrs Bennett. Thank you for coming.' Katrina spoke with a strong Russian accent.

'Hi, Katrina, thanks for having us over.' I didn't see Irina, and it wasn't apparent what was meant to happen next. 'Is Mrs Dimitrov here?' I asked.

'I don't know, Mrs Bennett. Please wait here, I will find out. Just a minute. I will take the girls to the playroom and will come back.' She took the girls away down another hallway and I noticed that Anastasia and Kaya were both pleased to see each other, shyly chatting and discussing what princess outfits they would wear for the play date.

I took a seat in a golden leaf-patterned, upholstered couch by the window that had a view onto the tree-lined street and of another mega-mansion across the street, and waited. And waited some more. I saw an army of Filipina women coming up and down the staircase and in and out of the hallway, like an active ant colony at work. I had noticed at drop-offs and pick-ups that Anastasia had multiple nannies: she had a Russian nanny, an English one and a Filipina one.

The sitting room where I was waiting had no personal items, no him-and-her photographs, or baby photos of Anastasia. There was a coffee table with a few generic coffee table books, perhaps displayed by the PA. It was impersonal and soulless and could have been mistaken for a hotel lobby.

Eventually, about ten minutes later, a matronly Filipina entered the room, clipboard in hand, stared at me up and down and without as much as a hello, asked, 'Do you have any experience cleaning or working with children?'

'No…' I was baffled; why was she asking me this question?

She cut me off abruptly and continued her questioning. 'Are you here for the housekeeper interview?'

'No, I'm Kaya's mother. I'm here for a play date with Anastasia. I am waiting for Mrs Dimitrov,' I said, using the most assertive voice I could muster.

Without another word, she turned around on her heels, stormed out of the room and left me hanging there, without an explanation or apology. My cheeks flushed with epic embarrassment. I realised that this woman was probably the head of staff who was waiting for a housekeeper to interview, and this was the staff's waiting room.

Two minutes later, Katrina came back.

'Sorry, Mrs Bennett. Mrs Dimitrov has gone shopping. Do you want to come down to the playroom? The girls are playing in the indoor playground.'

'Yes, of course,' I replied.

At this point, I followed Katrina like an automated robot, mortified about the mix-up, and also that I had spent so much time getting ready and researching Irina Dimitrov. I had been so naïve to think that Anastasia's mother would be present for: a) her daughter's first play date with Kaya, b) a Saturday mother-and-child afternoon, and c) to actually meet me. Given they had so much security and staff, wouldn't they want to make sure I wasn't a kidnapper or serial killer? Or perhaps this was the whole point: they didn't need to meet me because I was firmly locked inside this "castle" and couldn't get out, even if I wanted to.

As Katrina led me through a labyrinth of stairs, hallways and rooms, my head was spinning from the whole situation. I was locked up in a giant maze with towers, bodyguards and crystal chandeliers that probably had magical powers. I barely noticed the mega-basement that would make Kelly salivate with its indoor swimming pool, cinema room and spa rooms. My mind started to think of an escape route if Kaya so much as touched a strand of Anastasia's hair and we were deemed to be enemies.

When we arrived at the indoor playground, fully equipped with a slide, see-saw and soft play area, I sat down on the giant Olaf chair that was facing the *Frozen*-themed slide and the white icicles hanging from the ceiling. Although I was comforted by Kaya's squeals of delight as she slid down the slide with Anastasia close behind, both in full princess outfits, I hid my deep embarrassment in front of Anastasia's nannies, who chatted animatedly between themselves. Feeling so uncomfortable on my own, I moved to sit next to them. They looked surprised, as if this was the first time a non-staff member had ever spoken to them.

'Can I get you anything, Mrs Bennett?' Katrina immediately asked, as if the only reason I would be speaking to her was to ask her to do something for me.

'No, no. Thanks, Katrina. I'm fine.'

There was an awkward silence and two of the three nannies got up and left the room. Even the nannies were running away from me. Only Katrina stayed behind. She was young, probably mid twenties, and strikingly pretty.

'Have you been working for the Dimitrovs for a long time?' I asked her.

'Oh no, just a few months.'

'I just thought…Anastasia seems to really like you. You seem really close.'

'Yes. Her mother is away a lot of the time so I take care of Anastasia all day and all night. This morning she told me how excited she was about having Kaya over for a play date. This is Anastasia's first play date. She's never had one before.'

'She's never had a play date?' I tempered my voice so that I didn't sound so shocked. We weren't the only ones without play dates.

'No, her parents have never organised any. They are very busy.'

So maybe it wasn't quite the same, but nonetheless, I felt sorry for Anastasia, who never had a play date because her mother was too busy to organise any.

'She is always around adults and has never been around many other children.'

'Doesn't she get lonely?' I asked, bewildered.

'Anastasia has two other nannies apart from me, so I don't think so. There is always someone with her. Her parents live between Moscow and London so someone needs to look after her when they are away.'

'They live in Moscow?' I asked, now in complete disbelief.

'Yes, they live between Moscow and London.'

'So why doesn't the whole family live in Moscow? Anastasia would be better off living with her parents.' I bit my tongue then, knowing that I was already judging Irina without having even met her.

'They think that the education is much better in London. The children live in London most of the time, and then Anastasia goes to Russia during the holidays.'

I felt so sorry for Anastasia. She was being raised by nannies instead of her own parents. I couldn't start to understand how a parent could leave their child behind while they lived in another country. Maybe that was the price you paid to be a billionaire. Or perhaps it was a cultural difference. It sounded like the Dimitrovs still adhered to old-school family rules, where the children were seen and not heard.

After a few hours at Anastasia's house, I brought Kaya home, although Anastasia had begged for us to stay for dinner. I thanked Katrina and, as we were sitting in the taxi on the way home, I thought about the absurd life Anastasia was living and then remembered my embarrassment at being mistaken for a housekeeper. I may have managed to get a play date but I would always be an outsider.

Chapter Eight

Blogo...the Ring

'I went to my first play date yesterday and one of the many house-keepers thought I was there for a housekeeper interview!' I was finally speaking to Emma, my best friend from Canada, over the phone. We had exchanged a few emails, but this was the first proper conversation we had had since my arrival in London. I had been craving the security and familiarity of an old friend's voice that allowed me to be myself.

It was Sunday night and Michael was giving Kaya a bath. I could hear her high-pitched laughs and giggles against a background of splishing and splashing from the bathroom. He loved to give her her baths on the weekends because he had missed her bath time and dinner routine every weeknight since our arrival in London.

'Sophie! That is crazy! You're living the celebrity life with supermodels and billionaires in London! It's hilarious! I can't feel that sorry for you, can I?' Emma said.

'I don't think being mistaken for a housekeeper at an interview is that hilarious. Well, maybe it is. Not that there is anything wrong with being a housekeeper, but this represents exactly how they see me. Not one of them. It was humiliating! After they took Kaya to their giant underground playroom, I was brought into the staff quarters while I waited, no one really sure what to do with me. Then someone came in – probably their head of staff – and started to ask me about my past experience cleaning and working with children. Mortifying.'

'Sophie, I'm so sorry this happened to you. I'm sure you will laugh about it one day.' She chuckled. 'And the mums like that Kelly sound like real characters. You should write a blog about it. It would entertain a lot of people, I'm sure.'

'A blog? Why would I start a blog?'

'For one, so I can keep up with your stories, and also for you to make some virtual friends if you can't find some IRL. You'd be amazed at how much support you can get from the Internet these days.'

'Really?'

'Think about it. It's super easy. Just go on wordpress.com and sign up with a domain name.'

'And then what?'

'Then you start writing.'

'About what?'

'Anything. About how you're feeling. What's happening.' She paused. 'There's an entire world of mummy bloggers out there. You're not alone. It's a great community and source of support. And you never know, you could make real friends through the blog. A lot of people make friends through the Internet these days. Or you can use it as a way to vent. It's also a great way to keep in touch with me and tell me what you've been up to.'

'I guess I could give it a try. Do you have one?'

'No, but I follow a bunch of mums who write regularly. Some of them are really good writers. *You're* a really good writer – I mean, you wrote for a living, writing grants. You should try it. Maybe it could help.'

'I guess so. Thanks, Emma. At this point, I don't think I have anything to lose. I can't even find a job.'

'Really?'

'I've sent out a bunch of CVs and I haven't had any responses.

There aren't that many part-time jobs to start with, and I think it's also because I have so many holes in my CV between the move to Oakville and then to London.'

'What about working full-time?'

'I can't right now, especially with Kaya – she's found moving to London really difficult. I've got to be there for her.' I could hear my voice cracking as I said those last words. I couldn't hide how I was feeling.

'Hey, listen, motherhood's not easy – it can be lonely, isolating, and on top of it, you've just moved to a foreign land full of ice queens, witches, castles and two-headed dragons like Kelly,' Emma replied.

I laughed out loud, something I realised I hadn't done since I had arrived in London. Emma always had a way of making me feel better.

'I know. I've been feeling so lost and lonely.'

'You haven't met a single mother you could relate to?'

'No. I've tried to take Kaya to playgrounds to meet other children but she never wants to go and we fight every time I try to take her to a playgroup or class. And when we do go, she is so shy that she won't leave me alone for one second.' I paused. 'And I feel so intimidated by the mums at the nursery. They're like a different species to me. I don't know what to say to them and I don't think they could care less about me and my existence.' I sighed. 'I feel invisible when I'm with them,' I admitted to her. 'But Michael keeps telling me that they can't all be like this and that I'll eventually find someone that I get along with.'

'I reckon he's right. You've got to persevere. I know you're having a hard time now, but it's bound to get better. And if not, you can always come home. You'll always have a place in Oakville.'

'Thanks, Em. I can't tell you how much talking to you has cheered me up. I'm sure I will meet some friends soon. And maybe I will try this new blog thing.'

I sat in one of the heavy, worn leather armchairs at the back of Pain et Chocolat the next morning after dropping off Kaya at Cherry Blossoms. The smells of freshly baked dairy-free, gluten-free croissants and organic, ethically sourced Colombian coffee beans filled the air. Outside, the autumn air grew colder and wetter by the day. The café was filled with mothers with their babies in their strollers, chattering away, friends catching up over a coffee, and men reading their *Times* newspapers, staying dry away from the blustery winds and rains.

My coffee had gone cold and I sat staring at my laptop. It was about ten years old, and you could tell. It was originally Michael's, but when he had received a new laptop through work, he had handed it down to me. The screen had a small crack in the lower left corner and the keyboard was filled with crumbs and dust that even a computer vacuum couldn't get rid of. The letter H was wobbly and wonky and only typed every other time you pressed it. It made my emails seem like they were written by a four-year-old: "I am Sopie, I am thirty-tree years old".

I was engrossed in an article about the "blogosphere". Who even came up with that name? There was no sphere involved and Blogo sounded like a name out of *The Lord of the Rings*. 'Blogo, find the ring…' sounded just about right. I didn't know much about blogs, apart from them being someone's private online diary describing what toothpaste they used that morning (Colgate or Crest) and whether they ate Coco Pops or Cheerios for breakfast.

But when I researched 'blogs' and 'mums' I fell upon hundreds of blogs featuring mothers writing about the trials and tribulations of motherhood, some funny, some sad, some filled with mordant wit. I had occasionally stumbled upon a mum-blog, but hadn't realised the extent of the world of mummy blogs. For many, the common thread was that they wanted a community to share their thoughts, their highs and their lows, and somewhere to look for and give support.

There were many blogs on postnatal depression written by mothers who wrote about their feelings of unhappiness, instead of hiding them and perpetuating the taboo. There were a few blogs on being the perfect mother, but there were many more blogs on being an imperfect mother; the "imperfect mother who doesn't have her shit together most of the time and is just winging it the best way she can". That sounded familiar. And all of a sudden, I wanted to be a part of this community. I wanted to be one of them. I was ready to start my blog.

I browsed the Internet and found the WordPress website, the one that Emma had mentioned. First, I had to come up with a name for my blog. Lonelymom? I mean, Lonelymum? Too sad. Loopymum? Too crazy. Canadianmum? Too Canadian. Then I found the perfect name that summed up how I felt: Beta Mum. I was a Beta Mum lost in a sea of Alpha Mums.

I then had to create an email in order to sign up for WordPress. When I created my thebetamum@outlook.com email account and received the congratulatory banner, I felt a shiver of excitement and freedom. This was the first step towards creating my new self, my new identity in Cyber World. I could be whoever I wanted to be. Then came the time to choose a theme for my blog, register my domain name and five minutes later, presto! I had a blog to my name: www.thebetamum.com. For the first time in a long time, I was doing something that wasn't for: a) my daughter, b) my husband, c) my (now ex-) boss, or d) anyone else but me.

Now that I had accomplished creating a blog – which was already a very exciting personal accomplishment in my opinion – I had to start writing. I had seen other blogs which suggested that I should write an "About Me" section, to explain who I was and why I decided to write my blog. I sat looking outside while the October rain fell down, and thought about the picture-perfect mums and dads dropping off and picking up their children from nursery.

I began typing and soon became lost in my writing, trying to make sense of why I was writing and who I was. It was like I could write down everything I really thought but couldn't say out loud. The words and thoughts came pouring out. I needed to write. I needed to understand myself better, who I was and what I was doing in my little corner of the world. And the more I wrote, the more I knew that this was something I was meant to do.

The Beta Mum
About Me

On my first day of high school, I remember watching a sea of students in the cafeteria dispersed around various tables when it dawned on me that I had no one to sit with. I didn't know anyone, whereas most of the other kids seemed to know each other since kindergarten. As I walked through the rows of tables, I peered around to see whether anyone looked at me encouragingly, willing me to sit down with them, but no one did. On the contrary, they looked at me with stifled laughter. I knew my braces often locked in remains of my Cheerios breakfast for days, and that my hair was as untameable as Einstein's, but I didn't think it would come to this.

Later, I discovered that I had toilet paper stuck to my shoe that I had been dragging around all day – needless to say I was called TPG, "toilet paper girl", for months. But that first day, as I sat alone, by myself, at the last empty table, I had never felt more like an outcast, and never thought it could ever get any worse.

Until today. But now, instead of being excluded by the popular girls, I am excluded by the Alpha Mums.

Taking my daughter for her first day of nursery in Alpha-Land (a place where everyone is glamorous, rich, beautiful and super skinny, and I mean everyone), the same feelings of being an outsider came rushing back: no one to talk to, no friends, and being invisible.

But this was worse, because I had my daughter by my side to witness it all.

I am a thirty-something mum of one gorgeous girl, who I will call Posey, and wife to a wonderful husband I will call Mac. Some things haven't changed: my morning hair still lasts all day and I still feel socially excluded on a daily basis, but some have: my teeth are finally brace-free and I check my shoes every time I leave the bathroom to make sure they are toilet paper-free.

I have recently arrived in Alpha-Land, but I feel like a Beta Mum because: a) My life is far from perfect, b) I feel lucky if I put the right sock on the right foot each morning, and c) I have a small (loud) inner voice that constantly tries to remind me of my guilt and failures as a mum, but I try to keep it hush-hush on most days. Usually a chocolate biscuit or a red velvet cupcake will do the trick.

I try to find laughter and humour everywhere I go and I hope to share some with you. Here are my stories and my thoughts. I hope you enjoy reading my blog.

Thanks for reading!

The Beta Mum x

Postscript: For confidentiality's sake, I will keep all names in this blog private and anonymous. I don't want a lawsuit on my hands, and I want to keep my daughter's privacy in the best way I can. This blog is purely for entertainment purposes (mostly my own), and although my posts may be based on real events, details will be changed and fictionalised.

There. I pressed "publish" and posted my first blog post. It was a strange feeling, exposing my deepest thoughts and feelings for the whole world – or no one – to read. But it was done. I had used my brain for something other than reading three-letter-word books/ singing "Twinkle, Twinkle" for the thousandth time/bouncing my child up and down to the tune of Baby & Me music classes while pretending like it was the most exciting thing to do in the world.

It was liberating, writing freely about how I was really feeling, not having to pretend that everything was all right and perfect. I felt a feeling of clarity, as if I knew what I was doing here in London. Writing down those words validated me as a person and a mother. My identity, which had been out of focus like a photographer's dirty lens, was looking like it was coming into focus.

A few hours later after I had picked up Kaya from nursery and put her down for her nap, I checked my stats page, where it showed how many visitors had come to my page, how many views I had, and how many followers had signed up to my blog. I had one of each! One view, one visitor and one follower! I was thrilled! Someone was interested enough to read my blog! I wanted to call and tell Michael. Until, that is, I realised the visitor/view/follower was none other than the Beta Mum…me.

My enthusiasm waned, but I didn't feel discouraged. I had read that you should expect to write a few blog posts before anyone even noticed you were alive. I came up with my next blog post that afternoon and published it, right before Kaya woke up from her nap and started a WWF wrestling match with me because she didn't want to go to the playground when I suggested it. (Then two seconds later, was as happy as a lark biting into the organic cookie I had bought her from Pain et Chocolat.)

The Beta Mum
Alpha-Land: You Know You've Arrived in Alpha-Land When...

1   The annual gym membership costs more than most people's average salary.

2   The mum standing next to you at the school gates not only happens to be on the front cover of Vogue magazine, but on the front of every magazine at the newspaper stand.

3   The houses you visit will one day turn into museums with audio-guided explanations of their history and art collections.

4   The mums speak so loudly they make Pavarotti sound like a dormouse.

5   You know your child's nursery is the safest because it has bodyguards outside the school gates at all times.

6   The cars here are nicer than any of the ones on Top Gear.

7   Half of the nursery children's parents have appeared in the Forbes rich list.

8   The mums look like they've just walked off a catwalk at a fashion show – and probably have.

9   The men all have entire articles written about them in the Financial Times and the Wall Street Journal.

10 Everyone's favourite game is Monopoly. But the real kind.

I read over the post at least twenty times before I clicked the "publish" button. Nervously, I scrutinised every word and wondered how it read. Did I make sense? Did I sound stupid? Yes, I probably did sound stupid. Would I get any positive comments, or mostly the heckling and trolling that I had heard could happen in the blogosphere?

When I published the post, I felt stripped bare to my soul, but at the same time a cathartic feeling washed over me. There was freedom in writing anything I wanted without accountability. I was anonymous, I thought to myself. No one knew who I was, therefore I was hidden and protected from any criticism or from reality.

Chapter Nine

The Lonely Mums Club Band

'You started a blog?' Michael looked at me teasingly.

'Why do you look surprised, Michael?' We were sitting on the chosen-for-rental couch in front of the chosen-for-rental Samsung TV in our sterilely decorated living room and had just finished an episode of *House of Cards*. I still wasn't used to our flat, but at least there was no longer a leak, only its yellowed, stained walls remaining.

'I never thought of you as the blogger type.'

'Well, it's all about new beginnings for us right now, isn't it?'

'Yes…'

'And it happens to be very easy to start.' I proudly puffed up my chest like a frigate bird trying to attract his mate – in this case, my mate being Michael.

'That's impressive, Sophie. Can I read it?' He genuinely seemed pleased for me.

'I'm not sure I'm ready for that yet. It's so silly,' I said shyly. 'And it's still very new. And I only got one view today! My own!' I had to laugh at myself.

'I can be your second view.' He smiled encouragingly.

'I'll think about it.'

'What is it about anyway?'

'Pretty much, how I moved to London and feel like a case study of what it feels like to be an outcast in this crazy nursery.'

'Sophie-Bee,' he said in a disapproving tone, 'don't be so negative.'

'OK, OK. But it's an outlet for me. It's a positive thing. I need to vent my frustrations to someone and since I have no friends to talk to here, I might as well try my luck on the Internet.'

'Good point. But be careful with what you write. You never know who's going to read it.'

'I told you, the only person who's read it is me. And maybe you, if you're lucky.'

'What do I have to do to get lucky?' He flashed his sexy smile at me, teasing me.

'I think you can come up with some good ideas.' I looked at him with my sultry I'm-so-sexy look, which probably looked more like rictus from a stroke than a sexy invitation, but you couldn't blame a girl for trying. He grabbed my hand and started stroking it gently.

'Yes, I think I could come up with a few good ideas.' He started kissing the inside of my wrist, making his way up my arm, and kissed the nape of my neck slowly.

It had been months since we had had any kind of intimacy that didn't include: a) baby food, b) interruptions from a hungry/wet/scared toddler, or c) one of us falling asleep before reaching any kind of climax. A combination of his never-ending work hours, my libido-lowering loneliness and general running-after-a-three-year-old exhaustion had stood in the way between us and a happy ending.

Instead, it had been all working/organising/settling into London and planning Kaya's days to avoid the throw-myself-down-on-the-floor-and-scream-so-I-can-get-what-I-want strategy that has been perfected by most three-year-olds.

When we first met, the early days of our relationship had included a lot of dorm-room sex marathons and eating pizzas in bed. After that, there were plenty of hormones left on both sides to keep us happily in the three-times-a-week sex group for a few years. But after we had Kaya, we skipped the once-a-week sex group and landed straight in the once-a-month group. I quickly realised that there was an inverse relationship between how many times you had sex and the number of children you had.

Over the years, our relationship barometer had tilted more towards the "partners" side rather than "lovers", and as much as I hated to admit it, there was little lust left after a day's worth of cleaning up a child's poop/pee/pea soup. We had arrived at that stage which is reached in almost all relationships where sleeping is the most appealing and attractive use of a bed.

I had met Michael so young, but once he had won me over, we had very quickly formed an ironclad bond. When he had found me after that drunken night, I had said no when he'd asked me out to the university restaurant that was frequented by most of the students, but he'd continued showing up at my dorm, unannounced and "by accident". I had been so shy that I'd preferred turning him down to the prospect of being rejected by him if the date had turned out awful. What I hadn't known was that Michael was persistent and a people-pleaser. He asked me out three times before I agreed, and I had agreed only if we went out far away from the university local, and from the nosy, prying eyes of the other students.

Our first date had been at a Greek diner far from anyone we knew. It was painted in blue and white stripes, in honour of the Greek flag, and served delicious chicken souvlaki, tzatziki, moussaka and taramasalata. The owners were first-generation Canadian-Greeks who spoke in broken English, but with warm, welcoming smiles on their faces.

'The nine stripes of the Greek flag symbolise the nine muses of art and civilisation,' I'd said to him, trying to come up with something – anything – interesting to say to distract him from my shaking hands that I was hiding under the table.

'So, how do you know so much?' he asked, smiling, trying to put me at ease.

'My parents are both high-school teachers. My father is a history teacher and my mother is a biology teacher. Our house is full of books and magazines that they read to me since I was a baby.

During dinner, my father is always running back and forth from his library with encyclopaedias, wanting to teach me about everything and anything from octopuses to space shuttles.'

'So you must be clever,' Michael teased, smiling and showing off his adorable dimples. My first-date jitters had begun to evaporate.

'Not really, but they taught me to be curious and to love learning, and to laugh in any situation. I don't think I would have survived high school otherwise.'

'What do you mean?'

'I was pretty shy in high school, and I blended in the background. So I focused on studying and also learned to make a joke out of any situation. That really helped me through those terrible teenage years. What about your parents? What are they like?'

'My parents? I don't think my parents would have noticed if I had straight As or Ds and Fs. They divorced when I was seven after my father lost his job. But even before, they fought constantly. They just argued all the time over nothing. I don't think they were ever meant to be together. Even when I became president of my high school, I don't think they really noticed.'

'That must have been pretty tough.'

'Yeah. It was,' he said, playing with his moussaka. 'They were never that involved with me. I always tried to please them but it didn't help. I had to learn to be independent really young. I guess I can thank them for that. Your parents sound pretty great though.'

'Yeah, they're pretty great. But sometimes, they get over-involved. They want to know every single detail of my life. And when you're a teenager struggling to make friends, your parents are the last people you want to talk to.'

'I can't imagine you struggling to make friends. You're a lot of fun. And smart. And very pretty.' He leaned over and gently kissed me across the table. That's when I knew that he was actually the sweetest man I had ever met, and not just sweet-smelling.

'Thanks.' I blushed. 'I guess I still see myself as an awkward, lonely teenager. Even though I know I'm not that person any more, I sometimes forget.'

'You're really funny too, you know.'

'Really?'

'You made me laugh all night the first time we met. That's why I really wanted to find you the next day.'

'Well, that was mostly the alcohol talking.'

'It's still you. And you're not like the other girls who only care about make-up, jocks and going out to parties. You actually really care. About people and what's around you. I really like that.' He looked at me in a way I had never seen anyone look at me before. I never wanted that moment to end.

After that night, I had been scared that Michael was never going to call me again, but it wasn't so. He'd called me every day after that, until I'd broken down my barriers and let him in. I'd always worried that one day he would wake up and realise that it was a big mistake and I wasn't the girl for him, but that day never came. Instead, a few years out of university, he'd proposed on Lake O'Hara on a clear, cool summer's day when the sky and the lake met as if they were one, surrounded by the Canadian Rockies and subalpine fir trees as witnesses.

But now, we had been together for so long that it was easy to take each other for granted, and to become short-tempered at each other's flaws. Like many couples, it was easy to overlook each other's good qualities and fixate on our weaknesses. He wasn't always the most romantic of men, mostly because he didn't know how to be romantic and had never seen it from his parents but I knew his strengths lay in his loyalty, reliability and honesty, although lately it felt that these qualities were directed towards his work rather than me.

It was time to re-prioritise our lives, I told myself. Even if it meant more planning and organising towards a goal of getting out of the sex-once-a-month group and into the once-a-week group. These were baby steps, but at least they were steps.

I grabbed him and we walked (ran) into our bedroom and closed the door. Right then, I felt a renewed energy and empowerment from starting the blog. I wouldn't go down without a fight.

*

The next day I noticed a comment underneath my "About Me" blog post:

> I totally know about the imperfect life and the guilty mum inner voice! Congrats on starting a blog! Slum Mum.

I replied:

> Thanks, Slum Mum, I appreciate your comment and encouragement! The Beta Mum.

Elated, I checked my blog's stats page: I'd had twenty-eight views on my "Alpha-Land" post, with a map of the world showing where my views were coming from: Australia, the United States, France, Korea and Brazil. A sense of exhilaration and excitement filled me, which came from strangers connecting with me and my words over oceans and mountains. I was being read and heard over five continents. OK, it was far away from the million views that the popular bloggers got per month, but to me it was enough encouragement to write another post.

The Beta Mum
Part 1: You Know You're an Alpha Mum When...

1   As a new mum, you tell everyone in your antenatal group that your child was the first to sit up/crawl/walk.

2   Your child started reading the alphabet by the age of two, with the help of an ex-nursery school teacher/paediatric nurse/PhD literary student/nanny who has been practising letters and numbers since the age of one.

3   Your child was seen swimming, armband-free, by the age of two and a half, with the help of an Olympic medallist swimming instructor.

4   Your child can translate for you when you need to tell your cleaning lady that the washing needs to be done.

5   Your child played Beethoven's "Fifth Symphony" by the age of four, read Voltaire by the age of five and is at Suzuki level 300 in violin training.

6   You are convinced your child is a genius. And you tell all your friends about their off-the-charts reading level.

7   You fit into a size-two dress. Two weeks after giving birth to twins.

8   You wear five-inch Christian Louboutin heels for the school run, even though you're only going back home after.

9   You have a collection of handbags called Birkin, Kelly or Alexa, which are occasionally used to store dummies, wet wipes and Barbie dolls.

10 Your house has appeared in various house and design magazines, not because you submitted your photos, but because they begged you to include your photos.

As I wrote this last blog, I started chuckling at myself and at what I had written. I was having fun writing about the stereotypical Alpha Mums. My first two blogs had been stilted, self-conscious and awkward, but this post felt as if I had let go of my inhibitions and I was finally finding my "voice" in cyberspace. It was also a way of protecting myself against the painful rejections that had kept coming at me.

Half an hour later, I received an email from Ozzie Mum.

To: The Beta Mum
From: Ozzie Mum
Sent: October 03 2016, 16:00
Subject: Hello

Hi Beta Mum,

I love your blog! I completely relate to it and I live in Australia! We have plenty of competitive mums here, and I have struggled to fit in, just like you. You're not alone. It will get better, or at least you will get used to it. Have you read Liane Moriarty's Little Big Lies? If you haven't, you should... It should make you feel a little better. Keep writing and I will keep reading.

Your friend,

Ozzie Mum

I quickly replied.

To: Ozzie Mum

From: The Beta Mum

Sent: October 03 2016, 11:00

Subject: Re:

Thank you, Ozzie Mum! It does make me feel better that I am not alone. I never thought that Australians were also competitive. I always thought you were laid-back and super-relaxed. So much for stereotypes! And I will keep writing if you will keep reading. ☺

The Beta Mum x

The next day, I walked to the nursery in high spirits. Even if I hadn't managed to meet a single IRL friend, I had made two virtual acquaintances, Ozzie Mum and Slum Mum. We had bantered over emails and comments and they had been friendly and responsive. Instead of feeling sorry for myself (I had been having quite a few solo pity-parties recently), I felt close to these people, even though I didn't know what they looked like, how they sounded or where they came from, but only how they seemed from reading their words, which in turn validated my own.

The "Alpha Mums" post had generated forty-eight views from all over the world; the map of the world on my stats page had lit up in an array of rainbow colours, my views glowing from Australia, the USA, Brazil, China and Turkey. I imagined who these people were and what they were doing. Mothers between school runs, students researching mother groups, or techies browsing the Internet in pyjamas over a bowl of cereal. Whatever they did and whoever they were, they had landed on my blog, interested enough to read on. Like neurons connecting to one another, my blogs connected with others over forests, oceans, mountains and rivers. It was exhilarating. I pushed Kaya's stroller, humming to her and smiling to myself, my thoughts lost in cyberspace.

But as soon as I arrived at the nursery gates, I felt a deep, dark dread in the pit of my stomach when I saw that the gates were closed. Occasionally the nursery gates would open late, but everyone tolerated it because they loved Cherry Blossoms and Mrs Jones so much. But it meant extending the drop-off time. Nursery drop-offs and pick-ups had become my most dreaded moments of my day since I had failed to connect with any of the mothers. Usually, it was an in-and-out, military stealth mission: I dropped Kaya off and got out, or I grabbed her and left. When the school gates were closed, this meant only one thing: standing around with no one to talk to while the other mothers discussed their plans, play dates and Pilates sessions.

Often, I felt too anxious or shy to approach any of the mothers, worried that I would sound stupid, or be ignored, like the first time I tried to approach Kelly, who looked too bored to speak to me. I didn't have holidays to discuss, fashion tips to exchange or personal trainers to meet. Trying to make eye contact, say hello and start a conversation sapped so much of my energy that I had given up early on.

I shook off that anxious feeling and replaced it with the renewed self-confidence from the blog and the past forty-eight hours. It gave me an extra energy boost, leaving me ready to tackle anything or anyone. Today would be the day that I was going to say my hellos to all the nursery mums I recognised, just to see what would happen. First, I saw Francesca, the gorgeous Italian supermodel, and put a big smile on my face and introduced myself.

'Hi, I'm Sophie. Our children are in the same class.'

'Oh, really?' she said, giving me a look like she wasn't quite sure what to make of me.

'Lion Cubs? We were at the coffee morning together.'

'Ah yes, I was there, I remember you,' she acknowledged, meeting my eye, but her gaze quickly moved on, scanning the crowd to see if there was someone else she would rather speak to. It was obvious. She wanted someone else to speak to, rather than me, the out-of-town, plain-Jane mother. And then she found her. Alice Denham, her gorgeous supermodel best friend, who she'd told everyone about at the coffee morning.

'Excuse me. I need to talk to Alice one minute,' she said, and quickly moved away.

I attempted to say hello to Becky, but she was involved in another conversation with Poppy Sevigny-Bruce, a mother in our class who, I had learned, lived between London and the countryside. (I would only later find out that she was related to Princes William and Harry.) Becky nodded to me but I knew she was more interested in her conversation with Poppy. I could hear her say that Kelly also was thinking about starting a jewellery business, and that they should join forces.

I could see that various groups and cliques had formed at the nursery gates: the fashionistas wearing the latest trendy jumpsuits and silver-sequinned trainers discussing the British Fashion Council, the fitness fanatics talking about meeting their personal trainers at Body Beautiful at 6am, and the PTA mums discussing the various fundraising initiatives they were organising.

As I stood there on my own – yet again – with no one to talk to, I thought to myself, why did these women have the power to make me feel so much like a second-class citizen? Was I not good enough to talk to? Or did they only want to associate with those of similar or higher social standing, which I didn't happen to fit into?

All my original morning enthusiasm quickly waned and I realised I was where I started off: with no one to talk to, and with no one acknowledging me. For the past five weeks, I had stood on the sidelines of this microcosm, studying the social interactions of the Alpha Mums, feeling and being an outsider, closer to the nanny cliques than the mummy cliques. I had seen these cliques drawn together by their common interests, unwilling to let anyone else into their secret clubs. And I had enough of it. I was going to retaliate in my own way. I ran home after that drop-off and sat in front of my laptop and began to write.

The Beta Mum
The Dreaded Drop-Off in Alpha-Land

It is an almost universally acknowledged truth that the school run, the drop-offs and pick-ups, are stressful, dreadful and anxiety-fuelling chores, like going to a crowded supermarket on a Saturday morning. Not enjoyable, but something that must nonetheless be done. The only difference is that the weekly shop is once a week, whereas the school run is twice a day, five days a week.

Most mothers can identify with that feeling of dread: waking up the kids, dressing them, feeding them, taking (dragging) them to school, seeing all the gossipy, cliquey Alpha Mums in a circle talking about you (at least acknowledging your existence), or ignoring you (the worst). Saying hello in passing to anyone you know, or conversely putting your head down, pretending not to have seen someone you know. Then there is the idle chit-chat about nothing at all that usually ends up in gossip, because there is nothing else to say to each other.

The school run has become a heart-racing, chest-constricting, breathless-making daily ritual that has sent me right back to childhood. It reminds me of the "popular girls" who looked at me with a lack of interest during lunch, as if I were a piece of litter on the floor rather than a classmate. It takes me right back to the days of eating lunch by myself, pretending to look at my food as if it were a great science experiment about to win a Nobel Prize. Just as I was a lonely teenager, I am feeling like a lonely back-to-school mother.

Five weeks into this new nursery, I see the cliques formed around me: there are the "dropped-off drop-off mums" with their chauffeurs that congregate together as soon as they step out of their sleek Mercedes/BMWs/Bentleys; the Europeans who just returned from a jaunt to their homes in France/Italy/Spain; the super-fit who stand in their sleek, neon workout gear discussing the latest cleanses, workouts and "lifestyles"; the working mums, dressed in their power suits with their phones stuck to their ears; and the fashionistas, dressed in cool, shiny new trainers and ripped jeans, and who look so effortlessly cool and beautiful.

And I am the one standing alone in my own one-woman group, the T-shirt-and-jeans-wearing Lonely Mums Club Band.

That night when I checked the Beta Mum blog, I noticed that this latest post already had sixty views and three comments:

Slum Mum: I completely understand how you feel! I am very shy and I am always standing by myself during pick-ups and drop-offs. Can I join your Lonely Mums Club Band?

Ozzie Mum: In some parts of Sydney, the school run is like a fashion contest, with who wears who and what. There is a real clique mentality in some of the elite private schools and it sounds just the same where you are. A smile and some friendly banter could make the whole experience much happier for everyone.

Lillian: Glad I found your blog today! I love it. I just turn up at the last very minute to avoid all the school-gates drama. You should be glad you are not part of a clique; it can get so bitchy in these cliques. Half the time they end up exploding at one moment or another. I like not being one of the gossip mums. Stand strong is my advice to you. Have a look at this link: The Dreaded School Run!

I clicked the link, which sent me to a thread where there were hundreds of responses. Engrossed, I read comments by mothers writing about their experiences at the school gates, and who had felt exactly the same feelings that I had. What I was experiencing wasn't unique at all. There were hundreds of women just like me. Mostly, they were shy mothers who didn't know how to strike up a conversation or were too anxious to start one. My anger began to fizzle out and I felt calmer knowing that this was a perfectly common and normal phenomenon.

By the next day, I had gained twenty new followers on the blog and a hundred new views. My frustrations from the previous day had all but evaporated and it was as if writing could erase them. Also, knowing that I wasn't alone felt encouraging, convincing me that I was part of the majority rather than a minority. It felt good. Online, I felt like an insider, rather than the outsider I had felt like since starting at Cherry Blossoms. I had finally found a place in which I felt comfortable, accepted and welcomed.

Chapter Ten

I Want a Play Date With Oscar!

'Mummy, can Oscar come over for a play date?' Kaya asked me on the way home from nursery one day. I groaned to myself. Oscar was Alice Denham's son and I had soon sussed out that Alice was a celebrity/model/billionaire who seemed to live in a parallel universe from mine: she lived in a world where everyone was super-rich, famous and beautiful. Her husband was heir to a billion-pound dynasty that had spanned generations, investing in everything from real estate to supermarkets.

Her photo was often seen on the pages of *Tatler* or *Hello!* at some high-society or trendy party with Francesca on her arm. Initially, I was in awe of her. She was stunning, with long, blonde, lustrous hair and translucent blue eyes that reminded me of a crisp sky at the top of a snow-capped mountain. She seemed to have the perfect life: a beautiful son, Oscar, a rich husband, a successful career and a foundation helping sick children in Africa. She lived in a gilded bubble where she jet-setted from the Cannes Film Festival to photo shoots in Thailand, stopping by Burundi on the way to feed malnourished children, and all of this documented on her Instagram account.

Alice was rarely seen at the nursery, leaving the pick-ups and drop-offs to her nanny, Suri. The few times I had seen Alice and had actually spoken to her, she had seemed friendly, but only in the way that she was friendly to everyone she met so it was impossible to tell if she was really friendly or fake-friendly.

Her son Oscar was a smiley, cheery boy who seemed quite taken with Kaya, always wanting to hug, caress and kiss her when he saw her. They seemed close, but Alice was never around to notice. Kaya had asked for play dates regularly and when I finally tried through Suri, she suggested two days that could work. We had agreed on a date and time, but two hours before said date and time, Suri texted to cancel the play date. I didn't particularly want to try to organise another one, given they had already cancelled once and I didn't want to disappoint Kaya again if they did so again.

'Mummy, mummy! I want a play date with Oscar! Puuuulleeee-zeeee!'

I tried to make up an excuse. 'I don't think he can, Kaya. I think he is busy.'

'No, mummy. *I want a play date with Oscar!*' She looked at me with fierce, angry eyes that suggested she was on the verge of a complete meltdown. She had been so volatile since our arrival in London that I tried to appease her any time I possibly could. It wasn't often that she requested a play date with a particular classmate and since they had only cancelled once I should give them another chance, I thought to myself, and quickly conceded.

'OK, OK. I'll try to set something up for you.'

The next day, I saw Suri after pick-up and we walked together as Kaya and Oscar held hands, laughing and giggling, speaking in their undecipherable language.

'Hi, Suri, could we try to organise another play date with Oscar and Kaya this week?' I asked her.

'Oh yes, of course. He has nothing on Thursdays. I am the one to organise the play dates. You know, his mother is always away.'

'OK, great. Should we come to you?'

'Yes, 3.30 would be great – 80 Phillips Road.'

*

On Thursday morning, Kaya woke up and immediately began jumping up and down, screeching, 'Play date with Oscar! Play date with Oscar today!' Her big brown eyes looked at me with eagerness and love. Children's emotions were simple; they loved sleep, food, being loved and playing. There was nothing much more that they wanted. I could provide the shelter and food, but the playing part was where it got complicated. As much as I could pretend to play with her and her imaginary friends, it just wasn't the same as having real friends over.

'Yes, darling, I know.' I smiled.

Later that morning, I was getting ready to pick up Kaya when the phone rang.

'Hello, this is Oscar's nanny. Sorry but we will have to cancel the play date again. His mother already organised something and I didn't know. Sorry about that. Maybe we can do a play date another time.'

'Right.' I didn't know what to say. It was noon and the play date was meant to be in three hours. Kaya would be devastated. 'It's all a bit last-minute.'

'Yes, sorry about that,' Suri kept repeating, while my heart sank at the thought of telling Kaya.

When I picked up Kaya, I saw Oscar leave with Francesca's son, Luca, and Kaya looked at them leaving with sad eyes.

'I'm sorry, Kaya, the play date with Oscar was cancelled,' I tried to explain to her.

She looked at me, confused. 'Why can't I go with Oscar and Luca?'

'Sweetie, I'm sorry it didn't work out. Oscar's mum already had plans organised. We didn't realise.' I looked at her disappointed eyes. How could I explain that the nanny had made plans with us but Alice had probably found better plans instead? Kaya's eyes didn't understand what I was saying or why this was so complicated. As she watched their tiny figures disappear in the distance, becoming two bobbing points on the horizon, tears trickled down her face, which soon became big sobbing tears.

'Oh, Kaya.' I hugged her tightly, wanting to take away the hurt that her little body was feeling. There was nothing I could do. To her, this was one of the biggest hurts she had experienced in her three years of life and I was helpless to alleviate it. I wanted to tell her it wasn't her fault, that it was Alice and her nanny's fault. They were the problem, not thinking us worthy enough for a goddamn play date. And then I started crying. Not in front of Kaya, but silently in her soft hair, flower-scented from her baby shampoo, while she sobbed away.

I disentangled myself when I had stopped crying, wiping off the tears so that Kaya wouldn't see a thing. I had become more immune to the constant rejections – they didn't affect me as much as they used to and I had the blog to thank for that, but I couldn't bear to see my daughter in tears over a rejected play date. The super-rich had their own rules. It wasn't about anyone else but them, and you had to fit into their existence. I tried to rationalise that since they were high-profile, they had different rules and didn't have time for "normal" people, but it still didn't make Kaya or me feel any better.

'But you know what we'll do, Kaya? We're going to go out for mummy-and-me pizza and an ice cream together! Your favourite! Special treat!' I mustered all the enthusiasm of a child's party entertainer to distract her from her tears. 'Just you and me, it will be our special treat when we are sad about something. Pizza and ice cream!' Inadvertently, there I was turning my daughter into the stereotypical Bridget Jones, resorting to pizza and ice cream as an emotional Band-Aid. But I didn't have any better ideas and it was the best I could do. That was all I *could* do: try my best, walking through the social jungle that was Cherry Blossoms.

The Beta Mum
Part 2: You Know You're an Alpha Mum When...

1   You are running an empire/a model/a high-flying businesswoman/ running the world while simultaneously baking banana cake, chocolate-chip cookies and cupcakes for the bake sale.

2   Your child's entire educational trajectory has been planned from nursery to Oxbridge. The day they were born.

3   You (or your nanny) cook your children 100 per cent organic, freshly made, home-cooked food. At every single meal. And you say things like, "Processed foods are the definition of evil".

4   You never let you children watch TV or eat sweets. Absolutely verboten! So you can tell your friends that your darling Clarissa "doesn't know Mickey Mouse because she never watches TV" and has "never had chocolate before".

5   You're the president of the PTA/on the board of an art foundation/volunteer for a charity, and you tell everyone how busy you are.

6   You look like you woke up at 5am to blow-dry that perfect hair, apply that make-up and choose that perfectly paired vintage chic outfit.

7   You wear fur and leather to the school run. Even though it is sunny and 20 degrees Celsius out there.

8   You've already started donating to your alma mater to increase your child's chances of getting in, even though they are only two years old.

9   You have a colour-coded, two-page Excel spreadsheet of your children's schedules. Your nanny has a diary for each child and logs their each and every move throughout the day.

10   You cancel play dates at the last minute because you've been offered a much better invitation from a more favourable Alpha Mum.

Chapter Eleven

A Members' Club for the Super-Rich

'A hundred pounds each for a parents' evening? That's absurd! That's almost four hundred Canadian dollars for two people. Do you know what I could buy with that kind of money? I could go to Poundland, buy fifty bags of crisps (I had learned that "chips" were in fact fries in this country, and "crisps" were chips – very confusing), a hundred Diet Coke cans, fifty packets of chocolates and fifty pizzas and organise the whole parents' evening with just our ticket money,' I said to Michael, talking at 150 times my normal speed while he tried to stop my tirade.

'Slow down, Sophie! Yes, I know it's a lot of money, but we can afford it.'

I had recently discovered Poundland on Portobello Road and it reminded me of the ninety-nine-cent stores which were popular both in Canada and the US. I relished buying all the household products I needed for less than ten pounds. This was in stark contrast to the Cherry Blossoms parents' evening, which was being hosted at Serafina's, a private members' club in Mayfair. I knew I shouldn't be surprised at the cost, given the nursery cost thousands of pounds a year, and thankfully Michael's company was paying for it, but I didn't think they would charge so much for a parents' evening.

'I don't think we should go,' I said, hesitating. I was tired of being snubbed and rejected by almost everyone at the nursery, and the parents' evening was bound to be worse.

'I think we should. Besides, I haven't been involved in the nursery at all. I should show my face at least once. I don't want them to think that you have an imaginary husband.'

It was true that this would be our first outing as a couple, rather than me on my own, and it was the first time he was willing to join me at a nursery event. I also realised that the parents' evening could offer plenty of fodder for my blog, making the evening worthwhile for that reason alone.

'They better serve caviar, a lobster and oyster buffet and vintage champagne for that kind of money,' I muttered.

'I'm sure they will, Sophie. Come on, it will be our first night out in London. We've never been to a private members' club. It will be our chance to see what it's all about. And you said Miss Sarah offered to babysit.' Miss Sarah had made the offer when I told her that we weren't going to the parents' evening since we didn't have anyone to babysit for us.

'That's true.'

'And you promised to say yes to any invitation you received.' His eyes shined with mischief as he knew he had convinced me.

'OK, let's go.'

'Why don't you buy yourself a new dress for it?' he asked me.

'Why? You don't think I dress well enough?' I became instantly defensive, realising that I was a touch sensitive about my sartorial choices lately.

'No, of course I think your dress sense is fine. I just thought that maybe you wanted to buy something new. Maybe something more "London". You haven't gone shopping once since you got here. London's great for shopping.'

'Oh, right.' It was true that I hadn't had a chance to buy any new clothes since we had moved. I had barely returned to my pre-pregnancy size and I hadn't bothered much with new clothes since Kaya's birth.

'I want to treat you to some new clothes,' he said. 'And maybe a facial? A new haircut?'

'Oh, thanks, Michael. That would be nice,' I said flatly. But I was irritated. Michael had never been interested in the clothes I wore in Canada. He was happy when I was make-up-free and wore whatever I was comfortable in, but since we moved to London, he constantly made comments about what I wore and that I should dress up more often, as if he wanted to change me. He had also started shopping on Bond Street and came home with new suits regularly, and he'd brought home a new watch last week. It was as if appearances and image were starting to really matter to him.

'I know how hard moving to London has been for you and I want you to be happy. Go crazy.' He kissed me on the top of my head in a manner that felt more brotherly than anything else, not realising that it would take a lot more than a few new clothes and a spa day to make me happy. But I knew I should be grateful and more appreciative, so I hugged him back and nestled my head in his strong chest.

The next day, I took Michael's advice and decided to pamper myself, and went shopping for a dress. I walked along the trendy shops, looking at the slim-fitting, petite-sized clothes on the mannequins in the designer boutiques on Great Western Road, thinking that I would never fit into any of them. In fact, I was sure that I would look stupid in them. I didn't even like dresses or skirts, I said to myself as I stared at a red wraparound dress that probably cost as much as a small car.

The truth was that I had never been comfortable in dresses and skirts because I was so self-conscious in them. I had always been worried that someone would look at me and think that I looked ridiculous in them. I also hadn't had any girlfriends growing up who could have helped me with style. After many lunches on my own at school, I finally met Evelyn, my best friend in high school and a transfer student from Montreal, who preferred astronomy and Aerosmith to clothes shopping.

I stood outside the shop, looking at my reflection in the shiny, gleaming window and saw an out-of-shape, thirty-three-year-old woman whose confidence had been hit by our move to London.

When I had been pregnant with Kaya, my body had changed in so many uncomfortable and unusual ways that it had triggered the beginning of my identity crisis. I don't think I'd ever really felt as if I was back to being myself since she was born.

I wasn't fat, but right after Kaya was born, I hadn't had much time or energy to go hiking the way I used to on the weekends, and I was more jiggly jello than Body Beautiful. Clothes seemed more of a hassle than anything else, and were one more thing on my to-do list that I didn't want to worry about. I usually pulled out the same sweatpants and sweater every weekend, and wore an easy uniform of jeans and T-shirts when I looked after Kaya or went to GreenSpace (one of the bonuses of environmental non-profits is that they don't care how you dress). I hadn't given my clothes more thought than that.

But then, as I stood staring at myself, I thought about the success of my blog and all the positive comments came running through my head: "I love your blog, keep it going", "I know how you feel", "I also feel lonely at the school drop-off". And instead of hiding behind my reflection and feeling sorry for myself, I thought that I should go into the store and buy something new. New for the new me.

'Can I help you?' said one of the shop assistants as I browsed through the clothes racks.

'I'm looking for a dress in a size ten to twelve that would suit my body shape,' I said confidently.

'I think I have a few that would suit you perfectly,' the assistant said. She left and came back with a few dresses to show me. 'How about this one?' She showed me a sleeveless and backless red dress that came up to mid-thigh level.

'Definitely too racy.'

'This one is very Princess Kate,' she said, as she showed me a blue lace dress that went down to my knees and stopped at the elbows. It was beautiful, but I wasn't quite ready for blue lace.

Then she showed me the perfect dress; it was a black, A-line dress with short sleeves, cinched at the waist, and it flowed outwards, hiding any muffin top, thick thighs and cellulite city. When I put it on, it flattered my waist and managed to enhance my – very – flat bust. I didn't often feel sexy, having been a flat-chested teenager with muscular thighs from hiking and running, but this dress somehow made me feel sexy. It was the first time I had felt this way in a long time, and never before because of a dress. But I liked it.

I didn't know whether it was the perfume in the store enthralling me or wearing this new dress, but I began to feel exhilarated. I had clung on to so much anxiety my whole life and all of sudden I wondered why I had for so long. What had changed was that I felt a sense of belonging; of being part of something bigger. The blog wasn't only changing how I felt about London, it was changing who I was. In cyberspace, I had become this confident woman who spoke her mind, writing everything that was on my mind without censorship. I wasn't afraid or anxious to speak up, and in turn everyone had been very accepting. And now, I felt that I was becoming this woman in real life too.

Along with the dress, I bought myself a beautiful matching black calf-leather handbag. These weren't designer clothes, but high-end high-street clothes that could easily pass for designer. I looked at myself in the mirror and felt good about myself. I was finally ready for the parents' evening, like Cinderella was ready for her ball.

A huge life-sized, plush, golden giraffe with scattered spots stared at me, giving me the eye, as if to say, "I know who you are, Sophie Bennett. You're not one of them. You're one of us. You're an onlooker." The winding staircase of Serafina's members' club had led me down into a nightclub, where I found myself face-to-face with the giant giraffe.

I had read up on (Googled) Serafina's before coming; it was an exclusive members' club costing three thousand pounds a year and had welcomed everyone from Tom Cruise to Prince William through its doors. The club had three bar areas, two restaurants, one nightclub and sixteen hotel rooms. The restaurant had poached a chef from Nobu and served fusion-food classics including tuna tartare, lobster tempura and black miso cod. The bar areas channelled the dolce vita vibe, with white-uniformed barmen serving Martinis to show off their mixology skills, and drinks made with absinthe.

The nightclub had an upscale, louche, bordello-like feel to it, in keeping with the club's location, the old, respectable (or rather unrespectable) red light district in Mayfair. It was dark and windowless, with its burgundy walls draped with red velvet curtains. On my left stood a glittering bar where late-twenty-somethings with youthful aspirations were dressed to impress and stood drinking champagne and colourful cocktails adorned with edible flowers. On my right, I saw some familiar faces from the nursery pick-ups and drop-offs heading in the direction of a private room.

I squeezed Michael's hand as we followed them. My heart pounded just a bit faster than I wanted it to and my social anxiety increased with every step I made towards the private room. I wanted to be anywhere but here, ideally sitting in front of our TV in my *Roots* sweatshirt/sweatpants combo, or in front of my laptop, hiding behind a screen rather than exposing my vulnerabilities to the Alphas. This was not the usual parents' evening in the school gym with soft drinks and pizza slices.

'Champagne?' said a waitress in a fitted, black-and-white, cleavage-enhancing dress as we entered the room and found a spot near the door.

Another similarly dressed woman waved a tray across us. 'Fig and goat's cheese tartlet with manuka honey, or foie gras with grape and mango chutney on sourdough bread?' she offered.

We grabbed a flute of champagne each and I sipped the golden liquid, calming my nerves as I scanned the room. The women looked ready for a "hot-or-not" Oscars fashion-off; there were feathers, leather, lace and petticoats. The men stood dominantly in their suits, clearly not from Topman. Finding my perfect dress – the A-line black dress that hid my muffin top, bingo wings and post-baby belly – had been worthwhile. I still felt out of place, but the champagne and the dress were enough to give me a confidence boost to face the party.

Just at that moment, Laetitia saw me and stopped me. I hadn't seen her since the incident at the coffee morning and was surprised to see her coming towards me.

'Hello, Sophie. How are you? You look very nice tonight. Here is my husband Nicolas.' She air-kissed me once on each cheek, as if it were a reflex, and I almost kissed her on the mouth, not knowing where to turn or look.

'This is my husband Michael.' I introduced Michael to her husband, who was shorter than I had been expecting, but had a friendly face. They immediately chatted on while Laetitia turned her attention back to me.

'I have to apologise. I am very sorry about the play date. I did not know what you meant by "play date". I thought you said, "playmate" and thought it was very strange for you to ask if I wanted to be your playmate. It is not really my style.' She laughed, her short, gamine hair flying around. 'In France, there is no such thing as a play date. We have friends over and the children play together. That's it. Then one of my friends told me about play dates two days ago and I realised that you had asked me for a play date! I am so sorry!'

'No problem at all.' I gave her a big, bright smile, pretending that it was no big deal. That I hadn't cried to Michael and Emma about my lack of play dates, and feeling rejected and excluded since I had arrived. And it was all due to a Hugh Hefner-style language misinterpretation.

'The French have a very different way of doing things. Our education is very limiting, which is why we have chosen Cherry Blossoms. It is much more open. And this parents' evening is very *sympathique*, don't you think? I didn't think I would like it, but in fact, it is very nice.' She shrugged her shoulders, as if it were a surprise that anglophones would be able to organise a sophisticated evening that even the French would enjoy. 'We have to organise a play date soon, *oui? Très bien.*'

'Yes, that would be very nice. Thank you,' I replied, realising that this was the first normal conversation I had with one of the nursery mums. Laetitia seemed genuinely sorry, and seemed like a nice person.

Like a pawn on a chessboard, Laetitia moved on towards another mother and I had to make my next move. Meanwhile, Michael had joined a conversation with Nicolas and another father who appeared to be Becky's husband. Becky was standing next to him with Kelly by her side. Kelly wore a tight, cerulean, asymmetrical, skintight dress, and Becky wore a wrap dress in what looked like a flowery red, pink and purple print. I sidled up to them, seeing no other familiar faces and since they were standing next to Michael.

'Hi, it's nice to see both of you again. I wanted to ask you about the winter fair and how I could volunteer,' I said to them.

Kelly's face looked blank, not registering who I was, despite us having met numerous times.

'Hi, Sophie,' Becky said. 'We are planning on sending out an email about the winter fair in the next few days.'

'Oh, I didn't recognise you at all, Sophie, darling.' Kelly's face now showed some recognition. 'You look completely different in a dress and heels. You look…taller…and prettier. Don't you usually wear jeans and Converse?'

'Yes, but I thought I should try to *Keep Up With the Cherry Blossoms Mums* tonight.' I tried to crack a joke, which clearly went over their heads, as they continued to look at me as if I were commenting on the weather.

'You should dress up more often, Sophie. You look so much better in a dress. And you should wear make-up. It really brings out your eyes,' Kelly went on. 'And it's nice to see you wearing proper shoes. We're a bit too old to be wearing Converse, don't you think?' She gave me her pursed, condescending smile.

What I really wanted to do was roll my eyes at her, but I decided that it was too early in the night to start making enemies. Instead, I gulped down my champagne and took another one from a passing waitress.

'Kelly, I love your shoes!' Becky exclaimed, looking down at Kelly's shoes as if they were made of gold, diverting the conversation away from my apparently underachieving daily dress sense.

'Oh, thanks, Becky.' Kelly smiled contentedly. 'They're Zoe Phillips.'

'Who's Zoe Phillips?' I asked shyly, feeling ignorant.

'You don't know Zoe Phillips?' Kelly looked at me incredulously and patronisingly, wide-eyed, with faint disdain, as if I had admitted to never having heard of Nelson Mandela or Martin Luther King. 'They're Jimmy Choos but better. And much more exclusive. She's the hottest shoe designer right now. I had to wait four weeks for them to be made – bespoke – and to have my initials inscribed on the sole. Just in case I lose them.' She laughed. 'Do you know she's going to be a Cherry Blossoms mum soon? She has a one-year-old and lives in Notting Hill, so it's really close to her.'

'I live in Notting Hill,' I said, trying to make up for my embarrassment.

'Oh, I lived in Notting Hill once, but it was too dodgy. I realised that I am an Upper East Side girl at heart,' Kelly said. 'So now I live in Kensington and I feel much safer.'

She couldn't help herself; she had to criticise every word I uttered. I took another sip of my champagne and then moved on to a Martini to assuage Kelly's criticisms.

'How are your renovations getting on?' Becky asked Kelly.

'Can you believe we're being sued? We're building a sub-basement' – she looked at me as if I hadn't heard her go on and on about it at the coffee morning – 'and our neighbours have decided to fight against it now. They are so difficult! Already, we're paying millions for the renovations and on top of that we've got to pay legal fees! They're complaining about the dust, the noise and the view. I understand, but we kept the worst works for the summer, which I thought was very thoughtful. No one's here in the summer anyway. I think Chris has been speaking to David about it.' Kelly looked over to where Michael was standing with two men who I assumed were Chris, Kelly's husband, and David, Becky's husband.

'Yes, David mentioned it to me,' Becky said.

'Renovations take up *so* much time. I barely have time for my

Pilates classes or my mani-pedis,' Kelly emphasised while she stared at her perfectly manicured nails, as if this was a huge sacrifice she was making for the sake of her house.

Kelly's husband, Chris, was a Ken-doll lookalike: blond and handsome with a dazzling white smile. They were the perfect Ken-and-Barbie match. Next to Chris, Becky's husband was shorter, balder, and looked like he had crept out of a hobbit hole. Becky had mentioned that he was a corporate lawyer for one of the biggest law firms in the city.

'Look, it's Alice Denham's husband, Mark,' Kelly whispered like a sixteen-year-old girl speaking about her teenage crush. Mark Denham was a '90s boy band heart-throb who had made many sixteen-year-olds swoon. He was considered over the hill but was still gorgeous.

'He's made it into the *GQ* Most Gorgeous Men List at least twenty times,' Becky whispered to me.

'This is the best part about Cherry Blossoms, the celeb-watching and the networking,' Kelly said excitedly. I wanted to add, 'And the gossiping, by the sounds of it.' Mark Denham was standing next to Alice and Francesca, the Italian ex-model from our class, and another man.

'Look at Francesca's husband, Carl. He's really behaving strangely.' Becky gestured towards the man standing next to Francesca. He looked jittery, his eyes were bulging out and he kept running his hand through his hair and licking his lips. He then grabbed Alice's bum and squeezed it, trying to make sure no one was looking.

'God, he is high. Not again,' Kelly replied, rolling her eyes towards the ceiling.

'He's got one of the most gorgeous women in this room and he's still grabbing other women's bums?' I asked her in disbelief.

'Some men just can't keep their hands to themselves. The power and success has gone to his head. And the happy powder just makes it worse,' Becky explained.

'Maybe it's because Francesca thinks that the diarrhoea and vomiting bug is the best weight-loss programme. Not a lot of brain cells up there.' Kelly smirked. 'I just can't stand stupid people.' Kelly clearly had opinions about everyone. And not very complimentary ones at that.

'Doesn't Francesca get upset by his behaviour?' I asked, appalled.

'She's learned to live with it. She told me that at least she knows that he will come home to her bed every night and that's all that matters to her,' Kelly said. 'Then you've got mothers like Mary Wright who work all the time – it's a wonder her husband doesn't wander. I heard from my nanny that their son calls the nanny "Mummy". How tragic is that? I couldn't live with myself.' She shook her head.

'She's a partner at Accorcap Hedge Fund,' explained Becky.

'Maybe she has to work,' I suggested. 'London is so expensive, with school fees and mortgages. It's really impressive that she's a partner of a hedge fund.'

'At least she's not a Pilates or yoga instructor like Leila and all those Notting Hill mums. Everyone's a yoga instructor these days,' Kelly said, swirling her Martini.

'I think it's pretty great if they've found a passion. If they're happy, surely that's all that matters?' I said. Becky nodded her head, acquiescing slightly.

'That's not a real job. It's just a hobby,' Kelly said curtly. No matter who we spoke about, Kelly couldn't help herself; she had to put them down, one way or another. I realised that I wasn't the focus of her vitriol; she was the only one safe from it. Kelly was the type of woman who spoke badly about everyone around her.

As the night went on, she continued dissecting every other mother in the class: Laetitia, "the violent one" who spanked her daughter Chloe when she was being naughty; Poppy Sevigny-Bruce, the "bored, vacuous" heiress; Cecilia Cartwright, the divorcee of a tech entrepreneur who had "the personality of wallpaper. No wonder he divorced her"; and Alice Denham, who was "one of the most beautiful women in the world, but anorexic and a nervous wreck". No one was spared of her criticism.

I could only imagine what she said about me when I wasn't there.

I was surprised that she openly insulted of all the other mothers in front of me, given that we weren't even friends, but I was growing more uncomfortable by the second, feeling that listening to the gossip actually made me part of this mommy-gossip group. I drank some more champagne to alleviate my discomfort and could feel myself becoming more and more tipsy.

I think Becky sensed my mounting discomfort when I kept pushing hair away from my face like a nervous tic, and she changed the subject back to the winter fair.

'So, you're interested in helping out at the winter fair?' she asked.

'Yes. I'd be happy to help out,' I announced enthusiastically. It was better than sitting alone in a café all day with only myself to talk to. And I was determined to find another "normal" mother. Kelly wasn't the only mum at Cherry Blossoms. After all, I had been wrong about Laetitia.

'We need all the people we can to help out,' Becky said. A cloud passed over her face, but soon cleared. 'It's so much work and it can be intense, but it's really worthwhile. This year, we have chosen to donate the proceeds to a mother-and-child community centre for underprivileged families in north-west London. We managed to raise an incredible amount last year and hope to raise even more this year.'

'That sounds great,' I said. 'I worked at a non-profit a few years ago before moving to London. It was an environmental non-profit, promoting green spaces in urban areas and protecting endangered forests. I was involved in fundraising, but also in every aspect of the charity…'

As I spoke I saw Kelly quickly losing interest; her eyes glazed over when I started talking about my previous work experience, not hiding the fact that she didn't find it remotely interesting.

'As if Canada needed any more "green spaces",' Kelly remarked sarcastically. 'Oh, I've got to catch up with Poppy. I want to ask her to donate to the fair, either in kind or cash. I have to excuse myself. Nice catching up with you, Sophie, darling.' She gave me a half-smile, and took this opportunity to make her next move on the parents' evening chessboard. I didn't see her as someone who considered herself a pawn, but rather a queen. A Queen Bee. She turned on her Zoe Phillips heels and walked away.

After Kelly moved on to chat to someone more important, Becky and I tried to find Michael and David. As we walked through the crowded nightclub, I heard snippets of conversation:

'When my son flew commercial for the first time, he asked me, "Daddy, who are all these people on our plane?" Nowadays we are lucky if we turn left on an airplane...'

'Ferraris? They're for overweight, balding hedge-fund managers who need penis extensions. They're just slightly better than the poor man's Porsche Boxster, or the car salesman's BMW 5 series... DB5s are much more sophisticated...'

'We're in the middle of a five-hundred-million-pound takeover for Sweetdairy, the dairy and snacks company.'

'A bit risky nowadays, don't you think? What's your predicted ROI...?'

'In London, with ten million you're poor...'

'There's only one One & Only resort, and it's the one in the Maldives. Forget about the Mauritius resort, that one's dreary...'

It was so foreign to me that they might as well have been talking Chinese. Who were these people? I didn't belong and it wasn't getting any better. They made me feel so small and insignificant; I wanted to hide in our flat and never come out of it. I was hoping that as soon as I found Michael he would be ready to go home.

We finally found Michael and David, who were deep in a conversation with Frank Wright, Mary's husband, discussing the troubles with childcare.

'Mary's in Stockholm tonight, Copenhagen tomorrow and Frankfurt on Friday. The problem is when we are both travelling. We have one nanny that works from half past seven in the morning to half past six in the evening, and then we have another one who takes over until nine or ten o'clock if we both have to work late or have work dinners. Our night nanny sometimes has to stay overnight, but she's getting tired of doing overnights with us. So we have to find a solution. I think we have to look into 24/7 nannies from now on. There's too much uncertainty in our jobs.'

'It can't be easy starting up your own hedge fund,' David, Becky's husband, said.

'Finding investors is tough right now,' Frank agreed, 'and then finding the right investments is also difficult. The market's saturated. But when I was let go from SPG Fund, I didn't have much choice but to start my own. There are not a lot of places for fifty-year-old fund managers,' he explained.

'If you need legal counsel, you know where to find me,' David said, clearly seeing an opportunity, and he passed Frank one of his business cards. This was not only a "who's who" of the London financial world; it was also a networking event for the 1 per cent of London. And my tiny, suburban non-profit was not going to cut it in this world of millionaires and billionaires.

'See, it wasn't too bad, was it?' Michael said to me when we were in our black cab home at midnight. My feet had started aching, my jaw was sore from smiling so much and my voice had nearly gone from shouting over the DJ, who had increased the volume of the music at 11pm. It was relatively quiet in the streets of London on a Tuesday night and the taxi thundered on, swerving in between and around the few cars in its path.

'Maybe not for you. Kelly couldn't stop gossiping about every mother in the class,' I said, turning to him. 'It's like being back in high school, just instead of the mean girls, it's the mean mums. I can't imagine what they say about me when I'm not there.'

'Her husband Chris isn't that bad. He was friendly and I thought he seemed pretty down-to-earth. Although it seems that his fund is really struggling at the moment.'

'Well, then I don't know how or why he chose his wife. She couldn't stop criticising every single person in our class. She said that I was too old to still wear Converse shoes and that I look so much better in heels with a bit of blush and lipstick.'

'How about Becky, her sidekick? What do you think of her? Her husband David seems like a cutthroat corporate lawyer who doesn't mess around. He's been involved in some of the biggest M&A deals in the past ten years.'

'M&A?'

'Mergers and Acquisitions.'

'Oh, right. Whatever that means. I think Becky's all right, but she does and says whatever Kelly tells her to. She's a puppet behind the master puppeteer. She idolises Kelly for whatever reason.'

'At least you got a chance to get to know some of the mothers better. And the French mum said she wanted to organise a play date. It's a good start.'

When we got home, we quickly checked on Kaya, said goodbye to Miss Sarah and went to bed. Michael immediately fell into a rumbling, snoring sleep while I lay in bed with the room spinning from all the alcohol I had drunk. I sat up in bed, unable to sleep. His snoring sounded like a sea lion's roar and made my pounding headache worse. I had had one too many glasses of champagne and I was very tipsy, verging on drunk, but I couldn't get Kelly's condescending voice out of my head. I got out of bed, went into the living room, tripping over Kaya's red plastic toy supermarket trolley on my way, and sat in front of my laptop while my head continued throbbing. My fingers tingled, ready to write.

The Beta Mum
An Alpha-Land Nursery Parents' Evening: A Nursery Party or a Private Members' Club for the Super-Rich and Super-Famous?

With Taittinger champagne bubbling, foie gras canapés hand-ed out on silver platters, a fashionable DJ and a dance floor in one of the most exclusive members' clubs in London, it was one party not to be missed. The beau monde was dressed to the nines in Tom Ford and Ralph Lauren suits and Miu Miu and Marc Jacobs dresses. A few celebrity models and pop stars beautified the crowd, while the Fortune 500 movers and shakers discussed multi-million-pound deals and exchanged business cards for networking purposes. To get into this party, there is an annual membership fee of fifteen thousand pounds and a vetting process as strict as Harvard's undergraduate admissions process.

You wouldn't be the only one to think that this was a private members' club for the super-rich and super-famous, but this was the latest parents' evening at my daughter's nursery. Entry into this world requires a house worth an average of four million pounds (amazing what you can find out by using Zoopla and a class list), an Ivy League or Oxbridge education, a CV that includes a top investment bank/hedge fund/private equity fund, or an educational specialist to get you in.

The Alpha Parents discussed their first-world (super-rich) problems: where to get the best nannies and how many they need (weekday, weekend and night nannies), the difficulties of sub-basement renovations (and the nightmare neighbours and the number of lawsuits accrued), where and how they holidayed (the Alps versus the Indian Ocean) and how to get their children into Oxbridge (tutors, tutors, tutors). This is a socially segregated group of people based on wealth and status, who only like to mix with their own kind.

While the men compared notes on cars and investments, the Alpha Mums were out in full force, gossiping and glaring, backstabbing and talking behind people's backs. Forget the hedge fund managers and the locust private equity wheelers and dealers; it's the Alpha Mums you should be scared of. Their elbows are sharp but their tongues are even sharper.

That night, no one was immune to their vicious and vitriolic character dissections. As they sipped their watermelon Martinis and barely picked at their tuna tartare, they gossiped about "the anorexic mum who only eats green apples all day", "the mum who shouldn't have had that extra muffin at the coffee morning", "the mum who is as dull as wallpaper", and "the hot celebrity dad who everyone wants to bonk".

And which Cherry Blossoms daddy was seen pinching the bum of a famous mum? And what was that white powder sitting in his left nostril?

I'd better watch my back, because it's a tough and scary world in Alpha-Land.

The Beta Mum

After I finished writing the post, I quickly hit "publish", closed down my laptop, finally feeling tired, and went to sleep.

Chapter Twelve

I Am Not a Supermodel

'Before we have breakfast, I wanted to briefly mention the upcoming winter fair. Last year, we raised sixty-eight thousand pounds for a local homeless shelter. This year, we plan on raising even more for a local mother-and-child community centre. And we need all your help to make it the best ever.' Kelly spoke in front of two dozen mums who had congregated in the private room of an organic café around the corner from Cherry Blossoms for a class breakfast and an introductory meeting on the winter fair.

It was the Friday after the parents' evening and it had taken me two days to recover from my hangover (I wasn't twenty any more), using all my concentration skills to go through the motions of bringing Kaya to school and back, dressing, feeding and entertaining her.

'Today, I'll brief you on our general plan, and next week we'll allocate jobs and discuss strategy in further detail.' Becky and Kelly were co-chairs of the Cherry Blossoms winter fair, and had high hopes for the charity event. 'This year's theme will be "Winter Wonderland meets *Frozen*", so think lots of snow, ice, princesses, polar bears and reindeers.'

After Kelly briefed us on the plan of the winter fair, I ordered a croissant while the other mums went for egg-white omelettes and, of course, Kelly had a super-green juice. I was sitting next to Becky on my left and Mary Wright on my right, and Laetitia sat across from me. Mary Wright had been one of the power-suited mums I had seen on the first day of nursery, and had left the classroom as fast as Usain Bolt won the hundred metres. She was English, from London, and this was the first-class meeting she had managed to attend.

Our conversation quickly veered towards what all mums, from Timbuktu to Des Moines via Rio, talk about: schools.

'You haven't registered for any schools, Sophie? You need to get on it right now,' Becky was saying while I hung onto every word and Laetitia and Mary listened in. 'For the best schools, you're supposed to register at birth. Even if Kaya's coming from Cherry Blossoms, there is only so much Mrs Jones can do. You can forget the admissions-at-birth schools. They're full and have waiting lists of hundreds of children. That leaves the assessment schools, and if you want any chance of getting into any of those, you need to get a tutor now.'

'But our children are only three. Isn't it too much pressure at a really young age?' I asked Becky sceptically.

'If you want to increase their chances of getting into the top schools, you have to tutor your children,' she insisted.

That sounds like a first-class ticket to a mental institution for your child, I thought to myself.

'By the way, have you read the Beta Mum post about the Cherry Blossoms parents' drinks?' Becky asked us, causing me to nearly choke on a piece of croissant.

I tried clearing my throat, grunting and groaning, trying to dislodge the piece of croissant that had become stuck. I had been so tipsy after the parents' evening and I knew I had written a post at 1am after the party but it had seemed like a far-off dream, lost in my memory. What had I written? I tried to remember but I was sure that I hadn't mentioned Cherry Blossoms. I thought I had only vaguely mentioned a London nursery. Or had I mentioned Cherry Blossoms in the post? Had I been that drunk?

'She wrote a blog post on the parents' evening saying that it was at a private members' club for the super-rich.'

'*Non*. I have not heard of it. What is it about?' Laetitia asked, her interest piqued as she leaned forward, coming closer to Becky.

'There's a new blogger called the Beta Mum, who has been writing about "Alpha Mums", and she posted an entry about the Cherry Blossoms parents' evening at Serafina's. One of the other mums from the Bear Cubs class forwarded it to me and it's been circulating around the Cherry Blossoms parents. Everyone's been reading it and trying to guess who she is,' Becky explained.

Blood rushed to my head, making me feel dizzy, and I silently blushed. I stared down at my creamy cappuccino and the half-eaten croissant lying on my plate as my head spun. How had they found my blog? And who had read my post? How had it circulated around the whole nursery? I only had a few hundred views on my blog so far and did not expect anyone to be reading it apart from Ozzie Mum in Australia and my other random fans in India and Thailand.

When I had written the blogs, I thought that I had written in a cyber-world vacuum, far removed from anyone I remotely knew. I never expected anyone I wrote about to actually read any of my blog posts. I knew I was being judgemental and had unleashed my frustration and loneliness in my writing. I tried thinking about what I had written and whether I had said anything that was going to give me away, and I started to panic. How long was I going to be able to stay anonymous? And what would happen if someone found out I had been writing the blogs?

'It must be someone from the nursery. They must have been at the parents' evening. Someone says Annabelle Clarke wrote it, she's an ex-journalist who's quite opinionated and judgemental,' Becky continued.

'I was also forwarded the blog post,' said Mary. She shrugged. 'What she wrote is quite true.'

'But she is making enemies as we speak,' said Becky. 'No one wants to be the subject of parody and satire in these circles. It's a very tight-knit and private social circle, so for her to write about it is very risky. If anyone finds out who's been writing it, it's the end of her. Or them. They'll probably be expelled from Cherry Blossoms for invasion of privacy. Already the nursery doesn't allow photographs, and posting photographs on social media is a big no-no. And there's a reason why the nursery doesn't have a website.'

'Why doesn't it have a website?' I asked. 'I always wondered.'

'It's because Mrs Jones wants the nursery to be so private and exclusive that even paparazzi can't find any information about it online. She wants to keep it that way so that the celebs feel like they can send their kids here without intrusion. You know, Prince George was meant to come here before they decided to send him to a nursery in the countryside,' she said as if this was top-secret, invaluable information.

'I was told the Beta Mum was Lucy, a mum in another class who used to be an editor at a glossy magazine, and that she edits the blog and has a few writers providing the content,' Mary said.

'Ohh, it sounds very funny! I must read it.' Laetitia was wide-eyed and intrigued, while I kept my mouth tightly shut and my head down, fearing that if I spoke or looked at them, I would give away immediately that I was Beta Mum. I had never imagined that I was invading anyone's privacy. But from their points of view, it was very likely that I was treading on very thin ice. That would be a first: being expelled from nursery for writing a blog post.

I could already see myself begging Mrs Jones to let us stay at Cherry Blossoms, telling her that it was all a big mistake because I couldn't sort out a play date. I would be the laughing stock of the school. Was I really risking Kaya's nursery place by writing about the world of west London super mummies? I began to panic. Keep cool, Sophie. Keep cool. Don't let them see that you are the culprit. The villain. The mysterious, anonymous blogger known as the Beta Mum.

'I found it pretty entertaining,' Mary said.

'Yes. But she's also quite mean at times, don't you think?' Becky asked.

I had never thought I was being mean. I thought I was expressing my thoughts, my emotions, how I felt. Freedom of speech and all that. And everything I had written was true, I wanted to tell them, but I kept my mouth shut.

'She sounds perceptive, from what you are saying.' I finally spoke, thinking that the quieter I was, the guiltier I would look.

'Absolutely,' Becky said, 'but no one wants to be written about. Especially in a negative light. But at the same time, everyone is reading it because they want to know if she wrote about them.'

'Did you recognise anyone she wrote about?' Laetitia asked.

'It could have been about any of us,' Becky said. 'She made all the mums sound backstabbing, bitchy and gossipy.'

'I am sure there are mums like that,' Mary said, 'but they're a minority. Not everyone is like that. Although, I did feel like she was talking about me and my seven nannies and babysitters – I have so many I can't keep count.' She shook her head at the absurdity of it all.

After the breakfast came to an end and all the mums had gone their separate ways, I stood outside the café on the concrete pavement and reached for my phone in my new, black, over-the-shoulder handbag I had bought for the party and read through my blog post. There, towards the end, I had written about the "Cherry Blossoms daddy". I internally moaned to myself at my stupidity. I remembered carefully omitting "Cherry Blossoms" from the title, but I had been so tipsy that I hadn't picked up my mistake in the post. I quickly dialled Michael's number.

'Michael! You'll never guess what happened. The mums at Cherry Blossoms have all read my blog post. It's the latest nursery gossip!'

'Sophie, I don't really have time for this right now.' He sounded distracted, distant and mildly irritated.

'I know, but—' I said, but he interrupted me.

'I really don't have time for your nursery issues right now.' This time, he was firm, with a hint of anger, trying to signal to me through the tone of his voice that he wanted to get off the phone.

'Oh, right. I'm sorry, it's just that you've never had a problem with me calling you at work before. I didn't think you'd mind.'

'I know, but right now I am trying to manage some pretty big problems at work and I don't have the time. We can speak later.' He spoke tersely and then paused before saying angrily, 'Sophie, you really shouldn't be calling me during the day any more.'

'Of course. Sorry,' I said, repeating myself but wishing he had told me not to call him at work before so that we could have avoided this argument.

'Things have changed. I have fourteen people trying to talk to me, with sixteen different problems that I don't know if I can even solve.' His voice still sounded angry, and he hung up on me after that.

I knew I probably shouldn't have called him but this was so different to how it was in Canada. Back in Oakville, he would call me during his lunch break and we would catch up on Kaya's triumphs of building blocks and puzzle creations, while he would tell me about the latest engineering feats happening in the lab. We used to speak every day and share all the details of our lives. This was completely new territory. I knew he had a big, new job, but Michael was so stressed that he often became angry quite easily; not only with me but with Kaya too. When Kaya would have one of her meltdowns, within seconds he went from patient and understanding to angry and yelling at her. This was not how I had envisaged our life in London.

I stood there under an overcast sky and a cold wind that foreshadowed the winter that would soon arrive, before running to Cherry Blossoms to pick up Kaya, while all the other mums left for their spinning/Pilates/Zumba classes at Body Beautiful and the nannies picked up their children.

After picking Kaya up from nursery, I took her to the playground. Kaya had been warming to the idea of the playground lately and was happily playing on what she called "the pirate ship". Although the sky was still overcast, there was no sign of rain yet.

I looked at my blog and deleted the mention of Cherry Blossoms in the post. I then checked my stats page and there was a spike in the number of views since I wrote and posted the last entry: there were two hundred views in the last twenty-four hours, mostly from England. In the search terms, someone had Googled "Cherry Blossoms Nursery" and had found my blog that way. There was so little written about Cherry Blossoms on the Internet that a search engine had put my blog post right at the top of the search pages.

I took Kaya home after a fifteen-minute play and put her down for a nap. I rocked and sang to her until she fell asleep in her cot, gazing at the mobile my parents had given her as a going-away present to help lull her off to sleep. It had red double-decker buses, black taxis and policemen on horseback all rotating in a circle.

I checked my blog's stats again and the parents' evening post had gotten over five hundred views. It had gone viral! And the views kept going up. Then I checked my Beta Mum email account, and there were ten emails waiting for me. I had never received this many emails. I scrolled down and saw messages from three digital-marketing businesses asking me if I wanted to increase my SEO something-or-other and my digital presence.

One email was from Francesca Novelli. It was one line long: Who are you?

Another email came from Annabelle Clarke: Keep writing! It's really entertaining. I wish I had come up with this idea first!

Then came one surprising email from "Cyberdad":

To: The Beta Mum
From: Cyberdad
Sent: October 12 2016, 13:00
Subject: Your blog

Dear Beta Mum,
Let me introduce myself. I am a Cherry Blossoms dad and I saw your blog post after it made the rounds through the Cherry Blossoms email grapevine. Sadly, I am not a celebrity, nor a supermodel who beautifies the crowd, but I guess I am part

of the 1 per cent and I am a big fan of yours! It really made me laugh. Especially the post on the Alpha Mums. It was spot on. I am married to one such Alpha Mum and I think she ticks all the boxes. Sometimes, it can be exhausting being married to an Alpha Mum. Nothing is ever good enough for her and she puts so much pressure on herself, me and our children.

I also think it's a strange bubble we live in at Cherry Blossoms, so I understand where you are writing from. It's impossible not to be competitive where we live.

I hope you continue writing. I think your writing is wonderful and it is something I would like to continue reading. I look forward to your next post!

Best wishes,

Cyberdad

I was taken aback by the email. Why was a Cherry Blossoms father sending me an email about my blog post? I could understand the mums writing to me and wanting to figure out my identity, but I was surprised that one of the dads had decided to write. My writing was more geared towards bored and lonely stay-at-home mothers who surfed blogs and the web for virtual connections, like me. But there you have it. I had my first male fan.

I immediately wanted to call someone to talk about the emails, but I knew couldn't call Michael after remembering his reaction to my call earlier that day. He was not interested in my "issues", as he had called them, in Cherry Blossoms or in my blog. He wouldn't be interested in the emails I was receiving from Cyberdad, I deduced. He had his work to keep him occupied and distracted, and I had my blog.

So, who was Cyberdad anyway? I thought about all the dads I had met in the past few months at Cherry Blossoms. Had I already met him or was he a stranger? In his email, he admitted that his wife was an Alpha Mum. That could be anyone, I thought to myself. What clues hid in his email? I thought about Carl, Francesca's husband, who had been flirting with Alice at the parents' evening, but she wasn't one of the biggest Alpha Mums; she floated through life on her good looks and everything seemed to fall in her lap. What about Kelly's husband? Could he be Cyberdad? He did have the most Alpha of Alpha Wives. I could imagine how exhausting it must be to be married to Kelly.

I responded to the emails while Kaya's snores drifted through her half-closed bedroom door and into the living room. I answered Francesca's email, saying that I had to stay anonymous to continue writing so freely and liberally. Once my identity was revealed, I wouldn't be allowed such creative freedom. I sounded so important as I wrote those words, as if anyone really cared who I was. But she had written to me and she deserved an answer. In my reply to Annabelle, I thanked her for her kind words and told her I hoped she would continue to support and encourage me.

I then sat in front of my laptop, wondering how to respond to Cyberdad. Funny and witty? Flirty and whimsical? Or professional and distant, like an omniscient, godlike figure who knew all the secrets of Cherry Blossoms? I opted for funny and witty, but it ended up sounding more like an immature schoolgirl writing to her secret crush:

To: Cyberdad
From: The Beta Mum
Sent: October 12 2016, 14:00
Subject: Re: Your blog

Dear Cyberdad,
Thank you for your lovely and complimentary email. I always enjoy receiving emails from my fans, especially ones like yours that are so positive. I don't mind that you aren't a celebrity or supermodel; just having someone read my blog posts is good enough for me. ☺

I can only imagine how exhausting it must be to have an Alpha Wife. I am an outsider to the Cherry Blossoms community and I find it exhausting. How can I ever keep up with these

supermums with super lives? I can't match up to them and it is
draining trying to fit in. Any tips welcome!
Best,
The Beta Mum

I pressed "send", and then started having second thoughts. Maybe I shouldn't have added that smiley face. It probably made me seem childish, or too flirty. I really did feel like a teenager again. But it was completely innocent after all. No one was hurting anyone by emailing someone of the other sex. There was nothing to it, I told myself. Yet, in the back of my mind, I felt enlivened by the attention. No one can deny that after becoming a mother, there is usually less attention from men. Apart from Michael, there were literally no men in my stay-at-home mum's life.

As much as I still loved him, it oftentimes felt that we had fallen into a comfortable parenting partnership, rather than being lovers or the ideal soulmates. We were two people who had created a family that needed constant attention. And eventually we settled into our contractual duties. Within the family, I was contracted to provide most of the attention, nurturing and love for our daughter, while Michael provided the stability of food, shelter and clothes. We had slowly migrated towards this agreement, whether I liked it or not, and I did it for the sake of our family. It made me happy most days, but many days, I felt like my identity was slowly dissolving in my tears, especially since my job search had been absolutely fruitless so far.

Chapter Thirteen

Insanity-Prevention Parenting

'Someone forwarded my blog around to most of the parents of Cherry Blossoms and I have no idea who did it or how it happened,' I said to Michael. We were in Hyde Park the next day, feeding the ducks with Kaya around the pond near Kensington Palace. It was an early Saturday morning, with the morning haze barely off the hard, cold ground. There were only a few brave people around, who had courageously ventured outside to face the beginning of the winter weather.

Michael had arrived home late from work the night before and found that I had fallen asleep in front of a DVD. He had woken me up gently and I had groggily traipsed into bed, semi-sleeping, unable to speak coherently, in my pyjamas.

'How did you find out?' he asked.

'We were at a class breakfast and Becky started talking about the Beta Mum, asking if we had read her blog posts. I thought they were going to get up and start shouting, "There's a traitor amongst us!", and point fingers at me.'

'What did you write about?'

'Well…I might have written a drunken post about the parents' evening the other night after we came home from Serafina's. And it could have been misinterpreted in many ways.'

'Sophie, you have to be careful about what you write. It could really rub people the wrong way. Especially since you've been having trouble making friends and fitting in. If anyone finds out it's you, you're going to be completely ostracised. No one's going to want to talk to you because they'll think you're going to write about them. And no one wants that.'

'One of the mums mentioned that I could get expelled from Cherry Blossoms,' I told him, nervously laughing at what I was saying.

'This is serious, Sophie. It's not worth ruining Kaya's nursery place, or ours, for a silly blog that you write,' he said flippantly, as he threw a pebble into the water, which sank and left a column of bubbles in its wake. I finally realised that this was what he really thought about my blog: a silly pastime.

'Don't call my blog silly,' I snapped back. 'My blog is the only place where people actually listen to me. They support me and listen to me when no one else does. And I've tried looking for a job. I contacted headhunters two weeks ago but they can't seem to find any position that would give me time with Kaya so that one of us can be around for her.'

'God, Sophie. I knew you would say something like that.' He turned around brusquely, putting his back to me, and then turned back to me with an angry look in his eyes. 'I told you, you don't need to work. And you've got to understand that right now I'm working towards an important deadline and we found a huge flaw in the train-track prototype yesterday. I spent the whole day and last night trying to resolve it. Robert's still on my case about it and I may have to go into work today.' He gave me a reproachful look, as if it were my fault that there were problems on his railroad track.

'I understand that you have a huge amount of pressure and a new job but I also want you to remember that you have a family. And right now, all your focus is on your job. We were happy in Oakville. I had a job, I had friends, I had my family nearby. And now, I rarely see you. Kaya rarely sees you. I want you to see her grow up, I want you to be there to wipe her tears and be there for her when she has a scraped knee. Isn't that what life is about? Right now, you're never there during the week before she goes to bed, and on the weekends, you're so distant, tired or angry that I always feel like I'm walking on eggshells when you're around.' At this point, tears had welled up in my eyes and resentment came pouring out as I spoke.

'Don't you get it? I am doing this for us,' he said aggressively, 'for our family. This is a really important time for me in my career. I haven't told you, but if it all goes well, I'll be heading towards a management position at the company. That would mean a really high salary and a bonus every year.' His voice increased an octave and he sounded more and more angry. I could tell he was exasperated with me, but I wasn't going to back down. Not today. I had done so too many times and this time, I was immovable.

'I don't care about the salary and the bonus,' I interrupted him. 'I want you. Don't you wonder whether it's all worth it? The long hours, the stress? I feel like a single mother during the week. You haven't been home to put Kaya to bed in weeks. You're never around and you know how unhappy I've been.' My tears started streaming down my face, unstoppable, a deluge of loneliness, resentment and anger all coming out at once.

'Money is important. I saw what it did to my parents. It drove them apart. They never recovered when my father lost his job. You know this more than anyone else. I never want money to be an issue between us.' His shoulders were hunched over and he looked exhausted. I didn't want to fight, and I knew that he didn't either. Kaya was still feeding the ducks happily a few feet away from us, with a bag full of bread we had been saving all week to feed them.

'The only thing that's driving us apart right now is your work. I don't want to be a lonely mother who's kept happy by having designer clothes and handbags,' I muttered as the tears slowed down, until there were just a few left dripping from the tip of my nose.

Just at that moment, Michael's phone rang. He looked at it doubtfully, wondering whether to pick it up or not, and in the end, picked it up.

'Hello? Oh hi, Robert. No, it's fine. We can talk.' Michael walked away from me as if our conversation hadn't happened, and walked around the edge of the circular pond, as his voice grew smaller and smaller until it was imperceptible. I looked at Kaya, who was still happily feeding the ducks, oblivious to her parents' tumultuous arguing and fighting. I carefully wiped any remnants of my tears away from my face and nose, and went to help her feed the ducks while I waited for Michael to come back.

A few minutes later, he came back and apologised.

'I'm really sorry, Sophie. I had to take that call,' he said, but he didn't sound like he really meant it.

I bet you did, I thought to myself.

'I have to go in today,' he said blandly.

I looked up at him from my crouched position, next to Kaya. My look must have given away how I was feeling.

'I'm really sorry, Sophie.' He apologised again, as if another apology was going to sort out any of our problems. 'We can continue our conversation another time. But I really have to sort out the train-track prototype problem.'

How about sorting our marital problems instead, I wanted to say. But I kept quiet. I didn't want to launch into another tirade, especially in front of Kaya.

'Go. We can get ourselves home.' I barely looked at him as I said the words to him. I had too much on my mind, and perhaps a break from each other would be good to defuse the situation. I didn't want to say things I was going to regret.

We arrived back at the flat around noon. In typical fashion, we had left the house with a cloud-free sky, with promises of sunshine and a dry day, but by the time we arrived home, it was pouring with rain. And of course, I had forgotten to bring an umbrella. Such was the English weather, a trickster and fickle, always hinting at one thing and doing something else. My hair and clothes were wet, sticking to my face and body respectively. I was feeling completely sorry for myself, but tried to keep a brave and smiley face for Kaya.

Not only that, but Kaya was so grumpy she didn't listen to a word I said, both from being tired, hungry and wet and because she had dropped her favourite Berry the Bear, a soft, plush, stuffed animal, along the way somewhere and we hadn't been able to find it in the rain. As all parents know, the biggest obstacles between you and a happy toddler are: 1) hunger, 2) tiredness, and 3) a lost comforter/toy/pacifier of some sort. Most parents realise that there are routines and comforts that one should adhere to, to prevent a Third World War meltdown. And then we are accused of helicopter parenting, which I really think should be renamed "insanity-prevention parenting".

I mechanically and robotically fed her and put her down for her nap, carefully hiding my emotions and overcompensating with songs about little ducks going over the bridge, this little finger on my right, and wool for the little boy who lives down the lane. Internally, I was singing, "It must have been love, but it's over now, it must have been good, but I lost it somehow." OK, so I'm prone to a little exaggeration, but when I get down, I really get down. Sometimes, a good old cry can be quite healing. It's like watching the movie *Love Story*; even though we know we're going to be miserable and will cry for hours after the movie, we still want to watch it, and it feels strangely cathartic.

After Kaya fell asleep, I checked my stats to cheer me up. The thing with blogs is that we become obsessed with views, likes and comments. Another hundred views today. This was my most successful blog post since the inception of the Beta Mum. I opened up my emails and there was another email from Cyberdad. My heart raced a little. I wasn't sure if it was because of the fight with Michael, the hundred new blog views or whether I had been secretly hoping for Cyberdad to write back, but it jolted me out of my misery and into a state of mixed thrill and anticipation. Talk about volatile emotions.

To: The Beta Mum
From: Cyberdad
Sent: October 13 2016, 8:00
Subject: Re:

Dear Beta Mum,
Thanks for answering my email. It was lovely to hear from you. It made my day.

The mums really take the nursery seriously, don't you think? Who's who, who's doing what. Lately, my wife has been so involved with the nursery that I feel like a stranger to her. She is becoming more of an Alpha Mum and we've been growing more distant as each day passes. Although I come home to a house full of people at night, I feel more alone than I have felt in a very long time.

It feels safe writing to you honestly and I don't feel judged by you. Reading your blog, I feel for whatever reason that you understand me.

Can you tell me who you are?
I hope to hear from you again.
Cyberdad

I sat there stunned, reading his email over and over again. This was a lot more than I was expecting. It was so vague, yet so loaded. Was he trying to tell me that his marriage was in trouble? Or that he was lonely in his marriage? And what did he want from me? Just a friendly shoulder to cry on, or something more? I wasn't sure what to make of his email but it resonated with me because it reflected how I felt about the nursery, and how I was starting to feel towards Michael.

What I realised was that the anonymity provided by the Internet allowed people to open up to strangers through blogs, photographs and forums much more quickly than in real life. Instead of feeling that he was a strange, lonely man, I felt that he was someone looking to have a connection with someone he could open up to. And he was the first friendly person I had met since moving to London, which made me want to continue writing to him.

Although he knew a lot about me from reading the blog, I didn't know much about him. What I did know was that Michael thought my blog was silly, whereas Cyberdad was eager to read more of my writing and wanted to engage with me. And anyway, I still had no friends IRL and it felt great to be appreciated in cyberspace, even if it was for my writing about the Alphas.

Reading his email for the hundredth time, I realised that the blog was helping me connect with others in a way that I had never done before. Although it was very narcissistic, the blog gave me another identity than "Just a Mum" (JAM) and it helped me forget – just for a little while – that Michael and I were fighting more than we had ever fought before our move to London.

Even though Michael had warned me to stop writing the blog, I knew that I wanted to continue it. I didn't care that the Cherry Blossoms mothers were reading it. I would ensure that no one found out my identity and all would be well.

I wrote Cyberdad a brief email, unsure where to go with it, but knowing that I still wanted to continue writing to him:

To: Cyberdad
From: The Beta Mum
Sent: October 13 2016, 14:00

Dear Cyberdad,
I am so glad that you feel safe writing to me. I also feel that I can write freely to you. It hasn't been easy adjusting to this new life among the Alphas and it has been lonely too...so I understand how you feel.
    I can't tell you who I am, because I want to stay anonymous. It's part of the beauty of my blog so that I can continue writing freely, without judgement.
Feel free to write to me any time.
The Beta Mum

It wasn't the most eloquent or interesting email ever, but I thought it best to keep it at that for now. I wanted to keep a door open with Cyberdad but I didn't want him to read too much into my emails. I realised that my online friendships were growing much faster than they ever could in real life.

Late that afternoon, when Michael came home, we both acted as if the fight had never happened. We knew that fighting wasn't going to solve anything and although we had opposing views we knew that they couldn't be resolved at the moment. Neither of us liked confrontation. I knew that resentment was slowly and steadily building up in me, but I silently agreed that we would sweep this one under the carpet and try to enjoy a night on our couch in front of the TV.

Even though we weren't overtly fighting any more, I knew that something had shifted in our relationship over the past few months. In Canada, there had been lightness to our relationship, full of wit and jokes, but since Michael had been working so hard, it had all but disappeared. Occasionally our light-hearted banter would pop up, but Michael was too tired and stressed when he came home for work, and I was generally moodier and more sensitive than I ever had been (It didn't help that the Alphas were making my life miserable). Michael had become a workaholic that I saw less and less, and I had become a blogger: someone who wasn't scared of sharing my opinions with the World Wide Web on a virtual platform. We both lived under the same roof but led separate, distinct lives.

Michael and I went through the motions of putting Kaya to bed, choosing what to eat and what DVD to put on. Both of us were careful not to offend the other; I asked if he wanted to watch *The Godfather*, his favourite movie, and he said, 'No, let's watch *Children of Men*,' one of my favourite movies. We watched in silence, without our usual banter or post-film discussion. Perhaps we were also becoming strangers, sitting at either end of the same couch. Like Cyberdad and his wife, who were probably sitting across from each other in a restaurant, two strangers staring at each other, lost in their own sea of loneliness.

Chapter Fourteen

Mumsolini's Dictatorship

The Beta Mum
An Alpha-Land Nursery Winter Fair: A Very Professional Affair

Most school winter fairs and fundraisers involve raising five hundred pounds, which goes into improving the school and benefiting the children, like funding specialised classes, subsidising school trips, or buying new instruments. They involve a few homemade cakes at the cake stall, some second-hand toys to sell, a raffle and some mulled wine.

In Alpha-Land, it is an entirely different affair. Forget about mending broken school tables and chairs. The stakes are higher; homeless people are given homes and single, disadvantaged mothers are provided with a safe place to congregate. Who can say no to "the cause"?

At the helm of the winter fair is Mumsolini, a self-appointed PTA Power Mum Dictator who makes speeches about "the cause". She dictates what her committee members do and think. She looks down on her committee members with disdain and shouts, 'No second-hand or hand-me-downs at the fair! Only professional decorations, donations and doughnuts will do!'

The fair is run like a Fortune 500 company with Excel spread-sheets, PowerPoint presentations, predicted revenue streams and forecasted profits. There is a board with vice-chairs, sec-retaries and treasurers, and there are sales pitches, but instead of selling, they are pleading and scrounging for donations to the fair.

For tickets to the hottest shows in town and exclusive A-list events, forget lastminute.com – the Alpha-Land winter fair is the place to go.

It is, after all, for a good cause.

The Beta Mum

The following week, we were back at Pain et Chocolat listening to Kelly's speech at the first official winter fair committee meeting.

'As I said last week, we are hoping to break last year's fundraising record. Our goal this year is to raise eighty thousand pounds from our winter fair. It's something that's never been done and it would be a historical event for Cherry Blossoms. This year we are hoping to donate the funds towards building a mother-and-child commu-nity centre, which will provide a free, secure place for mothers and children from disadvantaged backgrounds to come for advice, sup-port and friendships. Like last year, I am the chair of the winter fair committee. Poppy Sevigny-Bruce is vice-chair, Mary Wright is the treasurer and Becky Goldberg is the secretary.'

I had received at least fifteen emails about the winter fair since the beginning of the school year, saying "how important fundraising is to the school's ethos and beliefs", and that everyone was "encour-aged" to participate (which I knew really meant had to participate). Already there were a myriad of emails about donations, volunteering and how to make it the best winter fair ever. With each and every email came an underlying pressure that you would be a bad mother if you didn't participate in the school's fundraising. To give the nurs-ery credit, this was a great cause and project.

'It is a collective effort and my job is to try to keep you connected, productive and committed towards our common goal,' Kelly continued.

'We will meet every two weeks until the winter fair to ensure that we are sticking to the timeline. Firstly, I would like to reiterate that we need a lot of donations to make this the most successful winter fair ever. We will need books and presents for the children's presents stall, but also fabulous prizes for the silent auction. Please remember that we do not take used goods. All the books and presents need to be new. And remember, the silent auction is one of the biggest fundraisers so we need you to tap into all of your networks to come up with some great prizes. In the past, we have had amazing donations like Wimbledon Tennis Finals tickets, a private dinner for ten cooked by Gordon Ramsay, a weekend away to New York staying at a five-star hotel, a villa in Tuscany for a week, and tickets to the BAFTAs. We are counting on you to get us some fantastic prizes.' Kelly was motivating the crowd, who sat in rapt attention.

'The winter fair will be divided into four areas: the food and drinks stall, the games, arts and crafts stalls, the Santa's grotto, and the silent auction and wishing-tree stalls. I will take charge of the food and drinks area, Becky will look after the games and crafts, Mary the Santa's grotto and Poppy will look after the silent auction and the wishing-tree area. We have split you up into four groups and we will start brainstorming ideas today and allocating tasks to try to make this fair the best winter fair ever!' She had more enthusiasm than the head cheerleader of a football team.

I was allocated to the food and drinks stall group, and yes, headed by no one else but Kelly. I didn't know if Kelly actually liked me, or just liked the joys of picking on me. We went over the general plan: there would be a "winter café" serving coffees, teas and hot food, with a seating area to have a drink and a bite to eat during the fair. Next to it would be a cakes and cookies stand where cakes, cookies and other pastries would be sold wrapped up, ready to take home.

'Does anyone have any ideas for the various stalls?' Kelly asked our group, made up of ten or so women.

With my newfound confidence, I spoke out.

'How about baking the cakes and cookies with the children so it includes them as well?' I suggested.

'Sophie. No, that wouldn't do. This is a Cherry Blossoms winter fair. We need the cakes and cookies baked by adults. We are trying to raise money. No one is going to buy a hard, stone, inedible cake or a cookie the shape of a blob,' she said, eyeing me patronisingly.

'OK. Then how about a biscuit-decorating area? We could bake the cookies and the children could decorate them on the day of the fair. I am sure we could charge a few pounds per cookie.'

'There isn't space for a biscuit-decorating area. One of the mums in the Fox Cubs class is a caterer. If she could donate some cakes and food, that would be ideal. Why don't you ask her?' Kelly didn't want any actual suggestions. She only liked to hear the sound of her own voice and her own ideas, but had to appear democratic. This wasn't brainstorming; it was Kelly-storming. At least I knew what to expect from her.

'But don't you think we should include the children? Maybe we could get them to help us with decorating the fair, painting winter scenes or cutting out snowflakes,' I insisted.

'Remember our goal, Sophie. This is about raising money for a community centre. This is not an arts and crafts fair. It needs to be the best it can be,' she said crisply, giving me a sickly-sweet smile, tilting her head as if she were talking to a toddler instead of a thirty-three-year-old woman.

The rest of the meeting was dominated by Kelly handing out tasks, which really was Kelly bossing all of us around. Later, after the meeting was over, she came up to me.

'Sophie, I loved your input today.' Kelly paused and smiled tightly. 'But I think there are too many chiefs and not enough Indians. I hope you understand but there's only one chief here, and that's me.' She flicked her shiny blonde hair in my direction.

I tried not to laugh. Kelly was a great character for my blog. She was actually amusing…hilarious, in fact. It was the first time I had looked at her without feeling intimidated.

'You're absolutely right, Kelly – you are the only chief.' I smiled back, unable to help myself.

*

'Kaya is doing much better, Mrs Bennett,' Miss Katie said to me as we were sitting on the multicoloured mini-tables at the parent-teacher conference. 'Did you get a chance to read the online report and see the photos and videos of her?'

'Yes, I did, thank you.' At Cherry Blossoms, a glue-and-paper diary report was not enough to monitor the future leaders of the world's progress; there was an online virtual diary of their every move with photographs, videos, journal entries and Early Years Foundation Stage achievements. Each week, a photo, video and journal log was uploaded and the online diary was accessible at any time. It was very impressive, and far from the yellow, cigarette-paper-thin report cards I used to have growing up. I loved watching the videos, which allowed me a peek into that sacred, mysterious world that Kaya occupied between 9am and 1pm, that I wasn't otherwise privy to.

Kaya's report was for the most part glowing; her language skills were developing appropriately, and her fine and gross motor development were in line with her age. Her interpersonal skills were still lagging behind, with only some occasional interaction with the other children. But there were some signs of progress. Even if she wasn't the initiator, when others came up to her to play, she now played along and started to role-play with them. She wasn't going to win a presidential election with that kind of behaviour, but at least she wasn't rejecting others either. We were off to some kind of start.

'Even though you may feel that she isn't progressing as fast as you would want on the social side, I have seen a huge change in her behaviour. Before, when others wanted to play with her, she would shy away and sometimes run away from them, and barely spoke to other children. Now, she is engaging with them. It shows that she is accepting of others and is learning how to make friends,' Miss Katie said encouragingly. 'And how about those play dates I suggested? Did you manage to organise any?'

'Yes, I organised one each with Anastasia and Chloe. They both went well, I think. Kaya seemed much more comfortable one-on-one than in a larger group,' I told her.

'Keep going with them. I think they can only help. We are very pleased with Kaya's progress. She is slowly coming out of her shell. It can take time. And I am glad to hear you are volunteering at the winter fair, I think she will really enjoy seeing you there. Do you have any questions for me?'

'I don't think so. She seems happier. Definitely,' I said. Despite the initial stumbling blocks, it appeared that Kaya was doing well and was enjoying the nursery more and more, and over the last few weeks, she had appeared livelier and happier. She smiled more often and even the colour in her face seemed rosier and brighter. Her general demeanour had changed imperceptibly into one that was more positive and engaging. Cherry Blossoms was working out for her after all.

The blog continued to do well and I wrote every few days. I checked my stats daily; some days I would get fifty views and would be ecstatic, and some days I would only get four or five views. On the rare day I would get a hundred views, I felt that I was part of something bigger than my small world of west London and Cherry Blossoms. I felt relevant. I felt part of a bigger group of men and women who shared and exchanged ideas on the Internet. It wasn't anywhere as big as the celebrity blogs, but I felt that I was still making a difference.

To: The Beta Mum
From: Cyberdad
Sent: October 18 2016, 20:00
Subject: Re:

Dear Beta Mum,
The post on the Mumsolinis of the winter fair was hilarious. Although, I'm afraid that my wife may be Mumsolini. You're right: for them, working on the Christmas fair is a full-time job. They become so invested in it; it almost becomes an obsession.

Good luck with it!
Best,
Cyberdad

I wrote back:

Dear Cyberdad,

Thanks for your email. I always appreciate receiving them. Now,
I really get what you are going through if your wife is Mumsolini!
It can't be easy!

By the way, do you know the number of a good plumber?
We have an ongoing leak that our landlord can't seem to fix!
Beta Mum

Cyberdad wrote to me every few days after each blog I posted,
commenting on the blog or telling me about his day. We had
developed an easy banter, discussing the Cherry Blossoms mums,
his wife, his children, Michael and his work, and how difficult
it was raising a family. I also asked him about practical things,
like if he knew a good plumber for our leaks, or a gardener for
our back garden we still had not used because of: 1) the rain, 2)
the overgrown rose bushes, and 3) the foxes that came regularly
looking for rubbish.

For the most part we had kept our emails light and airy, and we
had exchanged around five or six emails before I began opening up,
telling him that Michael (Mac in the blog) was a workaholic and
that I was feeling neglected. In return, he slowly told me about his
marriage troubles and his latest email told me everything I needed
to know.

To: The Beta Mum
From: Cyberdad
Sent: October 20 2016, 23:00
Subject: Re:

Dear Beta Mum,

I hope you don't mind that I write to you. I've been really enjoying our emails. They seem to flow easily. I feel like I could tell you anything and you wouldn't judge me or my family. I don't have many people I feel I can speak to so freely. I suppose once you get married, for a lot of men, your wife becomes your confidante and your friends disappear into their own family cocoons. There isn't anyone at work that I could turn to and I rarely go out with friends. Which is why I am turning to you. I hope you don't mind.

I feel lonely in my marriage. Work has been tough since the 2008 crisis. We don't make the money we used to and I've told my wife, but she continues shopping like there's no end to our funds. She doesn't seem to realise that the world has changed and that it is not all happy and cheery. She is also becoming more and more controlling at home. She nags at every opportunity and I don't feel that anything I do is ever good enough. Even when I try to help out with the children, when I dress them or when I try to make their dinner, she always finds a way to find something wrong. I don't feel I am allowed to make any decisions on my own.

Not only that, but her anxiety and control have been rubbing off on our daughter. Our older son is already in full-time school and with after-school activities he isn't around much, so he hasn't been affected as much by it. But our daughter always seems worried, as if something bad is about to happen to her at any time.

And now my wife's involvement in the winter fair is making her more and more stressed. It's not what we need now, and I am at my wits' end. I'm not sure what to do.

Thank you for reading,

Cyberdad

Cyberdad had to be Chris Miller, Kelly Miller's husband. It had to be him. Who else could it be? They had an older son and a younger daughter. She was overly involved in the winter fair. She was neurotic, controlling and I could imagine her rolling her eyes when he threw his clothes on the floor rather than in the laundry basket. No wonder he was coming to me to vent his feelings about her. Michael had mentioned after the parents' evening that Chris' fund wasn't what it once was pre-2008. And she was continuing to spend like they had a never-ending trust fund.

Not only that, but an invitation to Kelly's daughter's birthday party had arrived that morning. It had come in the post, in a large, thick, heavy, pale-cream envelope. It looked more like a wedding invitation with embossed, light-blue writing addressed to Princess Kaya Bennett.

Inside, the invitation read:

Princess Kaya is invited to Princess Olivia's
Cinderella-Themed Fourth Birthday Party
November 12th, 3–6pm
Dorchester Ballroom, Dorchester Hotel
Please RSVP: ClaireWilson@partypoppers.co.uk

This wasn't going to be a slice-of-cake-and-pass-the-parcel type of birthday. Kelly didn't do things by halves; 150 per cent, more like it. She had hired a professional party planner and had booked the entire ballroom of the Dorchester, just about the most exclusive and expensive five-star hotel in London. And her husband had just admitted that they were in financial trouble.

If Cyberdad really was Chris Miller, Kelly could never know. What would she say if she knew that her husband was confiding in me, that I had become his confidante and that he was telling me things that he wouldn't even say to her? I shuddered at the thought. She would make it her sole mission in life to destroy me.

Chapter Fifteen

Cinderella's Party in Alpha-Land

The cacophonous, headache-inducing screams of the children bounced off every wall of the grand ballroom of the Dorchester Hotel. The ballroom had been transformed into a fairy-tale amusement park; there was an eight-foot arch of intertwined pale-blue and white balloons framing the entrance, a giant pink-and-yellow bouncy castle in one corner and a merry-go-round with a pumpkin carriage, birds, mice and horses in another corner. The smells of freshly popped popcorn covered with melted butter hit my olfactory senses, taking me back to the local movie theatre where I had watched *Cinema Paradiso* for the first time as a teenager.

Kaya and I were left speechless, unable to move from where we were standing, taking in the noise, the colours and the action surrounding us. We had just dropped off Olivia's small present, a painting kit, on a specially dedicated presents table at the entrance of the party, which already had at least forty presents in Tiffany's, Harrods and Bonpoint bags piled on top of it. Kaya was offered a sparkly princess tiara at the entrance of the party; most girls couldn't refuse. This party was like being at your own private Disneyland.

Right by where we were standing was a chocolate fountain

overflowing with chocolate sauce and surrounded by white and pink marshmallow skewers to dip in the fountain. On another table, a pyramid of cupcakes was stacked five levels high, carefully iced and decorated with blue birds and ribbons made out of sugar. The birthday cake was a three-tiered castle cake with Cinderella and Prince Charming sugar figurines on top. There was even a candyfloss machine which made glowing candyfloss.

Kelly had invited the entire year – not just our Lion Cubs class, but all the other classes as well. This meant sixty children plus siblings and parents, which meant over two hundred people. There were more people here than there had been at our wedding. And of course, everyone said yes to the invitation, just to see Cinderella's castle in the Dorchester Hotel and drink the free champagne.

'Mummy! This is amazing! Can I go?' Kaya interrupted my thoughts and screamed at me as she wriggled one of her arms out of the sleeve of her Peppa Pig jacket and let me pull the other sleeve off.

'Yes, of course, Kaya.' This was actually better than Disneyland, I decided, because: 1) there weren't two-hour waiting lines for the rides, 2) I wasn't always two seconds away from a panic attack at the thought of losing Kaya, and 3) I could let her run freely without having to be by her side every single second.

I was blown away by the party. It was better than any party that I had ever been to – child or adult. There was a dress-up area with princess dresses and knight costumes, and next to it was Cinderella's room with brooms and buckets, small mice and bunnies to play with and blue birds chirping in cages. It was the ultimate little girl's dream turned into a reality; the live version of the Cinderella story, from rags to riches.

This party must have cost a fortune, and the excess of it all made me feel uncomfortable, but then I saw Kaya in the distance, running from the bouncy castle to spin in the merry-go-round, her face lit up with joy. I hadn't seen her like this in a long time, so relaxed, happy and carefree; as if, for a moment, all the difficulties of the past few months had disappeared. She looked as every child should look for as long as they can; their faces full of pure, unadulterated joy, free of the disappointments, tragedies and resentments that life piles on later.

I felt a sudden relief, as if the knotted muscles in my back were finally relaxed. I began to think that perhaps this move wasn't so bad after all. Perhaps she was finally getting into a more comfortable place, and perhaps I was too.

Mary arrived and stood next to me. 'Hi, Sophie, you look like you're having a good day.'

'It's quite a party,' I said, still stunned by the spectacle, but also thinking about what my mother would say if she were here: 'What a waste of money! Can you imagine how many mouths you could feed in Africa with this money?'

'It's a bit excessive, really,' Mary whispered to me. I was surprised to hear her say that. I thought that being the power woman that she was – a partner at a hedge fund – she was used to this type of excess and that it wouldn't faze her. This was the second time she'd surprised me, the first time being when I found out that she was the treasurer of the winter fair committee.

I hadn't seen Mary around much since her nanny usually did the morning drop-off (Mary went to work at 6am), but we had met a few times at the winter party committee meetings and what I knew about her, I began to understand. She was a hard-working mother who was trying to juggle motherhood and her career. Even if I hadn't made the same choices as her, I respected her. When she took on the role of treasurer at the winter fair, I was impressed that she was taking time out for it.

'I agree with you,' I said. 'This whole party…Olivia's not even going to remember it. And what's Kelly going to do for next year's party? And her sixteenth?'

'I heard of a dad who bought his daughter a new Ferrari for her sixteenth, even though she's too young to have a licence,' Mary said to me.

'Some people don't know what to do with their money – they should donate to some charity or something. I just don't see how this is setting a good example for their children,' I said to her, shaking my head.

'Well, you know it's about the parents and not the child when the party involves five-star hotels, unlimited champagne and professional photographs.'

'By the way, I was surprised to see you at the winter fair meeting the other day. I didn't think you would have the time to help out with that.'

'I don't really have the time, but I've felt so guilty about working so hard that I felt like I should be more involved at the nursery. Milo has been giving me guilt trips regularly about not helping out at the nursery or coming to read at the parent reading mornings, so I am taking a few days off to spend time with him and promised him that I would help out at the winter fair.'

'Is there a way for you to work less and spend more time with him?' I asked her.

'I wish I could spend more time with him, but my husband's fund isn't doing well and I am working all hours to maintain our lifestyle. His fund keeps him busy and gives him something to do, but it hasn't been making any money for years.' She had a look of regret in her eyes and sighed. 'I love what I do but sometimes I wish I could work less. It's not an option though. It's an all-or-nothing job, so I don't even think about it. There are only so many hours in the day, and so much time for me to do it all.'

'Maybe you could move somewhere less expensive?'

'There's no way he would agree to it. He was born in London, raised in London and his expectation is that we stay in London. It would be a big failure to him if we left. I know it's about his ego, but there's not much I can do about it.'

'Wow. I'm sorry to hear that, Mary. I didn't realise it was so hard for you.'

'That's why we only have one child,' she confessed. 'I wouldn't be able to handle more guilt about not seeing my children.'

It was the first time Mary had spoken to me so frankly and honestly. The first day of nursery I had wrongly assumed that she was a hard-ass, lunch-is-for-wimps career woman who put her job in front of everything else, when she left her son so quickly after dropping him off and he was left crying on his own, but now I could see that there was much more to her, and at play. She was trying her best to keep her family afloat in London in any way she could.

At that moment, Laetitia arrived and kissed us on both cheeks.

'Hello, how are you?' she asked us both.

'We were just talking about the party, work and the winter fair,' Mary explained.

'Oh, it is a great party.' She scanned the room, turning in a circle as her large, trendy, mohair sleeveless coat swirled around her, approving of what she saw. 'Very well organised.'

'I was just telling Sophie that work has been overtaking my life lately and I'm trying to make amends with Milo by volunteering for the winter fair,' Mary explained. Even though Mary and Laetitia weren't what I would consider friends – we didn't speak on the phone or see each other regularly for a coffee – they had become familiar and comfortable. We didn't have much in common – as a matter of fact, not much at all apart from having children the same age at the same nursery – but it seemed as if we were beginning to fit into each other's lives.

'Initially, I volunteered to be treasurer because I'm quite good with numbers, but then I was assigned the Santa's grotto without volunteering and now I feel like I may have to give up my day job to run it,' Mary joked.

'Have you read the Beta Mum's post on the winter fair? It sounds like it is very intense,' Laetitia said, as if she were giving us the inside scoop.

'You can say that again. And it's pretty clear who Mumsolini is.' Mary nodded her head towards Kelly in the distance as she said that. Meanwhile, I felt like I was shrinking again, and tried to hide my guilt.

'Now we know that the Beta Mum is a Cherry Blossoms mum, and is volunteering at the winter fair,' Mary continued, 'it narrows down the list of suspects by quite a lot. There were about forty mums at the meeting and we were split into four groups.'

'Do you think you know who it is?' Laetitia's eyes grew bigger out of interest, and I feigned the same interest, as I felt a layer of hot sweat accumulate on the back on my neck and my heart skipping a few beats.

'I don't know yet, but I am sure I will know by the end of the year,' Mary said.

'I keep hearing that Annabelle is the Beta Mum because she was a journalist before,' Laetitia suggested.

'Or it could be Becky. She's very involved in the fair,' I suggested, attempting to turn the attention away from me.

'Becky's too close to Kelly. And she is too much of an Alpha. She loves the winter fair. She's always very involved. I doubt she would write that about her best friend. Although, perhaps that's how she really feels about Kelly and can't say it out loud? Not a bad theory, Sophie,' Mary said.

'By the way, did you hear about Vladimir Dimitrov's assassination attempt last night?' Laetitia said, and I welcomed the change of conversation.

'What happened?' I asked. I had written an email to Irina Dimitrov's PA about organising another play date with Anastasia, as Miss Katie had suggested, but I had never heard back.

'Someone tried to break into their Kensington Palace Gardens mansion last night. They think the security guards were drugged with their dinner and fell asleep, but one of them woke up when he heard noise and found someone running in the back garden. He chased him away but the police found that the intruder left traces of aconite poison behind. Someone was definitely trying to kill Vladimir Dimitrov.'

All the security at Irina's house had been warranted after all, and the bodyguards following them around were for a reason. But it was not a normal way to grow up, and I felt sorry for Anastasia. She had not asked to grow up surrounded by security guards, or in fear.

We scattered when our respective children came to pull on our arms, asking about balloon sculptures, candyfloss and cupcakes. As Kaya stuffed her face with sticky, glow-in-the-dark candyfloss, becoming more hyper by the minute, I exhaled at the thought of the conversation about the Beta Mum. That had been a close call. The layer of sweat that had formed at the nape of my neck began dissipating. I was leaving too many clues and too many trails. It was only a matter of time until they found me out.

How would they react if they knew it was me, I wondered? Laetitia and Mary seemed like they were amused, but I couldn't expect them to be supportive once I was exposed. No one would talk to me if they knew I was scrutinising their every move and exposing them all over the Internet. Even celebrities wanted the final filter on their lives.

As the party continued, I saw Chris Miller standing surrounded by a few of the fathers who had showed up, smiling his white-teeth smile, laughing at what someone had said. He was handsome in that American-film-star kind of way: glossy, thick hair, charming smile, sincere and genuine-looking. You know, the Ryan Reynolds look that says, 'You can trust me.'

He was wearing the typical Cherry Blossoms dad's uniform of a white-collared, button-down shirt, which was tucked in his Diesel jeans. He had one hand tucked into his pocket and one holding a glass of champagne. He looked camera-ready. A shiver ran down my spine, and butterflies began fluttering in my stomach frenetically, as if they had been caught in a jar and couldn't get out. As if he knew I was looking at him, his eyes met mine and he smiled at me even more – if that were even possible – and raised his glass.

Was it possible that he knew I was the Beta Mum? OK, I was becoming paranoid. There was no way he knew; he didn't even know I existed, and I still wasn't even sure that he was Cyberdad. I relaxed a bit. Next to him, Mary Wright's husband was telling a story and David, Becky's husband, was hanging on every word, his chin slightly elevated to make himself look taller. I still wasn't sure about Chris, but I couldn't exclude him from my list. Just as all the mothers were trying to uncover the Beta Mum, I was trying to uncover Cyberdad. I wondered if he was also at this party, and whether he was also trying to find me.

By the end of the party, Kaya was so exhausted that she fell asleep in the taxi, her soft brown hair in my lap. She smiled and sighed intermittently as she slept and I thought of that phrase, "you're only as happy as your unhappiest child", and at that moment, I really believed it. Her smiling face was like a magic wand that instantly made me feel happy and at peace. It had been a hectic party, but Kaya had loved it. But this clearly wasn't the real world. It had been so excessive, but I was glad that Kaya had had such a good time and I realised that I had actually enjoyed chatting to Laetitia and Mary. Perhaps we were becoming friends after all.

'How was the party?' Michael asked later, after we'd gotten home and Kaya was tightly ensconced in her bed, listening to a lullaby playing on her baby monitor. We were sitting around the large dining table in the open-plan kitchen having a takeaway dinner from the local sushi delivery store.

'It was incredible. There were bouncy castles, merry-go-rounds, magicians, princesses, popcorn machines, birds and mice, all in the middle of this hotel ballroom. I don't think you could have more at a party. You couldn't even call it a party. It was an amusement park.'

'I missed a great party, by the sounds of it.' Michael had decided to stay home, saying that it would be only mums at the party.

'It was better than our wedding. Really. There were at least two hundred guests, champagne was flowing, there was a three-tiered cake and there was even a DJ and a dance floor to recreate Cinderella's ball. Except that they were playing Beyoncé and Pharrell Williams instead of the Viennese Waltz.'

'OK, you seem a bit excited.' Michael laughed. 'You actually seem happy.' It was the first time we'd had a light conversation in weeks. For the most part, that feeling of being disconnected and distant from each other had persisted and had only gotten worse.

'There were a lot of the dads there,' I offered gently.

'Sophie. Can we *not* do this tonight?' Michael replied, his tone quickly switching from laughter to anger in a split second.

'I didn't mean to upset you. I just wanted to tell you that there were a lot of dads and you wouldn't have been at all out of place.

That's all.' Everything I said seemed to trigger an argument these days. I didn't know what to say any more.

'I can't go on like this with you like that. Always resenting me all the time,' he said, his tone of voice still angry. He turned his face away from me and faced the living room, away from my eyes.

'I can't either.' I looked down at my hands, which couldn't stop fiddling with each other in my lap.

'Do you want us to go home, back to Canada? At this point, I'm willing to go back. Give it all up. You're right. It's not worth it. Let's go back.' He turned back to face me and spoke sarcastically.

'I'm sorry. I shouldn't have said that. I don't want to leave yet. I feel that Kaya is finally getting to a happy place, and I feel like I might be starting to make friends.' I had been the one telling him we needed to leave all this time, but for some reason I wasn't quite ready to go yet. I was finally getting somewhere with Kaya, and I was getting used to Cherry Blossoms, despite the Kelly-dictatorship and all. 'Let's wait and see how things are going by the end of the year when we go back to Canada over Christmas and New Year's.'

'OK. Come here, Sophie-Bee,' he said a few minutes later after calming down. He came towards me and hugged me, but it felt like a cold, hard hug instead of the overwhelming, soft ones he used to give me. Instead of feeling a rush of love, I felt nothing.

That night, after Kaya and Michael had gone to bed, I sat in front of my computer and began writing.

The Beta Mum
Rites and Rituals in Alpha-Land

In Alpha-Land, children's birthday parties are considered to be one of the most important rituals of the year. There are rules and traditions to be adhered to for these elaborate affairs:

1 First a date is decided upon and a "save the date" is sent, at least four to six months in advance, depending on the venue

or the entertainer's availability, to ensure that the date is fixed in everyone's calendar. This exhibits territorial dominance over people's time and attention.

2   The chosen venue should offer food, drinks and space for at least twenty children in the class, plus siblings, friends, parents, grandparents and others. This would amount to space for at least 120 people. Five-star hotel ballrooms, private gardens and private rooms in restaurants are all ideal options.

3   A theme is chosen, often based on a Disney movie (think Toys, Finding Nemo, Frozen, The Little Mermaid, Cars or Cinderella), and every detail of the party should match the theme – music, banners, balloons, cutlery, plates, cups, cakes, gift bags, entertainers, invitations and rides.

4   Invitations should not be homemade or handwritten if possible; thick, heavy 600gsm wedding-style invitations, videos or professionally designed 3D invites are best. Little treats, like candies or DVDs, accompanying the invite always make a good impression.

5   As mentioned, cakes should be professionally outsourced, matching the theme, a few layers and a few feet high, with sugar sculptures of princesses, dragons, cars, castles and Mickey Mouse.

6   Amazon-bought decorations from Amscan just won't do. Professional party planners are hired to create a fantasy world with decorations matching a film set; fake snow for a Frozen-themed party, DJs and coloured dance floors for dance parties, and props like real, live animals, such as ponies, baby bunnies or meerkats for a zoo-themed party.

7   Choosing food and drinks is a huge undertaking; first, children's food should be decided upon from a choice of grilled chicken,

pasta, sushi and crab cakes. Adults should also be provided for with proper French champagne (Prosecco will NOT do), and finger foods of beef sliders, roasted vegetable quiche and bruschetta are on offer. Gluten-free food should be available, as well as nut-free, allergen-free food, which should have its own table, so as not to cross-contaminate the allergen-full food.

8   Presents from an H store are optimal (Harrods, Hamleys, Harvey Nics) and should be carefully chosen as some parents acquire the reputation of giving the "best presents" and therefore their children are always invited to every birthday party (ten Barbies, a giant doll's house, a tablet or a camera will do).

9   Gift bags are expected at every party and plastic tat is deemed unacceptable. At the most illustrious parties, the value of the gift bag is higher than the value of the actual presents given; a pretty J.Crew necklace, a Disney Play-Doh ice cream-making set, or a bow-and-arrow set. Goldfish as a party favour are very popular and end up costing the invitee more than they expect: an aquarium, an air filter, fish food, a fish buddy and a holiday fish nanny.

10   Presents and present requests are also an etiquette issue, from parents requesting everyone to chip in for a tablet, or parties where presents are not required (for parents who already spoil their children enough), to parties where donations to charities are requested.

After I finished writing and published the post, I checked my email, and there was an email from Cyberdad.

To: The Beta Mum
From: Cyberdad
Sent: November 12 2016, 21:00

Dear Beta Mum,

It was a fantastic party, wasn't it? We were both there. In the same room. I wonder if we spoke. I looked around the room and thought about you. Do you sometimes wonder what it would be like if we met? Do you wonder about me?

I often wonder what you look like and sound like. What it would be like if we met.

Do you think about it too?

Cyberdad

I took the opportunity, as both Michael and Kaya were sleeping, to write back:

To: Cyberdad
From: The Beta Mum
Sent: November 12 2016, 23:45

Dear Cyberdad,

I do sometimes wonder about you, and I often wonder who you are. But we decided to keep it anonymous, didn't we? It would be too complicated if we ever met. We can't meet. It would be a bad idea. I know you still love your wife, and I still love my husband. Feelings could get muddled. Both of our relationships are strained right now and I don't know what it would mean for both of us.

I like the way we are. Let's keep it that way.

Beta Mum

Moments later, my laptop alerted me to a new message in my inbox.

To: The Beta Mum
From: Cyberdad
Sent: November 12 2016, 23:52

Dear Beta Mum,
You're right. Absolutely. I just couldn't help myself. I had to ask.
Good night,
Cyberdad

We decided to meet at the playground. I saw him from across the swings and see-saw as he moved slowly towards me. As soon as he reached me, he grabbed me, forcefully but gently enough to make me feel aroused but safe in his arms. His soft yet firm lips locked with mine and we kissed. He pulled me tightly to him, taking my breath away.

He slowly ran his hand up my thigh, up to the point where my thigh met my hip, pushing up my red skirt to reveal my black lacy underwear. His hand disappeared between my thigh and the intricate lace pattern of my underwear. He kissed the nape of my neck, slowly and gently, as if he were touching a statue he didn't want to break. His other hand was wrapped around my waist. He then softly caressed my breast. He smelled of a masculine, seductive aftershave mixed with his sweat. I breathed it in, feeling drunk from it and from his touch.

He ripped open my shirt and began kissing my breasts and my head swung backwards as I let out a small moan, losing myself in his hands and lips. My breath became shallower and quicker, and I could feel my skin tingle. My nails dug into his back, so hard that I was sure I was leaving scratch marks down his back that he would have to hide. Our lips met again and I followed his lead, letting his melt into mine. He stopped kissing me to look me in the eyes, his bright aquamarine-blue eyes looking deep in mine, vulnerable...

My phone's catchy tune rang and abruptly interrupted my dream. I had been meditating and had slowly drifted into a state of semi-consciousness, half awake and half asleep, when my fantasy with Cyberdad took over. The dream had felt so clear and real. In my dream, Cyberdad was Chris Miller and I had fallen in love with him. My feelings had seemed so real that I was blushing with embarrassment even though no one else was in our flat, and I was alone with my thoughts. I got up and ran for the phone.

'Hello?' I said as I put the phone to my ear. It was rare than anyone ever called me on my phone here, apart from automated voicemails asking if I had recently been in a car accident and if I had PPI insurance.

'Oh, hello, Mrs Bennett, it's Edward Calthorpe-Huntington calling,' he said. What a way to wake up from a fantasy: a phone call from your daughter's nursery consultant.

'Oh, hi, Edward. How are you?' I asked, flustered, trying to keep my voice as steady as possible, and not to give away my discomfort.

'I'm very well, thank you. I was calling to ask you precisely the same question. How are you, Mrs Bennett?'

'Good, good,' I said as I tried to get myself together.

'Am I calling at a bad time?' he asked, sensing my distraction.

'Uhm, no, not really.' Although I really meant, Yes, you really are catching me at a bad time. I was just having a fantasy about one of my daughter's classmates' dads.

'I was calling to see how you were doing and if you had any thoughts about switching nurseries.'

'Oh, right. As a matter of fact, Michael and I were talking about it last night.' I paused, thinking of how I would respond to his question. 'I think for now, we will stay where we are.'

'Does that mean you are – how shall I put this – enjoying it more?' he said. I knew that he was really asking if I was fitting in more.

'I think I am getting used to it. And Kaya seems to like it more now. I don't think switching now would do anyone any good.'

'That is good news, Mrs Bennett,' he said, his voice hinting that he was feeling very satisfied with his advice to me.

'Yes. I think so. Thank you, Edward.'

'Well, then. Goodbye, Mrs Bennett.'

I sank back into our sofa and exhaled, breathed heavily and then closed my eyes.

The Beta Mum

How To Get Into the Most Exclusive Nursery in Alpha-Land

Getting into the most prestigious and exclusive nursery school in Alpha-Land is akin to getting into an Ivy League university. Here are some of the guidelines:

1 Planning, researching and preparation must be carried out months in advance.

2 "Educational consultants" are called upon to help with the admissions process at five hundred to three thousand pounds per consultation. There are even special "cradle-to-Cambridge" packages if so desired.

3 Visits and interviews are scheduled and references given by the "right people", which include alumni and donors.

4 Early registration is encouraged, the day of birth being the most appropriate time.

5 Thereafter, letters of interest are sent regularly to increase one's chances of admission.

6 There is a secret, precise algorithm of admission based on postcodes, job profiles, attractiveness and connections. Each is given a certain number of points, with those scoring the most points gaining immediate admission.

7 The most contentious issue is the allocation of "morning" and "afternoon" spots. Morning spots are particularly coveted since toddlers usually still nap in the afternoon, therefore allowing mums to drop off their children in the morning, giving them time to run to their gym class, pick up their children for lunch, and then put them down for a lazy afternoon nap, while the mums

paint their nails and blow-dry their hair. Afternoon spots are a nuisance to mothers because a) mornings still need to be filled with activities, b) children are grumpy from their lack of a nap, and c) coordinating drop-offs and pick-ups is much harder with other siblings at different schools. Therefore, morning spots are extremely coveted and desired.

8   It is rumoured and confirmed that morning spots are reserved for a) the celebrities and supermodels, b) the have-yachts, and c) the PTA kiss-asses. (The afternoon mums seethe with rage, calling morning mums "snobs" when allocated an afternoon spot, while the morning mothers consider themselves "carefully chosen based on being like-minded individuals who would get along".)

Getting into the "best nursery in the world" is not an easy job.
Good luck!
The Beta Mum

The next day, I received an email from a Sarah Wellesley, a writer at the *London Post*.

To: The Beta Mum
From: Sarah Wellesley
Sent: November 16 2016, 9:30
Subject: Interview Request

Dear Beta Mum,
I loved your last post on getting into nurseries in Alpha-Land. I am writing an article about private nurseries in London.
    Can I interview you about it? My number is 08877678o.
Best,
Sarah Wellesley

My blog was so popular that journalists were reading it! It was thrilling. And they liked it so much that they wanted to interview me about it. I called her right back.

'Hello, this is the Beta Mum. You wrote me an email about nurseries in London?'

'Yes, thank you for calling me, Beta Mum. Is that what I should call you? The Beta Mum?'

'Yes please. I want to keep the blog anonymous, so it's best if I don't tell you my real name. And I don't want to give anything up that could expose who I am.'

'No problem. I completely understand. So, I've been reading your blog posts and I've found them fascinating. Really fascinating. I'm thinking about writing an article on nurseries for the elite and wondered if I could ask you a few questions.'

I felt flattered. I was being interviewed by one of the biggest media outlets in the world, and they wanted my opinions.

'Of course. But I've written most of what I know in the blog posts.'

'It sounds like there are some pretty bitchy mothers at this nursery of yours.'

'There are some very opinionated mothers, for sure.' I was careful with my words, not wanting them to be misconstrued.

'And it sounds incredibly hard to get into these nurseries.'

'It is. My last post explains it all, and you can probably get all the information you want from it.'

'How did you get in?'

'I think it was a lot of luck. I did have help, though, from a connection and an educational consultant.'

'And from reading your blog, it seems that you feel like an outsider?'

'For the most part, yes.'

'Have you felt that many of the women are bitchy and competitive?' she pressed, pressuring me into telling her any gossip she could use.

'Yes.'

'Can you give me some examples?'

'Uhm, I don't think so, but you can read about it in my blog. Sorry.'

'So why do you stay if the mothers are all bitchy and competitive?'

'It's a very good nursery,' I explained.

'Right. And can you tell me who the celebrities are?'

I stopped to think about my answer, but then realised how stupid I was, and that this journalist only wanted to extract the dirt and gossip on Cherry Blossoms and nothing more. I felt torn, feeling important because someone wanted to interview me, but at the same time guilty that I was doing something I really shouldn't be doing.

'No, sorry I can't tell you any more. There's everything you need on my blog. Good luck.'

I put the phone down and sat down on dining room chair. Saying too much was going to get me in real trouble, I thought nervously. And I had come too close. I was blurring the lines of what I could say, I realised. What if she called again, or came to the nursery looking for me? Having a blog was one thing, but speaking to the press was another matter altogether.

Chapter Sixteen

More! More! More!

'Please don't take it the wrong way, Sophie, darling...' Kelly said, looking at the bake sale stall with scepticism and wrinkling her little nose in disdain.

How else was I going to take it, I wondered? It was never good to start a sentence with, "Please don't take this the wrong way", unless what you were about to say was meant to be taken in the wrong way.

'...But the bake sale stand is not really up to the standard of the other stalls,' Kelly sputtered out, unable to restrain herself and her critical comments. 'The bake sale stand really needs to stand out, you see. Even though it isn't one of the biggest moneymaking stands, it still needs to be amazing. I'm sure you can do better.' Kelly smiled primly and patted my forearm. I was fixing a few last-minute decorations that had fallen off onto the table, and my arm became flaccid and limp in reaction to her comment.

I looked at the stand and scanned the array of chocolate-chip cookies, beetroot brownies, flourless chocolate cake, red velvet cupcakes and vegan, dairy-free oat and raisin cookies, and felt deflated. To me, it looked like a nice, perfectly adequate nursery bake sale stall, with white plastic tablecloths covering the hall tables and a few plastic wintery accessories. OK, so I had bought them at Poundland, which I had rationalised would keep costs down, meaning more profit for the fair. It was obvious that my stand looked a little sad to Kelly.

'Right. I will get to it right away,' I said, looking at her, knowing that no matter how hard I wanted her to be nice to me, it was never going to happen.

The Cherry Blossoms social calendar had kept me busy and the emails had started coming, fast and furious, on a daily basis from Kelly. Her email headings read, *More! More! More! We need more donations and more volunteers!* and *Come and Help!* She sent out an Excel spreadsheet with the volunteer slots that needed to be filled, another spreadsheet for the donations for each stall (and the donations that were still missing), and a final one with the projected profits for each stall.

For the bake sale stall, there was a breakdown of what goods were expected, the cost per cookie/cake/cupcake, and the projected sales figures. I knew that Kelly was a perfectionist and an organiser and she was pushing her team to deliver, but it was beginning to feel overwhelming. I just wanted it to be over.

The blog had also been taking up a lot of my time and my daily views were growing. My Australian fans kept the banter going, and I now had thirty Australian mums who followed me eagerly, and would always ask when the next blog post was coming out. I had been averaging one or two blogs per week. I kept writing because I felt I owed it to them, even if my regular fans only accounted for about fifty or sixty people in the world.

Cyberdad continued writing to me, especially at night, and I would read his emails when Michael was working late or when he came home from work and went straight to bed. We wrote more seriously now, about our children, our marriages, our fears and our difficulties in finding happiness. We had managed to keep our identities hidden from each other, hiding in the comfort of our anonymity.

The initial banter had become a deeper and closer connection that had been created out of words in cyberspace. I felt closer to him than anyone I had met since we had arrived in London. At times, I even felt closer to him than to Michael. I wondered what he thought about me, what we were doing and what would come of it. He'd admitted to me that things with his wife were worsening and that she barely spoke to him any more, blanking him when he came home.

I stared at Kelly and wondered again, as I had many times before, whether she could be Cyberdad's wife. I blushed, remembering my fantasy, and quickly left for John Lewis to buy decorations to redecorate the bake sale stall.

There, I found soft, cottony snow, shiny silver stars, glittery baubles, small Christmas trees and Christmas-themed cake stands. I rang the babysitter to beg her to stay on later than our agreed time, and then rushed back to the hall by 6.30pm and continued decorating past 9pm.

Kelly was still delegating, criticising and advising when I left. But before I left, she walked by my stand and commented on it.

'That's more like it,' she said, after I had spent over 250 pounds just on decorating the stall.

The next day, the winter fair was in full swing. I had to give it to Kelly: it was stunning. It was like walking into a mini Harrods with pyramids of glistening presents, bushels of food, and elaborate decorations everywhere you turned. One of the mums, a film-set creator, had borrowed props and had turned the hall into a veritable winter wonderland, with snow, a life-sized sleigh, live baby reindeers and Santa in the Santa's grotto. It was on par with a Harrods' Christmas window.

There stood at the entrance to the fair an eight-foot Norwegian Christmas tree with silver and gold baubles, which had prize numbers inside for both adults' and children's wishes. The silent auction, the biggest moneymaker, offered trips to New York, a pre-Oscars party in LA, a heli-skiing trip to Whistler and a week-long villa stay in Tuscany. It was much more than a nursery fair; it equalled the best fundraising galas you could imagine.

Kelly had pushed her worker bees to the point of stress and exhaustion over the past week, treating the fair as if it was a multi-million-pound affair. But it had paid off. The bake sale stand was much better off now than it had been yesterday, I admitted. But I still didn't know whether to think that it was an incredible feat, or that she really needed to find a day job.

I stood at the bake sale stall with Laetitia, who had been peer-pressured into volunteering for the day, while customers milled around in between the stacks of presents and hand-made and hand-decorated wreaths.

'It is a very good job you have done, Sophie,' she said in her thick French accent.

'Thanks, Laetitia. It wasn't quite up to Kelly's standard originally, but I managed to make it just about acceptable to her by nine o'clock last night.'

'Oh, that is very late. I wanted to try to help out more at the fair, but it has been a very difficult time since September. By the way, thank you for the play date with Chloe. She had a very nice time.'

'No problem. It was our pleasure. Maybe you could come to our place next time and we can have a coffee together?' I offered.

'It would be lovely, but I am often in Paris at the moment. My father has been sick so I have been back and forth to Paris each week.'

'I am so sorry to hear that, Laetitia. Is he OK?'

'Unfortunately, he has cancer. Lung cancer. From the time when we thought smoking cigarettes was healthy. It is quite advanced, and I've had to take over the company full-time as he cannot work very much any more.'

'I had no idea. That must be really tough,' I said, feeling bad for her and guilty that my problems seemed small in comparison.

'Yes, it is. He has chemotherapy every week and my mother is tired from taking care of him all the time. She needs more and more help from me. It has not been a very easy few months.' Her face looked tired, she had bags under her eyes and her skin looked ashen, as if for just a moment the perfect mask had dropped to reveal how she was really feeling inside.

'Please let me know if I can do anything, Laetitia. I could pick up Chloe from school if that helps, or take her home for play dates. Anything. Really, I have more time on my hands than I know what to do with,' I said honestly.

'The truth is that we have now decided that we must move back to Paris. I need to look after my father, my mother and also the company. It is a family company and someone needs to take care of it. There is no one else but me, as I am an only child. I have not told Cherry Blossoms yet but we are probably leaving at Christmas and not coming back.'

'That's such a shame,' I said, and genuinely meant it. Even though Laetitia and I weren't from the same world – she came from a prominent French family who owned one of the biggest fashion companies in France, making luxury cashmere sweaters, dresses and scarves, and was married to a French aristocrat – I realised that in the end we shared some of the same values. Our families were at the centre of our worlds, and we would do anything for them.

I now felt that I understood her better, and it made sense; all the times she had been distracted or not completely focused. It was the first time we'd had a real one-to-one conversation, and it felt like we had come one step closer in building a friendship, but I also realised that she was leaving soon for France and had a lot more on her mind than friendships.

After our conversation was broken by a customer, Laetitia put her smile and her brave face back on and handed out some gluten-free cupcakes and cookies in exchange for twenty pounds, as if our conversation had never happened.

The winter fair was a resounding success. We raised 78,880 pounds, and although we hadn't reached Kelly's target of eighty thousand pounds, it was still an enormous amount of money for our hard work. An anonymous donation raised another five thousand for the community centre, so in the end, we did exceed our target. After the winter fair finished, I felt relieved. I hadn't realised how much tension had been building during the fair, and how much pressure I had subliminally felt from Kelly breathing down my neck constantly.

Cyberdad had been writing to me more than ever, almost every day. In his last email, he had really opened up, admitting that his wife was having real anxiety issues.

To: The Beta Mum
From: Cyberdad
Sent: December 4 2016, 23:00
Subject: Re:

Dear Beta Mum,
I don't know what to do any more. My wife has started having panic attacks and is seeing a therapist. She has started taking anti-anxiety medication and antidepressants. The winter fair put so much pressure on her, and even though I told her to let it go, and it's not that important, she can't seem to see that it is just a nursery school fair. She can't sleep at night, she hasn't been eating and she talks so fast I can barely understand her. She's a different woman to the woman I first met and fell in love with. She seems like a stranger, obsessed with things that really shouldn't matter. She's panicking because our daughter still doesn't have a place at a school, even though it's almost a year away, and is even starting tutoring to prepare her for school assessments.

I think she is lost. She's lost her identity since having children, and since she stopped working. She overcompensates by planning and scheduling activities for the children and she is pushing our son to pass the 7+ and our daughter to prepare for the school interviews.

What worries me even more is that our daughter is really starting to show signs of anxiety. She seems afraid of everything. She won't leave our side and cries all the time. We are taking her to see a child psychologist in the next few days. I am sure that it is the pressure and anxiety that my wife is projecting onto her.

My wife has over-scheduled her to the point that she doesn't have a minute to play with other children.

I don't know what to do. What do you think?

Cyberdad

I replied right away.

To: Cyberdad
From: The Beta Mum
Sent: December 4 2016, 23:02

Dear Cyberdad,
I am so sorry to hear this, especially about your daughter. I think it's great that you're seeing a child psychologist and at least your wife seems like she is getting help. You're doing the right thing. Keep going with it. I'm sure your wife will eventually realise that these things don't matter, and that all that matters is her children and you.
I'm thinking about you.
Beta Mum

Could it be that Kelly was in fact anxious and depressed? She certainly looked anxious all the time. Olivia didn't seem to talk very much, which could be a sign of anxiety. And Kelly had told me that Olivia didn't have time for any play dates. I was being pulled into Cyberdad's world and had started caring – about him, about his daughter, and almost about his wife.

In the middle of these feelings, I knew that I was beginning to have real feelings for him. I wasn't sure what kind of feelings, but there were feelings. I felt like I was being pulled in his direction and away from Michael. I didn't know what Cyberdad truly thought about me, but I brushed away all these feelings and convinced myself that we both wanted a friendship; someone to talk to. Nothing more and nothing less.

*

A few weeks later, I was at a play date with Chloe and Laetitia at Lady Diana's Princess Playground.

'How's your father doing?' I asked Laetitia.

'Oh, not so well. He's lost his appetite, and lost so much weight. It's a cliché to say, but he is a shell of his old self. It's really difficult seeing him like this.' You could see the pain on her face as she winced saying those words.

'That must be so difficult,' I said.

'I am having to return to Paris next week and then the week after for his chemotherapy, and I will be missing the Christmas play. And my husband won't be able to make it either. It's a very difficult time.' She shook her head as she watched Kaya and Chloe playing in the sandpit.

'Oh, that's such a shame. Why don't I take some pictures for you? I would be happy to. And maybe Chloe can come over to ours after the play?'

'Thanks, Sophie, that would be lovely. I'll also be missing Kelly's charity Christmas dinner tomorrow night. I hear it's going to be a really big one this year.'

'Oh, what charity Christmas dinner?' My ears burned. I hadn't heard of the dinner before.

'Kelly's charity Christmas dinner? I am sure you were invited. She invites all the mothers from the class for a fundraising dinner. This year it's for the Syrian refugee appeal. Everyone donates however much they can. This year we can also bring clothes, canned food and toys for the refugees. Last year, she raised fifty thousand pounds for Great Ormond Street Hospital. She's very generous.'

'Are you sure we're talking about the same Kelly?' I looked at her, thinking that "generous" was not the first adjective that came to my mind when describing Kelly.

'Yes, it is Kelly.' Laetitia laughed. 'She can be quite bossy at times, but she's involved in many children's charities. She's a great philanthropist. I think, deep inside, she means well but doesn't always know how to show it. She brings toys and books to the charities and hospitals regularly.'

'I had no idea.' Maybe there was a lot more to Kelly than I thought.

'The Americans, they are so good at charity work. It is in their blood to fundraise, volunteer and donate. The French should follow their lead but we are too busy going on strike for that.' She looked mildly exasperated. 'Will you go to the dinner?'

I looked at her sheepishly. 'I don't think I've been invited.'

'I'm sure you have. Check your emails. All the mothers were invited.'

But I knew I hadn't been invited. I wouldn't have missed that email. And when I had seen Kelly earlier that day, she had said to me, 'See you on Friday at the Christmas play,' not mentioning her dinner to me. I was definitely not invited.

Even if Kelly was never going to be my best friend, I was hurt at being excluded from the dinner, especially when I would have really liked to help out the Syrian appeal. My face must have shown how crestfallen I was because Chloe quickly added that it wasn't a big deal and squeezed my arm, realising her faux pas.

I turned away from her as soon as I could to hide how terrible I was feeling. How could Kelly be so giving to some and so terrible to others? It didn't make any sense. Her work sounded impressive and I would have loved to get involved, but she clearly didn't want me to be part of it.

Chapter Seventeen

Why Didn't My Daughter Get the Solo?

The Christmas nativity play and the Christmas party were held on the last day of term at St Peter's Church, a local Anglican church a fifteen-minute stroll from our house. Having survived the winter fair, I thought the nativity play would be a walk in the park. I convinced myself that all I had to do was sit in my seat and survive fifty minutes of out-of-tune Christmas carols. Or so I thought.

When we arrived at the church, we were motioned towards the side entrance, where the children were dropped off to get changed into their costumes. There was a crowd of nannies and a few mothers pushing to drop off their children, like a protest except without the police to supervise the pushing. Kaya stood looking scared and afraid of being run over, just like the first day of school, when Kelly had bulldozed past her. She was eventually let in, and I went around to the main entrance, where a long line of nannies and parents had formed, all vying for front-row seats.

I caught sight of Kelly's nanny, who was first in line, keeping Kelly's place, ensuring that she would get the coveted front-row seats. Kelly had been boasting about Olivia's role in the nativity play for the past few weeks. Olivia had been asked to go into nursery for extra rehearsal sessions in the afternoons, with Becky's daughter,

Caroline, which could only mean that they had starring roles. The children had been asked to keep the play a secret and were not allowed to discuss it with their parents. It would all be a surprise, the teachers had promised.

Kelly had let the entire school know that her daughter had a starring role in the nativity play. Although I hadn't assumed that Kaya would get a starring role, I still felt sad that she had to listen to Kelly's boasting while we stood by the nursery gates at drop-off, knowing that she hadn't had any extra rehearsal sessions. It was one thing not to get the starring role in the nativity play; it was another to hear the star's mum boasting about it to all the other Alpha Mums.

When Kelly arrived, she wore a white chinchilla jacket, black leather trousers and studded biker boots with her coiffed blonde hair cascading down her back. She looked catwalk-ready, rather than nursery school play-ready, and took her place at the front of the line, where her nanny had been standing. Chris stood next to her, video camera in hand, ready to videotape their daughter's west London debut.

He looked dashing in his suit, I thought to myself, but erased that thought as I waited in line. I immediately felt guilty and thought about Michael, who yet again was missing a school event and couldn't come to the play or party for work reasons. Chris put his arm around Kelly and I felt a pang of jealousy. It was absurd and I knew I shouldn't feel that way, but I did. I had barely even spoken to him all year, yet all those emails made me feel like I knew him, inside and out. I couldn't be 100 per cent sure that he was Cyberdad, but the hints he had dropped convinced me more than ever.

I sighed to myself, lost in my daydreams, until I heard a mother standing behind me talking to another mum.

'Did you read that article in the *London Post* this past Saturday?' the woman asked the other.

'No, why?' the other mum replied.

'There was an entire article about Cherry Blossoms. It quoted the Beta Mum, who called it "the most exclusive nursery in the world", but said it was "infested with bitchy, backstabbing Alpha Mums".'

'Mrs Jones isn't going to like that. You know how she is with privacy. She prides herself on keeping the privacy of Cherry Blossoms as tight as possible.'

'She's got to find out who it is and get rid of her. No one wants a gossipy type in our nursery,' the other mother concluded.

I stood, paralysed with fear. I had never said that it was "infested with bitchy, backstabbing Alpha Mums", and I had never even mentioned Cherry Blossoms during the interview, and had deleted the drunken mention of the name from my blog ages ago. She must have found out somehow. I was sure the journalist had paraphrased what I had written in the blog, and even if I had written those things at the time, lately I had begun to feel differently about the nursery. It was slowly growing on me and I had started to like some of the mums more and more as I got to know them, like Mary and Laetitia.

I wanted to turn around and apologise to those women and say, 'I didn't mean it that way – they paraphrased my blog and I don't really think those things. Well, maybe a little. But I'm really sorry.'

I couldn't even remember half of the things I had written, and I certainly didn't mean for anything I had written to get into the papers...even if, at the end of the day, writing a blog was just like writing in a newspaper, open for anyone to read. I was making very personal stories very public.

The blog seemed to have taken its own direction and had become an entity of its own. Even though it was mine, and I had written every word of it, it seemed like a stranger to me. When I reread some of the posts, I felt completely different than when I had originally written them. It was as if the blog had grown bigger than me, its master, and I could no longer control it; I had blasted my thoughts and opinions into cyberspace, but now they were out of my control.

What if they found out I was the author of the blog? What if I dropped too many hints and someone found out who I was? The news that I was the Beta Mum would spread like wildfire and I would be confronted by two hundred angry mothers, wanting to burn me at the stake. I was downright frightened by the thought, and a cold sweat formed all over my skin.

At that moment, the doors of the church opened wide and we were led into the church hall, and the hordes of mums lunged towards the front-row seats, reminding me of my first day at Cherry Blossoms. I found a seat in the third row, with my view obstructed by a very tall man whose oblong, balding head blocked most of my view. There was no preferential treatment given to anybody here, apart from the celebs and the super-rich.

The church hall fell silent as the play started. It was magical, with a real wooden manger, stacks of fresh hay and live donkeys, goats and sheep, probably from a farm in Wiltshire, taking me away from my thoughts about the blog to the town of Bethlehem. Stars flickered in the cardboard background and the costumes were as good as any from a West End play.

The children came out singing Christmas carols in unison, obedient and well behaved, although most were only three or four years old. They sang "Rudolph the Red-Nosed Reindeer" in sign language and "Jingle Bells" in French. This was the Cherry Blossoms way. I looked for Kaya but couldn't see her. I hoped that she hadn't been too distressed at the thought of coming out onstage, intimidated by the hundreds of parents intently watching.

When Joseph and Mary came onstage, I was taken aback. Kaya was dressed as Mary. But where was Olivia? She was meant to be Mary, surely. It took me a few seconds to register that Kaya had one of the starring roles. There she was dressed up as Mary, reciting her lines perfectly and singing a duet with Joseph about the birth of their son, Jesus Christ. Kaya spoke and sang proudly with confidence, her voice reverberating strongly throughout the church hall. Even if it was just a few lines, I crumbled in tears as I saw her turning from a shy, inward little girl to a girl confident enough to stand up in front of two hundred people to sing a solo. It was magical.

Kelly's daughter, it turned out, was part of the chorus. I wished I could see the look on Kelly's face, but since she was sitting in the front row, it would be left to my imagination. All I could see was her camera in the air, which was visible for everyone to see, blocking everyone else's view with complete disregard.

'Sophie, Kaya's singing was brilliant! I didn't know we had a Beyoncé in the making.' Becky congratulated me at the Christmas party held in the next-door restaurant, La Traviata, where the parents milled around drinking champagne and eating mince pies. The children were being entertained in the private room at the back by Mr Whizz, the recognisable children's entertainer who all mums had on speed dial.

'Neither did I. Honestly, I had no idea Kaya was going to sing a solo. She hid it from me so well,' I said.

'She didn't say anything to you?'

'No, it was a big secret. I don't know how she hid it from me. Usually she can't tell a lie if her life depends on it. Not even when Michael sneaks in a secret cupcake or cookie when he's not supposed to.'

'Well done, Kaya,' Becky said, looking impressed.

Kelly saw us and walked over to us with a large, fake smile across her permanently tanned face.

'So, Kaya is quite the singer,' she started. 'Even though she was out of tune a few times, she was very brave to sing in front of such a large crowd.' Her fake smile stuck to her face like superglue, unwilling to show her embarrassment or humiliation.

Before Kelly could continue, Mary Wright joined us too.

'That was amazing, Sophie – Kaya was the star of the show!' she said to me as Kelly winced, as if in pain.

'Oh, but they were all stars,' Kelly said quickly. 'Olivia, Chloe and Caroline were especially cute. I mean, *they* have something special. I think Mrs Jones chose Kaya so that the same girls don't always get all the attention,' she said, looking at us innocently but implying that Olivia always got the attention.

'Kelly, seriously? Can't you shut up for once?' I said to her, but she pretended that she hadn't heard me. I looked at her, transfixed, my eyes wanting to burn into her. Did she just say that my child wasn't as special as the other girls? What planet was she on where it would be acceptable to say such a thing? Especially about a three-year-old child? I had the urge to slap her, her and her pursed lips, her permatanned face, and pull her blonde, silken hair, but I controlled myself. The last thing I needed was the headline "Mothers' Catfight at Cherry Blossoms' Christmas Play Ends in Tears and Tantrums" on the front page of the *London Post*. I breathed deeply.

'So, what are you doing for Christmas?' Mary cut me off, steering the conversation in another direction completely, to avoid the awkwardness of the potential altercation.

'Christmas is going to be so busy,' Becky said, also trying to calm down the two raging bulls that Kelly and I had become. 'I have to organise a Christmas dinner for twelve adults and twelve children. That's how big my family is, and my housekeeper won't even be there. I don't know what I am going to do.'

'Are you staying in London?' I asked.

'We're going to our chalet in Verbier without any help. I will have to do all the shopping and cooking. David insisted on giving the housekeeper and nanny holidays because they wanted to go home to see their families for Christmas for the first time in five years. Can you believe it? But what about me? It's going to be two weeks of cooking and cleaning. I won't even have time to go down three pistes.' Becky looked utterly flabbergasted and frenzied at the thought of hosting her own family in their beautiful five-bedroom chalet. It all sounded quite lovely to me.

'We're going to St Barts,' said Kelly, having composed herself and returned to one of her favourite subjects: holidays and name-dropping. 'We've been going every New Year for the past ten years. You have to book at least one year in advance. This year, we've rented a sailboat from St Maarten to go to St Barts. Not a huge one, just ninety-six feet. Last year, we anchored right next to Bill Gates' yacht and our boat was the size of the sailboat that was *on* Bill Gates' boat.' She laughed as if that were the funniest thing she had said all year. 'We saw Leonardo DiCaprio, Jay Z and Beyoncé, Rihanna and Puff Daddy all in one day. What about you, Mary? Aren't you going to the Maldives?

'Yes, we are. It's been a really long year, and I just need two weeks to decompress at Soneva Fushi. No news, no shoes. I just need a break from London's rat race.'

'Oh, it's such a shame you're not going to the One & Only Reethi Rah, but there is a two-hundred-person waiting list for New Year's,' Kelly replied. 'Friends of ours who spent one hundred thousand pounds there over Easter still couldn't get a reservation. Over New Year it's the fashion crowd that take over. The Beckhams, LVMH's Bernard Arnault, Naomi Campbell and her crowd and all the Italian designers: Ferragamo, Armani and Donatella. Last time I went, I was literally next to Naomi Campbell on the treadmill. Talk about feeling fat and ugly next to her.' Kelly was back on form, doing what she did best; flaunting her life with the rich-and-famous crowd, as if it elevated her status to more than just what she was – whatever that was. I now knew that I was so far removed from it all that I was becoming used to it.

'What about you, Sophie, what are you doing?' Mary asked me – she seemed to have gotten a bit bored with Kelly's ongoing name-dropping.

'We're going back to Canada for two and a half weeks, but Michael is staying in London for one of those – he's got to work.'

'But isn't going to be cold in Canada? I mean, what are you going to do for two and a half weeks with Kaya? Are you at least going skiing?' Kelly asked.

'No, I want to see my family and my friends. It's been four months since I last saw them. I'm quite excited.' I defended myself while Kelly's eyes glazed over as if I were talking about the dullest place on earth.

'Well, I've got to run,' said Kelly. 'I've got another Christmas party to go to. This one's an adult one, thankfully. Chris' boss has rented Somerset House and created an entire winter wonderland out of it. He's having the Royal Opera House ballerinas from *The Nutcracker* performing and an ice palace carved out of three hundred kilos of ice, or something like that. There's even going to be an ice slide for vodka shots. He's reserved the entire Somerset House ice rink too, so we can skate without some spotty teenager bowling us over. And *everyone* will be there.' Her eyes twinkled with excitement, as if her Christmas present had come early.

'It sounds amazing,' said Becky with admiration.

'It really is – we've been invited for the past five years and I wouldn't miss it for anything. We even changed our flights to Saint Maarten for it. But don't get too much FOMO!' She laughed. Kelly was one of those people who couldn't help herself. She wanted others to envy her and her life; she needed to be adored and adulated, to the point where it felt that she was convincing herself. It seemed like it was the only way to keep herself happy, I thought to myself, otherwise why would she do it? I had finally realised that Kelly would never be satisfied with being "average" – she had to be "exceptional" and she had to win every one-upmanship competition that she could.

'FOMO?' I asked, and Kelly looked at me like I was an ignoramus who didn't know who Barack Obama was.

'Fear Of Missing Out. Don't you read the papers, Sophie?' she quickly retorted.

'I do, but clearly I haven't been reading the tabloids enough.' I paused. 'And anyway, I suffer from JOMO.'

'JOMO?'

They all turned to me, really not knowing what I was talking about.

'The Joy Of Missing Out – it's the new trend, didn't you know?' I smiled back at them.

After Kelly left to go to her super-party and Mary returned to work, Becky and I stood sipping our mulled wine as the party continued. I had realised that when Kelly wasn't around, Becky seemed more like a normal human being rather than trying to be an Alpha Mum like Kelly. I was much more comfortable around her when we were one-on-one.

'I find Christmas so stressful,' she said. 'I have so much to do before we go to Verbier. I've got sixty cards to write and send out to my family and friends, I have to pack for the four of us for three weeks. David doesn't pack for himself any more. And I promised the children I would get them a Christmas tree here in London before we left for Verbier. I need to buy them all presents too before we go. And then I need to buy presents for my family, who aren't that happy about being in Verbier because we were originally supposed to go to the US but David doesn't want to go any more.' She spoke so fast that I had to concentrate to keep up with her. 'We usually alternate years but he doesn't want to go this year. I just don't know how I will fit everything in.' She looked overwhelmed and shell-shocked at the prospect of her lengthy bullet-pointed list.

'It's just Christmas, Becky. Surely you can prioritise? Maybe don't do the Christmas cards this year?' I tried to find solutions to her self-created stress.

'Each day, I receive these gorgeous personalised cards from my friends and family with their perfect families, and I can't *not* send out mine. I'll feel too guilty and they'll think I've snubbed them. Some of my friends hire professional photographers for the Christmas-card photo, and others show off their exotic holidays where everyone looks like swimsuit models. I don't think I have even one photo where we are all smiling.' Her face fell and she looked like she was about to start crying.

'It's OK, Becky. I'm sure they would all understand. And anyway, you know that these family photos are all contrived to make the rest of us feel like crap. It's like Facebook or Instagram. They just show you the version of themselves that they want to show you, not how they really feel every day. Don't believe it.'

'And then I will have to write thank-you cards to my in-laws so that I don't create a family rift. Can you believe David insists that I write thank-you cards to everyone who has sent me a card?' Her lips trembled as she spoke and she looked like she was going to shatter in a million pieces. I realised that this wasn't just about Christmas cards, but about how she was feeling at the moment, as if not being able to send Christmas cards was like failing at her job. Her wrinkles deepened and I noticed that her eyes were red and sunken. Instead of looking healthy and strong as she had appeared when I first met her, she looked gaunt and fragile. All of a sudden, Becky looked more vulnerable than I had ever seen her. Instinctively, I hugged her.

'I think you need one of these,' I whispered in her ear, feeling sorry for her. This was the first time I had seen real emotions coming from Becky, and it touched me. I had always thought that she was happy to be one of the Alpha Mums but it seemed that she had her own problems too, and that she also wondered where she fit in that world.

'Yes, thanks, Sophie.' Her eyes welled up ever so slightly, before her tears went back to their tear ducts. 'I'm just feeling really tired these days.'

A few days later, I saw my mobile ringing with a call from Cherry Blossoms.

Oh no, I thought, I hope it's not Mrs Jones calling me about the blog or the article in the *London Post*. My face flushed and I felt my heart pounding.

'Hello?' I tried to answer cheerily, my voice faltering slightly.

'Hello, Mrs Bennett, it's Mrs Jones.' Shit. It was her.

'I wanted to call you personally to talk about...' That was it. We were going to be kicked out of Cherry Blossoms. Michael would be fired and it would all be my fault. '...Kaya. She was absolutely wonderful at the Christmas play and I feel that she has really come a long way from when she first started at Cherry Blossoms.'

'Yes!' I almost shouted, thankful it wasn't about the blog or the newspaper article. 'She has really blossomed at Cherry Blossoms! Sorry for the pun,' I continued as cheerily as I could.

'Oh, but that's really what we want to achieve here. For each and every one of them to blossom into themselves.'

'Thanks for giving her the chance to sing in the play. I'm so proud of her, I couldn't stop crying.'

'Me too. I had tears in my eyes during the play, my dear. She is a wonderful young girl.'

'Thank you, Mrs Jones. Have a wonderful Christmas.'

'Happy Christmas to you too, Mrs Bennett.'

Chapter Eighteen

Catfish

Christmas in Canada was bitterly cold with temperatures of minus thirty degrees Celsius, so cold that cars needed to be plugged in so they didn't freeze. Children were running in the streets throwing boiling water into the air to see it transform into a beautiful ice-crystal cloud. Although I hadn't forgotten the coldness, the mild London weather had begun to sway me and on the coldest Canadian days, my toes and earlobes were screaming to go back to London. We stayed in many of the days, except for days of crisp, cold sunshine when we took Kaya ice-skating or to visit friends.

We stayed with my family since our house in Oakville was rented out, and my father droned on about things like "where everyone's moral compass had gone", and bemoaned "what the world was turning into", while my mother praised the new Prime Minister as being "like an angel come from above". Both were intellectuals who actually, truly believed that Canada was the best country in the entire universe, with its universal health care, its excellent public high schools and its high social consciousness. They were the last people I could speak to about excessive wealth, competitiveness and one-upmanship. All they wanted was for me to come home.

Michael's unstable home with divorced parents who were too

busy arguing and fighting over money had made my stable, Canadian socialist family seem like a happily-ever-after family.

My brother was fifteen years older than me so we were never really close. My parents had him when they were really young and hadn't had any money to have another child soon after. It was only years later when both of them had found stable jobs in the public school system that they were able to raise me, a few years before he left for university, and I hadn't seen much of him after that. He wasn't spending Christmas with us, but with his own family.

My parents' home was a small, detached house in a middle-class neighbourhood, but they had never needed more. The house sat next to the Korean corner shop-owner's house, which in turn sat next to the Greek diner-owner's house, which in turn sat next to the Vietnamese nail shop-owner's house in complete harmony. It was an immigration experiment that had gone very, very well, as my father liked to say. In his view, there was nowhere but Canada.

I missed Canada, but being in my parents' home didn't feel like being at home. We all quickly fell into our roles in the family structure. My father would preach to me, while my mother prepared dinner and praised his enlightened thoughts. And I would sit in the middle of them, agreeing, because disagreeing would lead to a family argument, which neither of them was going to tolerate. In our household, we lived in an idealistic, utopian world where everyone was there to serve others. Sometimes, I wondered whether I was quiet growing up because my parents never let me speak as they were too busy listening to each other talk. I loved them all the same, and they were adoring grandparents to Kaya, so I was happy for her to receive all the attention for once.

When I visited Emma in Oakville, it felt as if I had never left. Immediately, I told her about my relationship with Cyberdad. I couldn't hold it in any longer, and I had no one else to talk to about him.

'Emma, I know I should stop emailing with this dad, but I just can't seem to stop it,' I told her while we caught up over a cup of tea and warm, freshly baked banana bread that Emma had made with her daughter that morning. Kaya and her daughter were happily playing a game of dolls and babies together, while we sat at their kitchen table.

'You're playing with fire, Sophie. I know it must be exciting to have an admirer and someone to confide in in the way the two of you have done, but you have to remember that it's a virtual relationship. You don't really know this guy from Adam,' she said as she cut four slices of banana bread, two for us and two for the girls.

'But we've been emailing for two months now, and he seems to understand me even better than I understand myself! It's hard to believe, but we've created such a connection over email that I don't know what to think any more.'

'You're projecting what you want to believe onto him. I doubt he's as wonderful as you want him to be in real life. And you have a real relationship with Michael, that's what you have to work on, not a virtual relationship with a man you've never met. Haven't you heard of those scam artists on *Catfish*?'

'No, what are they?' Emma was a walking encyclopaedia of gossip, movies and celebrities.

'It's a television show that follows couples who have created online relationships but one person isn't what they appear to be. For example, one young, gay teenager posed as a gorgeous, blonde girl and started various relationships with good-looking jocks that he would normally only dream of meeting. *Catfish* brought the jock to meet his so-called "girlfriend", revealing that the girlfriend was a young, gay teenager. Cyberdad could be anyone. You have to be careful.'

'You're probably right, but he sounds so…authentic.'

'Don't say things like that, Sophie. It made me vomit a little in my mouth,' she said to me, her face deadpan.

We both laughed as I realised how ridiculous I sounded, and then she looked at me seriously.

'What's going on with you and Michael anyway? You wouldn't be having these online relationships if you were blissfully happy with Michael, would you?'

'I don't know what's going on with us. We feel so…disconnected. Ever since we moved to London, it feels like we've lost the laughter in our relationship and all we do is argue. For him, it's been work, work, work. And it makes him tired, stressed and he has a really short fuse. Not only has his work taken over our relationship, but our relationship has felt like hard work too.'

'All relationships go through ups and downs,' Emma tried to reassure me.

'Not this way. I've never felt like this with Michael. We lead two separate lives right now. He spends hours at work, coming home late at night – we can't even have dinner together. And when he is home, he is preoccupied with work in a way that I can't relate to. Now I've found this online community that has been supporting me through what has been a really difficult transition and he hasn't been a part of it. I'm trying not to let the resentment build up, but it has been since our move to London. I want to blame him for everything: for us moving to London, for Kaya's difficult behaviour, for my lack of friends in London, for the bitchy women like Kelly who have made my life hell.' My face fell. I couldn't hide all the anxieties and frustrations I had accumulated over the past three months.

'Sophie, I know it's not easy, but Michael is your husband. And I know you will get through this. Just don't let a fling get in the way. You'll regret it. I promise you will. You have to focus on your relationship with Michael.'

'I know, Emma.' I sighed. 'You're usually always right about these things.'

'Promise me you will.'

'I promise.'

When he flew in from London, it took Michael a few days to de-stress and towards the end of the holiday, he became as charming as could be. For Christmas, he bought me a brand-new MacBook Air and promised to set up an iCloud – whatever that was – so that I could blog from any of our tablets, computers or laptops. It wasn't the most romantic gesture (he was an engineer, after all), but when I saw the excitement shining in his eyes, I could see that it was the Michael I once knew: a loving, caring, loyal husband and father.

Just a week away from his work and his focus and attention were completely on us. He put Kaya to bed every night, read her stories and took her out to play in the snow. With me, he avoided talking about work and little by little, the cold barrier I had built up around me began to thaw.

On Christmas Day, we laughed about the first Christmas we spent together when Michael had mistakenly left a note on my father's car saying, *I love you*, which was meant for me, but my father had truly believed that it had been intended for him. I watched Michael playing with Kaya and her new toys and remembered what a good father he was. Later, I stood in the hallway watching him and my father sitting together in front of the fire discussing world politics, and I felt so happy seeing them together. It was the Michael I knew. I realised that I had never really fallen out of love with him. I had just forgotten what it was like to love him, and only needed reminders, like this, to feel it again.

For the entire duration of our time in Canada, I barely opened my laptop or checked my email. The blog didn't seem to exist in this context; I didn't need it to feel strong or confident here. We seemed happy and our family was in harmony once again.

I had mixed feelings about returning to London. On the one hand, returning home had felt comfortable, like an old blanket with frayed edges and a familiar smell, but thinking about London felt exciting. Something was pulling me back there, as if I would be missing something if I didn't go back.

Chapter Nineteen

From Mr Singh in India

When we landed in London after two and a half weeks in Canada, I quickly reached for my laptop as soon as I finished turning on the heat in the flat and went to check my emails on the Beta Mum account.

There were a few emails from my cyber-friends, Ozzie Mum and Slum Mum, asking why I hadn't posted in a while. There were other emails from Mr Singh in India, who promised to put my blog on the first page of Google Rank. There were a few emails from Cyberdad with the heading "Hello?" I hadn't replied to any of his emails, which was very unusual for me, and I knew that he was wondering what had happened to me. Then my eye caught an email from him with the header *I miss you*, dated January 3rd. I checked that Michael wasn't around – he was still playing with Kaya in her bedroom – and quickly opened the email.

It read:

To: The Beta Mum
From: Cyberdad
Sent: January 3 2017, 09:10
Subject: I miss you

Hi Beta Mum,

It's been a while since you posted anything on your blog, and a few weeks since I heard from you. Why haven't you written? Are you OK? I've missed hearing from you – you and your advice, your support. My life and my marriage feel like they are in tatters. I need you. Not hearing from you has led me to think only one thing. I need to see you.

Please, can we meet?

Cyberdad.

I quickly logged out of my email and shut down my laptop. That email filled with me trepidation and made my stomach churn. I checked to make sure Michael was still in Kaya's room. Did I really have feelings for Cyberdad, even though I had only "met" him through email exchanges? He knew more about my deepest thoughts than even Michael did. Having an email relationship with a stranger had allowed me to open myself up in a way I couldn't even do with my own husband, I realised.

Prior to our trip to Canada, I didn't want to admit that I had developed feelings for Cyberdad and I resisted the thought that he had developed feelings for me. It seemed that not emailing him had only encouraged his feelings for me. I had occasionally daydreamed of him in the comfort and secrecy of my mind, while Michael had taken Kaya ice-skating along the river that had frozen solid, which was unusual for warm winters, but common during harsh, cold winters, or when he had taken her to see his best friend who lived in Rosedale in Toronto and I had pretended to be sick so I could be alone with my thoughts and fantasies.

In my mind, I had created an image of Cyberdad; he was handsome, ruggedly so, but not so handsome that it made him arrogant and demanding. He was generous, both in and out of bed, and listened to my feelings and desires. He would have soft yet firm hands that he would use to expertly caress my breasts before stroking down to my belly button and hipbone. He would then gently but firmly pull back my hair so that my head would tilt backwards, and kiss the nape of my neck until I could no longer stand it.

Was it wrong that I had once succumbed to fantasising about Cyberdad during sex with Michael to help me reach an orgasm? It was wrong! Completely and utterly wrong! Yet, there was an intense pull in me that wanted to see him. We had connected so much over the past three months that I couldn't ignore him. I had to decide what I wanted from him, if anything at all.

But since our trip to Canada, things with Michael had changed. We were in a better place. I didn't know if it would last, but our relationship was happier than it had been in a long time. I knew I had to stop this relationship before it was too late and someone got hurt. But there was a small part of me that was aroused by Cyberdad's attention, and wanted to see him too.

Chapter Twenty

Goldilocks and the Three Pigs

The first day back at nursery was one of those dark, cold winter days, with a soft drizzle that would last all day but never really turn into proper rain. The heavy, grey, clouded skies descended and turned into fog that made you want to stay indoors all day, wrapped up in a thick, fluffy blanket. It was true what I had heard: in London January really was the lowest point of the year. Christmas and its holidays were behind us, and it would be months before the hibernating sun made its appearance to try to give us our fill of Vitamin D.

In front of the nursery was the usual line of Mercedes and SUVs with drivers waiting aimlessly for their employers or nannies. Mummies and nannies walked in and out of the nursery gates for drop-off, wrapped up in furry jackets and mink coats. It was a normal day in the life of a yummy mummy. I entered the nursery and the Lion Cubs class, but there were no other children, just the teacher, Miss Katie, the teaching assistant, Miss Sarah, Kaya and me. It was strange; we were not early – it was 9.10am and the other classes were buzzing – but our class was quiet.

'Happy New Year!' Miss Katie said to me, as I walked in the classroom. She looked bright and perky although her skin was pale from months of sun deprivation.

'Happy New Year,' I replied, conscious that we were the only ones there. 'Where is everyone?' I asked her, trying to assess whether I was right that something strange was going on. Kaya, on the other hand, didn't seem to notice that she was the only child in the class and quite happily went to the puppets in the puppet show area and began an imaginary tale of what would happen if Goldilocks met the three pigs.

'Oh, there are a few families still on holiday, and a few also had to leave the nursery for various personal reasons.'

'Oh, that's a shame. Who had to leave?' I asked curiously. I went to hang up Kaya's coat on a bright yellow elephant's trunk peg with her name underneath it.

'Three. Anastasia has moved to New York, Chloe had to return to Paris because her grandfather is sick, so Laetitia moved the children back, and Arabella's family has moved to the country this term, but they may be back next term. I am not really sure why, though.'

I had obviously missed an episode of *The Private Lives of the Super-Rich*. I hadn't had a chance to say goodbye to Laetitia properly because she had missed the nativity play and hadn't been able to come back to London since then. I assumed that things must have progressed for the worst for her father. I was sad for Kaya, who had started to become close to Chloe, and I was also sad not to have Laetitia around.

I guessed that Irina and Vladimir Dimitrov decided to move to New York after the assassination attempt. It was too dangerous for them to live in London any more. It was a strange existence for them to have, to always be running away from something even though they were the richest people on the planet.

Arabella was Francesca and Carl's daughter. I could think of a million reasons why they would leave London; he had cheated on her one too many times and she had had enough and moved the family to the country, or he had checked into Drugs Anonymous and this was part of his "new life" programme. And all along I thought that I was going to be the first one who dropped out of Cherry Blossoms.

Right at that moment, Becky came in with her daughter, Caroline, and Olivia, Kelly's daughter.

'Good morning!' Becky greeted us as she came in. 'Miss Katie, I think you received an email from Kelly saying that I would be dropping Olivia off for the next week or so? And that I will be the interim class rep?'

'Yes, Mrs Miller informed us that you would be dropping off and collecting Olivia for the next few days. And we will send any class rep-related emails to you until Kelly returns.'

'OK. Good. I've got to run off, but it'll be Wilma, my nanny, who will be picking them up after school. Thanks!'

Becky walked right out of the gates at the same time as I did, and I stopped her to catch up.

'Hi, Becky, did you have a good Christmas holiday in the end?'

'Oh yes, it was lovely, but so busy. There were too many people, I had to "work" the whole time, entertaining, cooking, cleaning. It really wasn't a holiday.' She sighed.

'So, where's Kelly? I thought she was supposed to go to St Barts and then come back right after New Year's for the renovations?'

'Oh, you haven't heard.' Becky's smiley façade broke down instantly, revealing an edgy, strained look on her face, as if she was unsure whether she should confide in me or not, and she wasn't quite sure if it was appropriate. After a split second of deliberation, she decided that she did want to speak up and whispered in a hushed tone.

'Chris, Kelly's husband, was arrested over Christmas for insider trading. The day before they were due to leave for St Barts, the police barged into their house, handcuffed him right in front of Kelly and their children and took him straight to the police station for questioning. He couldn't even take his phone. They took it from him as well as his laptop, memory cards and everything in his office that could have been related to his work. Then other police officers searched their house from top to bottom.'

'No! Did Kelly know anything about it?' My eyes grew in astonishment.

'I don't think so. She called me crying, saying that she had no idea and didn't know what she was going to do. It turns out that he had been burning money and pretended to be getting these huge bonuses, but it wasn't true. He had massive debts so he started siphoning money off the fund and made a few dodgy deals. Now the FCA has accused him of insider trading. Their entire lifestyle was being funded by illegally acquired money.'

If Chris had been arrested and in prison, he couldn't be Cyberdad, could he? Although he had mentioned in the emails that his life had fallen apart.

'Where is Kelly now?' I asked, enthralled. After all she had made me endure, I couldn't feel too sorry for her. A part of me felt like she'd got what she deserved. This was karma biting her in the ass.

'She's at the Mayr Clinic in Switzerland for a detox. She couldn't handle the pressure. She needed a break from the investigation. After Chris was arrested, he stayed in jail for two days, but was then released on bail – one million pounds – and she had to remortgage their house a second time for his bail, so he was freed. She then kicked him out, sent him to live in a short-term rental studio around the corner and he has to check in regularly at the local police station as part of his supervision.'

'Is he guilty?'

'I would think so, if it's come this far. The FCA – that's the Financial Conduct Authority – has been trying to crack down on illegal trading and is coming down really hard on anyone doing risky deals. David's been giving him legal advice on top of Chris using his own lawyer, but it doesn't look good.

'What exactly was he accused of? Do you know?' I enquired, engrossed by this story of lying, deception and betrayal. Becky furtively looked around her to make sure no one else was around. The drizzle was still falling, and we had moved under the awning of the restaurant next to the nursery.

'I think he was accused of shorting a stock that he knew was going to plummet and made millions of pounds from it.'

'OK, I have no idea what you just said. You could be talking

Mandarin for all I know. Apart from the fact that he made millions of pounds from it.'

'Someone apparently gave him information about a stock that he shouldn't have known about.'

'What about their beautiful house with its four-million-pound sub-basement renovation?'

'That's all going down the gutter. They're going have to sell it, if it's not taken away from them. Chris had been spending so much money that he didn't actually have. He got a massive mortgage to buy the twenty-million-pound house, and then used the money he took from the fund to pay for their sub-basement renovation.'

'Didn't she have any idea of where the money came from?'

'Kelly says she didn't know very much about it. Chris was always very secretive about his salary, his bonus, and how much he really made. He had been acting a bit erratic lately, being really high and happy one day and then low and stressed the next. But he made it seem to her that they had enough money to buy any house they wanted and build as big a renovation as she wanted, so Kelly didn't question it, she just went along with it.' Becky shrugged her shoulders.

'And so she did,' I said, thinking of all the times Kelly had mentioned their four-million-pound sub-basement renovation. The renovation alone was more than ten times the cost of an average home in London.

'It's all over the newspapers. I'm surprised you haven't read about it yet.'

'We just got back from Canada two days ago and I haven't had a chance to look at a newspaper yet. I will now. I've clearly missed a lot since I was away. What about the kids?' Even if I didn't have that much sympathy for Kelly, I felt really sorry for her children, who were at the centre of this mess.

'They're at the half-built house, living with the nanny and sometimes staying with us as well. Kelly got rid of all the builders when she realised she couldn't pay them. Chris is only allowed to see them two hours a day for now while the investigation is ongoing.'

'Did the police say that? That's unusual.'

'No, Kelly enforced that. She only wants him to see the kids under supervision for a maximum of two hours per day. And he accepted her demands. He's caused enough problems.'

'He certainly has. I can't believe this is the same Chris we're talking about.' I paused, thinking that I was so wrong about him.

'Well...' She hesitated, and her eyes darted right, then left, nervously, as if someone were watching us. She didn't seem like she was telling me the whole story.

'Is there more to this story? You don't have to tell me, I understand.' I tried reverse psychology. This story was too good to miss.

Becky looked like she calmed herself down, and spoke under her breath.

'When the police ransacked their house, the FCA took every electronic device they could find. Laptops, iPads, tablets, telephones. They went through all of them and found emails from a Katrina Ivanova. Turns out he had been seeing escorts. Prostitutes. And the lawyer or whoever was questioning him threatened to tell Kelly unless he gave evidence against his sources. Eventually he gave in and told them, but also came clean with Kelly too.'

'What? Chris? With escorts? I can't believe it. He's so...but he looks like Ken! From Ken and Barbie, Mr Nice Guy. I always thought he was a good, family guy,' I said, shocked. I always wondered what Chris saw in Kelly (well, apart from the long legs, the perfect body, and her Californian sun-kissed blonde hair), since she had the personality of a troll. No wonder he looked elsewhere for love. Kelly was certainly not the warmest, most loveable person I knew.

This confirmed it. He wasn't Cyberdad. He wouldn't be wasting his time with me if he was paying for the real thing. He was living out his fantasies in real life. I was disappointed, thinking all along that Chris was the mysterious Cyberdad and all the time he wasn't at all what I had imagined he was. And I was still really in the dark about Cyberdad's real identity.

'I know. I couldn't believe it either. He's so handsome, good-looking, and Kelly's so gorgeous. She's a superwoman. I always thought they were the perfect couple.' Becky looked amazed that Chris could have cheated on his picture-perfect wife. 'There's more,' she continued. 'Katrina Ivanova is none other than Anastasia's nanny.'

'What?! But how could Katrina be an escort? She's their full-time nanny and works there twenty-four hours a day!'

'She works seven days on, seven days off. On her seven days off, Katrina was an escort living in a flat in Chelsea, where many Russian escorts live.'

I was shocked. Katrina was so pretty and sweet. It had never crossed my mind that she could be an escort. I had really liked her, and it was so sad that her circumstances had led her to becoming an escort.

'So,' Becky continued, 'Chris had been seeing her and really fell for her hard. He wanted her to stop working as an escort so they could be together, and he became obsessed with her. But Katrina didn't want to stop working for the Dimitrovs or as an escort. You can imagine Chris wasn't too happy with that. That's when he tried to break into Vladimir Dimitrov's house to try to convince her that he was going to leave Kelly to be with her, but then the guards chased him out.'

'What? Chris was the one who tried breaking into the Dimitrovs' castle? What about the poison they found?'

'The poison, aconite, was from one of their exotic plants that shed its pollen. It's from a plant called monkshood and Vladimir apparently had a whole hedgerow planted, and when they warned him that they were poisonous, he insisted and no one dared to contradict him.'

'So why did they move to New York if it wasn't a murder attempt?'

'Who knows? But they probably don't want this kind of attention.'

'Does Kelly know all of this?'

'She's the one who told me. No one would have ever guessed that her husband would fall for an escort and, not only that, want to leave her.'

This was more riveting than any TV series I was watching. These men were rich, successful and had beautiful wives, but couldn't help themselves. They always wanted more.

As soon as I arrived home, I Googled "Chris Kelly Miller arrest insider trading" and dozens of articles appeared. I opened the *London Post*'s article dated a few weeks ago and in front of me unfolded Kelly's husband's story.

Chris Miller Arrested in Insider Trading Scandal at Aquarian Hedge Fund

London, December 28th 2016

Chris Miller, a hedge fund manager at Aquarian Asset Management LP, was arrested yesterday morning at his house in Ledbury Square Gardens in Kensington, the affluent west London neighbourhood. He has been accused of insider trading, placing one of the fund's largest bets on Solenium Pharmaceuticals, which has been trialling one of the most advanced cancer prevention treatments.

The Financial Conduct Authority has been investigating a £200 million windfall into Aquarian's fund when they shorted the pharmaceutical company's stocks in 2013, two days before the announcement of the Phase Two results, which were not as good as expected. The coincidence of the stock short and the subsequent stock plunge after the announcement were suspicious, and were flagged up to the FCA. There, an investigation was started, trying to link Aquarian and the Solenium Pharmaceutical Group.

It has emerged that one of Chris Miller's childhood friends from Boca Raton, Florida, Matthew Mottola, was on the board of GMG Group, the umbrella company of Solenium Pharmaceutical Group. They were often seen spending their holidays together and were at the same New Year's party on St Barts, ringing in 2013 together, just a few days before the announcement of the Phase II trial results. Silently and efficiently, Aquarian offloaded all of their stocks of Solenium

Pharma between the 1st and 3rd January 2013.

After going through hours of telephone calls and thousands of emails, it became clear that a firm connection was made between Miller and Mottola's calls and emails and the buying and selling of the firm's Solenium stocks.

During the investigation, Chris Miller was found to be millions of pounds in debt, having spent his money on a £20 million mansion and lavish yacht holidays in St Barts, the South of France and Ibiza, as well as flying private jets and paying for high-end escorts. He was arrested on four counts of securities fraud, wire fraud and conspiracy. He was later released on a £1,000,000 bail.

Chris Miller grew up in Boca Raton, Florida, before moving to Philadelphia to study at University of Pennsylvania's Wharton Business School. He then worked on Wall Street for Coleman Lazaar, where he met his wife, Kelly, before moving to London to set up the London office of Aquarian Asset Management. He has been instrumental in growing the European fund to £15 billion.

This is in the background of the Financial Conduct Authority's firm resolve to go after white-collar criminals in the aftermath of the 2008 credit crisis.

Chapter Twenty-One

The Nightmare of Alpha Mum and Alpha Dad

'Can you believe Chris Miller was arrested for insider trading?' I asked Michael that night when he came home early for once and we sat down to eat our M&S easy-cook dinner.

'Yes and no. The FCA is really trying to crack down on insider trading. The US has managed to charge over eighty people since 2009, but the UK has barely managed to arrest and charge anyone. Looks like Chris will be their first golden apple.'

'Kelly's house is going to be repossessed – she'll end up on the street. And she might end up with nothing. I mean, on-the-streets nothing.' I said these words, imagining Kelly having to sell her red-heeled Louboutins, Prada handbags and Chanel sunglasses. 'That story would make a great blog post,' I joked out loud.

'Sophie, you better not write about it in your blog.' Michael looked at me, knowing how my brain worked even better than I did.

'Oh, I won't,' I said, realising that it would be a terrible idea to write about Kelly, especially with children involved.

'Sophie.' The lilt in his voice wasn't a questioning lilt; it was a firm, don't-mess-with-this kind of lilt.

'OK, OK. I won't write about it, but—'

'No buts, Sophie-Bee. Really. It's their business. Not yours. Let it go. I know you think she's the world's biggest bitch, but it's not worth your time or ours. It will just get you into trouble.' Michael gave me a threatening look, and when he finished his dinner went to our bedroom, saying he was tired and needed an early night.

I went to watch *Game of Thrones* reruns, but instead of concentrating on the gory battle scenes, sex and death, I couldn't stop thinking about Kelly. She had fallen from grace with a husband arrested for insider trading, her house was being repossessed, and who knew what the future would hold for her? I almost felt sorry for her, but then, in a way, it felt like divine retribution.

I thought back on all the times she made me angry, the times she humiliated me, and made me feel like a second-class citizen. Look who's the second-class citizen now. Her life and marriage were really in tatters. Her husband was likely going to jail, and her reputation was ruined. Not only because her husband was arrested for insider trading, but because she would always be known as the wife of the guy who was paying for high-class hookers with insider trading money.

After the show was over, I checked on Kaya, who was fast asleep. I could hear Michael's snoring through our bedroom door as I passed by. I sat down in front of my laptop, and a story came to me. The impulse was so strong that even though I tried to stop it, hearing Michael's warning over and over in my head, I couldn't help myself. I had to write it.

The Beta Mum
The Fairy-Tale (Nightmare) Story of Alpha Mum and Alpha Dad

Once upon a time, Alpha Mum was a young girl who dreamed of meeting Alpha Dad. She dreamed of her dream wedding, and of her dream house and her dream children.

To achieve her dreams, Alpha Mum attends an excellent university and starts working at a top investment bank in New York, where she meets Alpha Dad.

Alpha Mum is educated, headstrong and a "go-getter". She is also very pretty. You could almost mistake her for a C-list model or a former Miss California. She exercises daily at 6am – for two hours – and has a perfect body (it helps that she hasn't had any carbs since 1981, which may be why she always looks irritable). She dresses in designer brands that flash their logos.

Meanwhile, Alpha Dad has been climbing the corporate ladder after business school, becoming a managing director at twenty-eight, then a partner of a hedge fund at thirty-two. His favourite words are "P&L", "EBITDA" and "bonus". His favourite car is a Porsche 911 GT and his favourite watch is a Rolex Roadster. His dream is to be on the executive committee of his fund.

Alpha Mum and Alpha Dad fall in love after a whirlwind romance on the beaches of St Barts, the canals of Venice and a safari in "exotic" South Africa. They marry at the Villa Ephrussi de Rothschild in Saint-Jean-Cap-Ferrat in the Côte d'Azur, France, her in a Vera Wang dress and him in an Armani suit, surrounded by four hundred of their closest friends, colleagues and family. Everyone comments on how beautiful they are as a couple, only to mutter under their breath that "money helps".

They move to London to find a stunning, wedding-cake-white, stuccoed mansion on one of London's finest squares and plan to do what all aspirational Alphas do: procreate and build a subterranean basement. While on holiday in Barbados at the Sandy Lane, they manage to conceive when she manages to "lose" his phone in the sand.

Two hours after Baby 1 is born (in September, the right month to be born), Alpha Dad is at the "right" school, application in hand, waiting for the doors to open to personally deliver the application to the headmaster by hand. Further letters, chocolates, cards and telephone calls ensure entry into the best school in London. A few years later, Baby 2 is born and the same ritual occurs.

Alpha Dad is not involved much in the baby period, as he doesn't feel the need to bond with the babies. Luckily, Alpha Mum has a maternity nurse who stays on for six months, and privately thinks that a nanny and a maternity nurse are much more helpful than Alpha Dad when raising a baby. When she confronts Alpha Dad for not spending enough time with Baby 2, he responds curtly, 'You can't go back on the deal, you've signed on the dotted line.'

It was always clear to him that Alpha Mum would run the household and look after the kids while Alpha Dad would be earning the money for their luxurious existence of Bugaboo prams, black Range Rovers, a second home in Saint-Tropez, and their twenty-million-pound home backing onto a private garden.

Alpha Dad is not involved in his children's schooling, except on sports day, when he gets to ogle the supermodels and yummy mummies and show his "competitive spirit", determined to win all the races in front of the other dads. Alpha Dad is very competitive, not only at work, but also socially; he loves to mention that he owns four polo ponies and name-drops as often as possible. He likes to show off his vast wealth – probably to compensate for some childhood inadequacies.

Alpha Mum becomes head of the PTA to compensate for her empty life. She runs her PTA empire like a FTSE 100 company, bullying her employees, terrorising them and putting them down to ensure productivity and to scare them into loyalty. No one is immune to her wrath and all those around her follow her like diligent, military-style soldiers. She is the Queen Bee after all.

Alpha Mum loves being the Queen Bee and can't help herself but criticise everyone around her to make her feel better about herself. She uses aggressive methods to maintain her dominance: pushing, threatening, and lip-pursing like a macaque monkey. Her witch's brew, the green juice, keeps her strong and at the head of her tribe.

But the fairy tale must end, when Alpha Dad is arrested for insider trading at his multi-million-pound house, in front of his beautiful children and his beautiful wife, Alpha Mum. He has been caught stealing from the cookie jar. Not only that, his dangerous liaisons between the sheets with "professionals" have been discovered. (Looks like Alpha Mum wasn't able to keep her husband's jewels in his pants.) Alpha Mum is devastated and retreats – well, to a retreat in the Swiss Alps.

In the blink of an eye, everything that defines her is destroyed; she loses her husband at the hands of the FCA, her house is at risk of repossession, and her personal grooming assistants are about to lose their jobs. Perhaps karma has finally caught up to her.

Poor Alpha Mum, whose dream has been shattered, when Alpha Dad did what he does best: philander, gamble and cheat. But all the employees at Alpha Mum LLC are rather happy to see the downfall of their CEO, Alpha Mum, whose reign of terror has ended with her empire's demise.

It was midnight as I sat staring at the blog post. It had taken me two hours to write it and I was almost delirious from concentrating so much. I pressed "publish", closed my laptop and went to bed, thinking that no one knew who the Beta Mum was. The secret was still safe.

The next day, when I walked to the nursery with Kaya, I noticed a mum, who was taking her baby out of her pram, staring at me longer than the usual up-and-down look. Could it be that she knew who I was? No. There was no way. No one was reading my blog anyway. By now, I had a few hundred followers and a few hundred views each day, but they were mostly from Australia, India, Brazil and the Philippines. The blog was beginning to take off, but most of my comments and follows were from strangers. I shook that thought away; it was just paranoia speaking.

After I dropped Kaya off, I noticed an email.

To: Sophie Bennett
From: Becky Goldberg
Sent: January 9 2017, 09:00
Subject: Emergency Lion Cubs class meeting

Today, back room of Sweet Bites Café, 10am.
Becky.

No one else was cc'd in on the email apart from me. Usually the class emails were sent from the class group email. Kelly was still in Switzerland and Becky was covering for her until she came back. I started walking towards Sweet Bites Café. I was surprised the meeting was being held there instead of an organic café like Plantaria, a plant-based restaurant that was popular with the yummy mummies as it offered courgette spaghetti, lentil burgers, and pomegranate and quinoa salads. Sweet Bites Café had opened as a backlash against all the organic/raw food/juicing/cleansing restaurants that had sprouted like mushrooms, and it served all sorts of full-fat and full-sugar cakes, cookies, crepes and cupcakes.

When I walked into the back room, a separate room from the rest of the café, I saw the entire Lion Cubs class sitting down in silence with Kelly at the head of the table. On the table was an array of cupcakes and cookies that no one seemed to have touched. It took me by surprise. I had thought that Kelly was still in Switzerland. But clearly she wasn't.

She sat staring at me with her cold, blue eyes boring into me. Her usual blow-dried hair was stringy and oily, as if it hadn't been washed in days. She was wearing an old tracksuit that hung loosely on her small physique. She looked gaunt and skinny, as if she had lost a lot of weight and hadn't slept in days.

I would ask for my money back from the Swiss retreat if I were her, I thought. She didn't look detoxed; she looked worse for wear. This was an older, skinnier, sunken, sallow version of herself. But what really gave it away were the un-manicured, naked, sick-looking nails on the ends of her fingers that clutched a cappuccino instead of a green juice.

They all looked at me like it was the first time they had ever seen me, not sure what to make of me. Kelly's cool, glacial stare continued as she stood up to face me.

'Good of you to come, Sophie.' She spoke slowly, her steady gaze holding mine.

'Of course. Becky said it was an emergency. Kelly, I didn't realise you were back from Switzerland.'

'Oh, cut the crap, Sophie. Don't pretend like you care or give a damn about me. I know who you are. This is why I called this meeting.' Kelly's eyes were piercing into mine, full of palpable anger and hatred, which I could almost physically feel. 'I know you are the Beta Mum blogger.' She seethed as she said those last words. I stumbled backwards, as if her hatred had pushed me and I needed to steady myself. All the women's faces dropped, as if they had seen a ghost. Of course, she had brought me here to "out" me in front of the entire Lion Cubs class.

'Kelly, I am so sorry,' I didn't know what else to say. My ears were starting to burn, and I could feel myself turn scarlet.

'Oh, shut up, you idiot.' Kelly couldn't stop herself, spitting the words out and gesticulating wildly. 'Do you think I am that stupid? That I didn't know it was you? But now you had to go ahead and write about my personal life for the whole world to see. You took pleasure in my downfall, didn't you? You think you are better than all of us. You and your tree-hugging righteousness. Writing that we are the devil. But you. *You!*' She pointed at me with her un-manicured index finger, poking at the air between us. 'You think you are so saintly and perfect. But you're worse than all of us. We may be everything you write about, but you are constantly judging us. You take joy in other people's misery. You are the lowest of the lowest pond scum,' she spat out. I could see her trying to control herself, trying to regain composure, flattening her tracksuit that was riding up her waist from her gesticulations.

'Oh, yes. I had my doubts right after reading the blog after the parents' evening. So, I put you in my group at the winter fair to keep an eye on you. And then you confirmed it, when you wrote about our conversation on the blog. About the winter fair, and then Olivia's birthday party. Why do you think I didn't invite you to the charity Christmas dinner? Do you think I wanted you to write about me? I needed the right time and place to expose you, but then my life fell apart and you had to rub it in my face.'

I couldn't believe that Kelly had been reading my blog, and had actually been running her own investigation to uncover my identity.

'Kelly, I am so sorry about what's happened to you,' I said, realising that I had really gone too far.

'Really? You're sorry? It didn't seem that way after you wrote all of these blogs about me. Spreading the word that I am a bitchy Alpha Mum who talks about everyone behind their backs. That my husband was arrested, and that my perfect life isn't so perfect after all. It seems like you were happy that Chris was arrested. Is that it? You thought I deserved it, didn't you?'

'No! Not at all!' I pleaded. I realised how awful I had been, and how selfish I was. I had become worse than them.

'I may be a bitch and I may bitch behind people's backs, but at least I don't take pleasure in other people's misfortunes. And you? You bitch about everyone for the world to see. Do you really think that's much better? Oh no, it's not better, it's worse!' Kelly's eyes were bulging out, her neck veins were throbbing and her hands looked like they wanted to slap me or strangle me, I wasn't sure which one. She kept repeating herself; I didn't think this excruciating inquisition was ever going to stop.

'I didn't mean for any of this to get out of hand. I didn't think any of you would be reading it,' I said lamely.

'Because that would make it so much better?' Kelly yelled again. I felt her wrath descending on me like a thunderstorm, constantly battering down on me. 'What are you going to write about now? Describe my husband's infidelities with prostitutes? That we haven't had sex in three years?' she hissed. The whole room went silent. 'Will that make you feel better?' Her head dropped slightly, as if she were defeated, but then she raised it again, staring at me once more. 'And here I thought you were some uninteresting, suburban mother whose worst quality was a lack of dress sense but, in reality, you are a prime Alpha Mum.' Kelly started laughing manically.

'Kelly, please – I am sorry. No one deserves what you went through. I should never have written any of it.' I tried to stop her shouting, in vain.

'Oh, Sophie. You're so naïve. Why don't you go back to Canada if you hate it so much here? You have no idea how things work in this city.' Kelly's tone softened, but was filled with threat. 'You should really be careful.'

'Please, I promise I won't ever write anything about you again,' I said to her.

She stood with her legs slightly apart in front of me, like a wrestler ready for a fight. For a moment, I thought she was going to throw a punch at me or slap me, or yell, 'Off her with head!' like the Queen of Hearts in Alice's Wonderland. But instead, she started crying and her body crumpled over onto the table with her head folded over into her forearms. She let out a blubbering sob into her arms.

When she stopped crying, Kelly picked up her brown calfskin Hermès bag and stormed out of Sweet Bites, muttering incomprehensibly. Becky soon followed suit. I stood there speechless, not knowing where to look, what to do or how to defend myself. The women at the table looked transfixed, as if they had witnessed a zombie vs. alien battle. When I tried to gauge their reaction, they turned their stare away from mine and gathered their handbags and mobile phones and scurried away. I didn't have a chance to speak to any of them.

I continued standing there, while tears formed in my eyes. What had I done? I had mocked all the mothers in Kaya's class, and had unleashed a raging tiger in Kelly. It was a big mess. Michael was right. I should have never written about Kelly.

I headed home with a heavy heart. Once I was home, I put down my coat and handbag on the couch, sat down and looked at the empty flat, filled with loneliness. I had become one of them, an Alpha Mum, bitching, gossiping and berating. Kelly was right. I was worse than all of them. I was worse than Kelly. How had I arrived at the point where I had lowered myself to this level? I hated myself for it and wondered how on earth I would get myself out of this mess.

I heard the door unlock. It was only 11am and Michael was the only one with a key.

'Hi, Michael, is that you? I did something terrible,' I yelled out as I turned around to see him.

I was surprised to see that his eyes were red, angry, and his usual smile had fallen downwards into a grimace. He looked angry.

'Michael, I know you didn't want me to write about Kelly, and I know I've made huge mess, but I'm going to fix it, I promise.'

'Who the hell is Cyberdad?!' he yelled at me with such force that it scared me.

'What?' I couldn't answer; I was frozen in a blind panic.

'Don't lie to me! Who the hell is Cyberdad who so desperately misses you and wants to see you? Have you been cheating on me all this time we've been living in London?' For a second, his face contorted with pain, before returning to its original angry state.

'Michael, I don't know what you know, but it's not what you think.' I tried to justify myself, to explain something he probably would never understand.

'Oh, I know that you've been emailing him. I know that he misses you and cares about you and wants to see you. That I know. And how do I know?' He turned away from me, shaking his head, his eyes on the floor. 'I was stupid enough to think that I could set up the iCloud for you to blog from wherever you wanted. I did it for you. To support you. And then today an email popped up on my phone. Except it wasn't from you. It was from Cyberdad.'

'How…?' I was so confused.

'When I set up your new computer on the iCloud, I linked my computer to the iCloud as well so the email from Cyberdad – what kind of idiotic name is that anyway? – arrived on my phone.'

'Michael, please. Listen to me. There's nothing going on between us. We're like pen pals. You know, people who just write to each other occasionally.'

'Occasionally? You received five emails from him over the past three weeks! That's not occasionally.'

'OK. But he contacted me through the blog when I was so down, and we got chatting. He kept me company when I was so lonely after we arrived in London.'

'And I wasn't enough company?' He was shouting now, his body shuddering with rage.

'You were never around! You were always too busy with work! We had so many fights!' I started crying, which soon turned into sobbing. He looked at me as if he didn't know whether he should hug me or stay away as far as possible. 'I moved here for you and you were never around. I moved and changed my whole life for you and you were too absorbed in your work to even notice me! You didn't support my career, my blog or anything else. What was I supposed to do?'

'Certainly not start an affair!'

'I didn't have an affair! Please believe me,' I cried desperately.

'How can I believe you? How can I trust you when you've been hiding this relationship for months?'

'I know, Michael, it looks bad, but trust me. Nothing happened. Michael, the move was so hard for me. You know that. I struggled for months, and I didn't feel like I was getting any support from you.'

'Support? I gave you plenty of support. I listened to you complain and complain some more about everything. I can't help you learn how to make friends. That's on you.'

His words stung me, and I felt more inadequate than ever. He was right. I didn't know how to make friends, and I had made a mess of it all.

'Are you in love with him?' he asked me.

'No! I've never even met him!'

'But you wanted to?'

'No, I didn't,' I lied, but this little white lie had the potential to save the relationship I was losing. 'I never wanted to meet him. I was going to tell him I wanted to stop writing to him. As soon as he mentioned that he wanted to meet me, I knew I had to tell him that it couldn't go on any more. Please believe me.' I grabbed his arm, begging and imploring him to believe me.

'Then why didn't you bother telling me about him if it was so innocent?' he responded angrily, thrusting his arm away from me.

'Because I knew you would take it the wrong way and you would never have allowed me to continue writing to him. And I didn't think you cared. It was companionship. And the blog was the only thing that was my own. Not yours, not Kaya's. You have to believe me. There's nothing going on between us.' I could see that Michael had imagined the worst: that we had been having an affair, or that I was in love with Cyberdad. Our relationship was still vulnerable and we had only started feeling strong once more over Christmas. He grumbled something I couldn't quite understand, but he still wouldn't look at me.

'I love you, only you. It was a stupid mistake. He was just a crutch at a time when I felt I was losing you. Please forgive me.' I looked at him, but he kept his face turned away from me. I didn't know how else to convince him that there was nothing going on between us. Even though we hadn't had a physical relationship, the emotional relationship we had developed was threatening to ruin my relationship with Michael.

The phone rang. It was Cherry Blossoms.

'Michael, I've got to pick it up. It's Kaya's nursery. They only call when it's an emergency.' I looked at him pleadingly, but he mostly ignored me and turned his back to me.

'Hello, Mrs Bennett, we're calling because Mrs Jones would like to see you in her office,' Mary Studnick, the administrator, said.

Oh no, I thought. I groaned to myself. Was this about the blog?

'Um, of course. I can come in. When would you like me to come?'

'Can you stop by when you pick Kaya up?

'Yes, that's fine.'

'Miss Katie can look after her during the meeting.'

I hung up and looked around to speak to Michael, but I couldn't see him in the living room. I ran to our bedroom to see if he was in there, but it was empty. Kaya's room was also empty, and the kitchen was silent apart from the humming of the refrigerator. I went back to our bedroom and searched the room frantically. What I found confirmed my fear: his suitcase was missing and he was gone.

Chapter Twenty-Two

In Real Life

After Michael left, I fell onto our bed and cried until I had no more tears to cry and my eyes became two small slits between my puffy eyelids. I never thought that Michael would find out about Cyberdad, and I never imagined that he would take it so badly. He left with his overnight suitcase as if he didn't know when he was going to come back. Kelly was right: I had become worse than any of those of Alpha Mums, bitching and gossiping like the best of them. And now I would probably be expelled from Cherry Blossoms.

I dragged myself out of bed and left to pick up Kaya at the nursery. I arrived late deliberately, not wishing to see anyone with my red-rimmed, puffy eyelids and swollen face, and I knew that Miss Katie would be looking after Kaya for a while.

I entered Mrs Jones' office, where she was sitting at her desk, reading over some papers.

'Mrs Bennett. Have a seat,' she said frostily. Oh no, not another showdown. I didn't think I could face another one.

'Yes, thank you.'

'I wanted to discuss an issue that has been raised by the parent body. It appears that you have taken on journalistic skills since starting at Cherry Blossoms?' Her steely grey eyes looked at me, questioning.

'Mrs Jones, I'm really sorry. I…didn't mean to hurt anybody.'

'Mrs Bennett, I am sure you are aware that our nursery prides itself very highly on its confidentiality, privacy, and that of our families. Our reputation is famous for this. Now, none of the parents have come forward to complain about your "articles", but if they do so, you are at risk of being placed on probation, and therefore at risk of expulsion.'

'Mrs Jones, please. I am so sorry. I didn't mean for anyone to be hurt by this.'

'So far, I haven't been made aware that anyone has, but if I hear of any more indiscretions, we will be meeting again very soon.'

'Thank you, thank you.' I shook her hand with relief.

'Perhaps a wiser way to spend your time would be to give the children computer and coding lessons, since you appear to be so tech-savvy.' She raised her eyebrows as she looked at me with piercing eyes.

'Yes, sure… Well, actually…the truth is…I have no idea how to code and I really don't know that much about computers,' I admitted, embarrassed. 'But there is something I could do. I could teach the children about ecology, evolution and conservation. The private garden is so beautiful and full of teaching opportunities – the trees, the plants, the butterflies, worms and bees. There's so much I could teach them. And this is something I actually know about,' I offered, desperate for her to accept my offer.

'That sounds like an interesting idea,' she said, looking at me. 'We've always wanted to put the environment on our curriculum but we've never managed to find the time. I'll put you in touch with Mrs Rafferty, the garden's secretary, and you could discuss it in further detail.'

'Thank you, Mrs Jones. Thanks for your support,' I said as I walked out, shoulders hung over, tired and exhausted, and glad she hadn't kicked us out of Cherry Blossoms.

Later that day, I sent a few texts to Michael:

I love you. Please forgive me.
It was all a big mistake. I should have told you sooner.
I promise, nothing happened. He's just a friend. You have to believe me.

That night I tossed and turned and cried some more. He didn't reply to any of my texts and I tried calling him as well, but he didn't answer. I knew that it could only mean that he was still angry. Angry enough not to answer any of the phone calls or texts. I was frantic. I couldn't lose him. At 4am, after hours of staring at the ceiling, it was clear what I had to do.

At 9.14am I sat in the back of Aquas Frutas in one of their plastic chairs with a carrot, orange and ginger juice. Run by a Brazilian family on Queensway, Aquas Frutas was a fresh juice shop that I sometimes went to when I needed a break from the yummy mummies of west London. It was dark and had been open since 1986, with local residents old and young, hailing from all around the world, from Africa to South America, sitting around in its old, creaking chairs. It was a safe haven I knew that no yummy mummies would ever come to.

I had sent an email to Cyberdad in the middle of the night, agreeing to meet him.

To: Cyberdad
From: The Beta Mum
Sent: January 11 2017, 03:00

Dear Cyberdad,
Yes, let's meet. I need to see you. I've made a mess of things. My husband's disappeared and won't return my calls and the mums at the nursery have found out that I am the Beta Mum blogger. No one is speaking to me. Can we meet at Aquas Frescas on Queensway tomorrow at 9.15am?
Thanks.
Beta Mum

He quickly replied that morning at 5.05am. He would meet me there and I shouldn't worry. It would all work out. I sat nervously waiting for him, wondering what he looked like. The first man that came in looked too old. The next, too tattooed with slouchy, hipster jeans. Then he came in. Cyberdad. The man I had been communicating with for months and had fantasised about. Who I had imagined was Chris Miller, and had thought that we had connected on so many levels. He walked towards me in recognition, and all the tension and anticipation I felt about meeting him drifted away.

Cyberdad was Becky's husband, David. David, with his balding head and growing paunch, and whose voiced squeaked more than it should. David, with whom I had spoken to at birthday parties and school events, and who, like me, also sometimes seemed out of place in a world full of beautiful people, coolness and excess. I had never thought about it, but it was Becky who was always emulating Kelly and Kelly's life, and David always followed along. I had never really thought of him as anything apart from as Becky's husband, but now that I thought about it, he'd never really fitted in either.

'David, it's you.' I smiled at him in relief, as if it had been someone else, I wouldn't have known how to react.

'Sophie.'

'It's nice to meet a fan,' I joked.

'Absolutely! I am a fan. A rather big and plump one, really.' We laughed in unison.

'Thanks,' I said meekly.

'I heard from Becky that you were the Beta Mum last night.'

'You already knew and you still came?' I looked at him, perplexed.

'Yes. I still wanted to meet you. We've written to each other every few days for months now. I've grown attached to having you as a confidante. It's not often that you feel completely safe writing to someone you don't know.'

'It really has felt like having a confidante, hasn't it? You were like my best friend, but only online. You helped me out in a difficult time.'

'I can say the same. I don't know…I felt like my life was spiralling out of control and you helped me anchor it.'

'We had a special friendship, didn't we?'

'We still do,' he offered. 'Did you ever feel anything more?' he ventured. I didn't know whether he hoped I had or not.

'It's difficult to know what I was feeling. I was feeling like you listened to me, you engaged with me, and you seemed like you cared. I really appreciated that. I guess it would be easy to misconstrue those feelings with something else. But I love Michael and I always will.' I was playing with my straw, which was sitting in my half-full glass of juice, trying to collect the orange and carrot foam that had accumulated on the top of my juice.

'Right.' He looked a little disappointed, as if he were hoping for a different answer. 'He's a really good guy.' He nodded his head in approval of Michael. 'So where is he? You said he disappeared in the email.'

'He found your emails saying you wanted to meet me. He was furious and left yesterday and hasn't answered my calls or texts.'

'He'll come around. He loves you very much. I've seen his face light up whenever he talks about you and Kaya. You're the most important things in his life.'

'It hasn't felt like that lately.'

'Men often lose themselves in their work. I know I have. But I'm sure that with Michael it's temporary.'

'And Becky loves you, David.' It was good to get that ambiguity about our relationship over and done with.

'She's so caught up with being a certain person here in London. What she has, who she's seen with, what she wears. And she's been obsessed with Kelly. She follows Kelly like a puppy dog and sees herself as Kelly. I can't stand it. It's like she wanted to be Kelly. As if her own self is not good enough, and I can't convince her that she is. We've started seeing a marriage counsellor, and I hope it's going to sort us out.'

'Well, I don't think she'll want to be Kelly any more now that Chris may go to jail and Kelly may lose everything. Maybe that will be a wake-up call for her.'

'I hope so. Chris has found himself in a real mess.'

'Do you think he'll go to jail?'

'Probably. If the FCA has anything to do with it, they'll send him to jail. Maybe not for long, but at least to show all the other guys that they are serious about cracking down on illegal trading. All these white-collar criminals, sometimes they convince themselves that what they are doing is not really wrong, or that everyone else is doing it, so why shouldn't they?'

'What do you think will happen to Kelly?'

'I think she'll probably divorce him. No point in sticking around to see your ship sinking. Better to get on a raft and find another ship. Especially while she still can.' I knew he was inferring that Kelly was still attractive enough to find another husband.

'I feel terrible about what I did: writing about it in the blog. Kelly hates me, and probably the rest of the class does too.'

'Kelly has other problems to worry about. She's been really unhappy this past year, which is why I think she's been so horrid to you. Now her life is falling apart and she needed someone to blame, and you happened to be there at the right time and under the right pretext. This will blow over. The mums are not stupid, they know what Kelly is like too, and secretly some of them probably feel the same way you do.'

'You think so?'

'Trust me, it will blow over when the next big drama happens. No one will even remember that you wrote that blog post. And anyway, everything you wrote was true.'

'I've been mocking them, exposing them. It's a big betrayal.' I sighed. 'I'm thinking about stopping the blog.'

'I don't think you should stop. Your writing is funny, witty and spot on. I hope you continue writing it.'

'Perhaps.' I blushed, feeling flattered and embarrassed, unable to own my writing for what it was.

'You'll always have me as a fan.' He grabbed my hand and squeezed it. His hand on mine felt like a brother's or a friend. It didn't feel at all like I had imagined it would during the many times I had fantasised about Cyberdad.

He had become a fantasy in the way we fantasise about celebrities or superstars; we feel close to them. Familiar. Even though they are unattainable, they are kept on a pedestal. Cyberdad, it turned out, was just another father who struggled with his marriage, his work and his children. We always imagine the "other" as being better than what we have. The grass is always greener. But I realised that we had to ride the bad times as well as the good times in a marriage, and I had been distracted from mine by a fantasy that didn't really exist.

We chatted some more, and I felt like we knew each other so well. Our conversation flowed like pieces of a puzzle falling into place and fitting together perfectly. Without any expectations. We were a man and a woman who had created a friendship. When we said goodbye, I didn't know where it left us, but I knew that we wouldn't be emailing daily like we had done. I knew he was working on his marriage with Becky, and I had to work on my marriage with Michael.

After I picked up Kaya and put her down for a nap, I heard the key clinking in the lock and in came Michael. His eyes were red and sunken. He looked haggard and ten years older. He put down his black suitcase and hung up his jacket on the coat rack. His actions seemed so slow, as if he had aged overnight and couldn't possibly move his arms any faster. He turned to look at me, and with the same slowness, came towards me and put his arms around me. He engulfed me with his broad shoulders, almost suffocating me, and put his rough, unshaven cheek against mine. His familiar smell instantly broke me and tears streamed down my cheeks, mixed with his.

When we broke apart, we held hands and sat down on the sofa side by side.

'Michael—' I started.

Michael stopped me. 'Wait, let me go first. I know how hard it's been for you. I asked you to move to London, change your life, leave your family, your friends, your home so that you could follow my dream. And since we've been here, I've been so caught up in making the right impression, impressing my bosses and wanting everyone to accept me, that I forgot about the most important people in my life. You and Kaya.'

My body, which had been tensed up like an ironing board for the past twenty-four hours, started to relax. In his eyes, I could see regret. He looked so tired. As if the past four months had caught up with him: the eighty-hour weeks, working weekends, and the constant stress.

'I kept thinking that it would get better, that you would eventually like it here,' he continued. 'I never thought it would go on for months. And then the fighting started and the more we fought, the more I turned to work. At work, even though I was stressed, I was doing well, but at home I felt like you were never happy. It's not an excuse, I know. I'm sorry, Sophie.' He squeezed my hands, and looked down at them, as if he were ashamed.

'I'm sorry too. I didn't mean to keep the emails from you, but you seemed so wrapped up in your work that I didn't think you would care. But I promise that nothing ever happened. Do you believe me?' I croaked through the tears that had formed in my eyes.

'Yes, I believe you,' he responded with a grimace.

'What about yesterday, when you said you didn't trust me…do you still feel that way?'

'Yesterday, I was angry, hurt and I felt betrayed. I needed some space to think it through and digest it. When I arrived in my hotel room alone, I realised how much I could lose because of this job. I was sitting on the hotel bed and thought that this is what would happen if I lost you: I would be living on my own, in a cold, empty hotel room, and then it dawned on me that I took you for granted. That you would follow me. That you would adapt yourself to me – to my goals, my aspirations. That you would still be waiting for me, no matter what I did. I never thought you would have a relationship with another man.'

'It wasn't a relationship! It was…a friendship.'

'I never imagined you would feel like you needed someone else apart from me. I don't know if it's naïve or self-obsessed to say that.' He smiled tiredly, but it was still that charming, dimpled, lovely smile that had made my heart flutter the first time we met. 'At first I was so angry. I couldn't cope with the thought of you with someone else. But then our conversations came flooding back through my mind. All the times that you were calling out to me, that you needed me, but I always had an excuse for working late or not being there for you. Then I started understanding why you wanted to write all your thoughts on your blog, and why you started writing to your "man".' He said the word "man" teasingly, which made me feel that everything would be all right. That he hadn't quite forgiven me, but that perhaps one day he would be able to move on.

'He's not my man! You're my man, Michael. I hope you know that.'

'I know. I read through all your emails and saw that there wasn't anything but an online friendship,' he said sheepishly. 'I also realised that I was partly to blame for your friendship with "Cyberdad". I still don't know what to make of your online friendship, but it's the twenty-first century – you should be able to have male friends.' He paused. 'But I never want to feel this way again: on the brink of losing you. Nothing is as important to me as you and Kaya. Not my job. Not my career. Not anything.'

'Thank you, Michael. I really needed to hear you say that, and to know you felt that way. The past few months, I've felt that your job always came first and that we came second. I felt like I was losing you.'

'You never lost me. I was just distracted.' He looked at me apologetically.

'I'm glad you're not any more.' I went to hug him, holding him tight until I could no longer breathe. 'We still have a lot to work on. Our relationship, I mean.'

'I know. I promise to change things. Like coming home at a reasonable hour, and not being so angry all the time. Also, I want us to explore London. We've barely had a chance to see what London has to offer: music, theatre, the arts. I've been overwhelmed by work and you've been settling Kaya in nursery and in London, but I have been building up a team that can take some of the pressure off me.'

'That would be great,' I acquiesced.

'And I also found something that you might enjoy doing. I was surfing the Internet the other day and I came across something that may interest you. There's an ecology centre in Holland Park that carries out practical conservation. They're always looking for volunteers. I know it's not much and not a job, but maybe you could meet like-minded people there and it could lead to something bigger? I was going to sign you up for one of their conservation days and surprise you. But then I received the email from Cyberdad and I thought our marriage was over.'

'There is no way Cyberdad could remotely compete with you.' I smiled and kissed him softly on the lips. It was a gentle, sweet, tender kiss, as if I were kissing him for the first time, full of excitement and anticipation for things to come. I hoped that it marked a new start in our relationship.

'It would be hard, but we can move back to Canada if you want?' he suggested after the kiss, as he held me in his arms.

'Oh, Michael. We may have to.' I pulled away from him. 'Kelly has known all along that I am the Beta Mum and she's told everyone at the nursery. She confronted me yesterday in front of the whole class. Becky called an "emergency class meeting" and Kelly accused me of being worse than all of them for writing about her and her problems. I don't know what we're going to do.'

'I'm sure it will blow over quickly.'

'I posted a blog post about her and her problems, which infuriated her.' I winced, embarrassed by what I had done.

'Maybe that wasn't the smartest thing to do.' Michael gave me a look, but knew better than to tell me, "I told you so".

'All those horrible things she said to me…maybe it was a manifestation of how she felt inside? Maybe she was so unhappy at home that she projected her unhappiness onto everyone around her?'

'I wouldn't be surprised. It sounds like she has plenty of her own problems to deal with, but it almost sounds like you feel sorry for her.'

'It's funny, I never thought I would feel sorry for her. I always thought that she was so superior to me. Or at least that's what she made me feel, and I believed it. Now, I feel bad for her and I feel awful about having written all those things about her and what she's going through.'

'It's horrible what's happened to her, but I wouldn't worry too much about Kelly. She's not your problem. And we can always change nurseries, or we can go back to the Sunshine Nursery in Oakville.'

'Some of the mums aren't that bad after all,' I murmured under my breath.

'Am I hearing you correctly, Sophie? You sound like you might approve of some of these mothers.'

'Apart from Kelly, whom I do not envy right now, and a few other Alpha Mums, the majority are not that different from us. They have problems like us. Family problems, health problems, financial problems. Just on a different scale. But I understand them better now.'

'Does that mean you're willing to stay in London another two and a half years?'

'Maybe. But first, there's something I need to do. And then I'll let you know.'

The Beta Mum
To All My Followers

These past few months online have been a wonderful time of exploration, discovery, learning about myself, and making new friendships. Without the support of you, my readers and followers, I don't think I would have survived without having a full-on, nervous-wreck, IRL breakdown. I've met people from around the globe, from Australia to Argentina. I have connected with you and it has given me so much strength, confidence and belief in myself. I thank you for that. With every view of my posts, I have gained immeasurable satisfaction and pride.

But the reason I am writing this post is that I would like to apologise if I have ever hurt anyone through the blog. It has come to my attention that some of my posts have hurt others, which was not my intention at all. I am the first person to know that not only do sticks and stones hurt, but words can hurt too. It is not for me to judge others, to tell them what is right or wrong, or to mock them. I know that most of us just try the best we can.

So, I have decided that it is time for me to stop my blog for now. I have realised that I need to focus on my real life instead of my "virtual life", because I have so much more to lose in my real life. I almost lost everything I care about recently, and it is time for me to face my reality. It turns out that it is not as bad as I have made it out to be.

I will keep the same email to continue the friendships I have made, which you can find in the "contact me" section, so please continue to write!

Yours,

The Beta Mum

It was 4am when I pressed "publish" and knew deep inside me that it was the right thing to do. Unlike print journalism, blogs have no accountability and I had underestimated the impact of what I had written on people, both positive and negative. I had never thought that my blog would be read by hundreds of people and that they would form such strong opinions on it, or that I could hurt people through it. I also felt a sadness that I had created this "being" and was now letting it go.

But it had served its purpose. I remembered the day I had started it, feeling low about not finding any play dates for Kaya, my panic that she would become cripplingly shy as I had once been, and how far we had come. She had bloomed into a happy, well-adjusted child.

The next morning, when I brought Kaya to nursery, she was skipping into the building, laughing and giggling, excited to walk into Cherry Blossoms. I looked around to see if anyone looked at me differently, but no one seemed to notice me. Even when I saw Becky, she nodded to me. As I left the nursery, I crossed paths with Kelly, whose head was down, fixing her daughter's collar on her floral dress. Behind her, a group of paparazzi had formed and were taking pictures of her. I could see that Olivia had tears in her eyes, and that her dress was torn on the edge.

'Kelly! Kelly! Do you have any comments about your husband?' one paparazzo yelled out.

'Did you know he was embezzling money from his fund?' another one said.

'And did you know that he was seeing prostitutes?'

I saw her exhausted, shamed face look up at the paparazzi, but she was too tired to fight back. She scooped Olivia into her arms as if to protect her from them.

'Hey!' I yelled at them. 'This is a nursery. Can't you see there are children here? And can't you respect people's privacy, especially when they're with their children? Get the hell out of here!' I swung my handbag at them and shooed them off like they were a pack of hungry flies. Kelly and I had had our differences, but this was different. We were both mothers trying to do the best thing for our children. It was the least I could do for her after what I had done.

She raised her head and our eyes met and she nodded at me. Instead of hate or anger, which I was expecting, she looked at me with a mixture of exhaustion, despair and shame.

It wasn't about me or my blog any more. She had bigger problems than the blog. She had her whole future to think about. Whether to stay with the father of her children, what to do with their sub-basement renovation, how they would survive financially and what this would mean for her entire life. And now that I had stopped the blog, there was nothing more to say.

I saw her walk towards Mrs Jones' office and I wondered whether she would be having a "personal conversation" about paying school fees. Despite all of her tyrannical behaviour, Kelly really loved her children and wanted the best for them. Even if it meant facing the embarrassment and humiliation of the paparazzi in front of the nursery, she was willing to face it for her children.

As I walked away, someone rushed to stop me.

'Hey! Sophie. I wanted to talk to you.' It was Mary. 'I heard about what happened yesterday. I couldn't believe it was you! It was really gutsy of you to write the blog. Sorry I wasn't there for you. They must have seemed like a pack of wolves looking for blood.'

'Thanks, Mary,' I said gratefully, knowing that I had at least one ally. 'It was pretty awkward.'

'Look, many people felt that way about Kelly. Some people love her, but she's also bossy, she's mean and she's irritating. Just know you're not the only one who feels that way. We just knew to leave her alone.'

'I guess I woke up the wrong beast. But what's happened to her – it's terrible.'

'It is. But life goes on. And there will always be a Queen Bee. I think Becky will happily take over her place.'

'Really? Already?'

'Oh, Becky has already volunteered to take over the PTA the minute Kelly lets it go. Life goes on.'

After I left Mary, I went home and checked my emails. There were twenty new emails since I had posted my last ever post on the Beta Mum blog.

The first email was from Ozzie Mum, who had probably been the first to read the post since it had been daytime in Australia when I had posted it at 4am.

To: The Beta Mum
From: Ozzie Mum
Sent: January 15 2017, 08:00
Subject: Don't stop your blog!

Dear Beta Mum,
I am so sad to hear that you are stopping your blog! I loved it! And I loved having you as my cyber partner in crime. I completely understand your predicament though. I always admired you for taking the chance and writing about these women. I would never have the courage to do what you did.
Let's keep in touch.
Ozzie Mum

There were a few other short emails from other fans telling me that they were sad to see the blog come to an end. I noticed that there were no emails from Cyberdad, and although I was glad, I also felt somewhat sad, as if I had lost a friend over a petty fight.

The last email was from Annabelle Clarke. The email address looked familiar but I couldn't quite remember why.

To: The Beta Mum
From: Annabelle Clarke
Sent: January 15 2017, 07:55

Dear Beta Mum,
You can't stop your blog! You need to continue writing it! I love it and always wished I had been clever enough to start it. It is brilliant. I used to write a similar column for the London Post until they found me too redundant and not relevant enough.

I'm one of those mums who feels guilty when I work, and also a void when I don't. But then I love my mad children and the chaos that comes with them. And then I worry that I'm not a perfect size eight (or six in these parts of town), and not wearing the latest trend. It's a struggle being a mum. Especially in west London.

I know it sounds a little strange, but I feel that we are more similar than not, and I'd love to meet for a coffee. I hope you don't think I'm too forward, or that it's too strange. I am a Cherry Blossoms mum so I've been fully vetted, ha-ha. Pain et Chocolat? After drop-off? Tell me when.
Best,
Annabelle

My memory finally unmeshed where I had heard the name Annabelle before today. She had written to me after the blog about the parents' evening, but I had been too intrigued by Cyberdad's email to really connect with her. And then I had heard Mary talking about the rumour that Annabelle, an ex-journalist, was the author of the Beta Mum.

This was the first time since my arrival in London that someone had asked me out for coffee (apart from Cyberdad). And not only had she asked me for coffee, but she wanted to meet me and get to know me for who I was, not because our children were in the same class or because the Cherry Blossoms social calendar dictated it. Annabelle's email sounded friendly and down-to-earth. It seemed that there were more people at Cherry Blossoms who thought like me than I had originally thought. The blog had not only found me some virtual friends, but it had possibly found me an "in-real-life" friend. I sank back into my chair and looked out of the window. It was time to get out of my cyber world and start living.

Chapter Twenty-Three

Queen Bees vs. Wannabes

A few weeks later, Michael, Kaya and I were headed to the ecology centre in Holland Park for one of their family volunteer days. It was a rare clear, sunny day in February, with a blue, crisp sky, making promises of spring days. Kaya was running ahead in her purple boots adorned with yellow butterflies, jumping in muddy puddles and running in between the trees.

Michael and I walked hand in hand in silence, listening to the rustling of the leaves swishing in the trees and under our feet with each step we took. The past few weeks hadn't been easy. I had tried to rebuild our trust and convince Michael that I had never stopped loving him, despite my actions. Each time I was on the Internet, he would snoop over my shoulder and sulk for a while. I had to show him that I was to be trusted, but I knew it was going to take time.

We still had more to work out, but our first priority of spending more time together was helping us feel more connected. These days, Michael made the effort to come home at around 8pm so that we could have dinner together. Even if it meant that he had to wake up an hour earlier, it showed me that he was willing to make concessions and compromises as well to make me happy. I felt less alone, and instead of feeling like roommates living under the same roof, we were starting to live the same life instead of leading separate, parallel lives. I tried to be more understanding about his work hours and he tried not to let the stress affect our home life.

We began a routine that resembled our previous life in Canada, including our weekly Saturday night movie/box-set night. Whereas before we had been missing out on Canada's trees, space and fresh air, now our new Saturday tradition was making up for it. Our Saturdays now involved taking walks in the parks in London, to give me the trees, space and air I yearned for. Each week, we explored a different park: Regent's Park, Hampstead Heath, Richmond Park, Kew Gardens and, of course, Hyde Park and Holland Park. Holland Park was the nearest park to us and we were becoming closely familiar with it.

I had started volunteering at the Holland Park ecology centre and had met Hugh Jones-Llewellyn, who managed the centre, and soon we became fast friends. He had been working at the centre for over twenty years and had created a little paradise in the middle of one of the biggest urban centres in the world. And he didn't care what shoes, clothes or bags I wore, or that I had no idea who Zoe Phillips was.

I had also started planning "garden school" lessons for the children, which I enjoyed more than I expected to. Surprisingly, Alice Denham decided that she wanted to help out and was donating time and money to build a small greenhouse for the children to grow their own plants in the garden. It turned out that she had fired her nanny, who had never even mentioned that Kaya had wanted a play date, and hadn't mentioned a lot of other things, like the time she had been texting on her phone and Oscar ran across the street full of traffic. A friendly Cherry Blossoms mother who had witnessed it had contacted her to let her know that her nanny wasn't to be trusted.

At Cherry Blossoms, despite a few strange stares in the aftermath of shutting down the blog and Kelly's "intervention", most of the mothers had stopped staring and had returned to ignoring me, just as they usually did. I had never thought I would be grateful for being ignored. But being in the limelight wasn't all it was hyped up to be.

Becky had quickly filled Kelly's PTA shoes, once it was clear that Kelly would no longer be able to run the PTA or be a class representative. There were rumours around school that Kelly was divorcing Chris and that she had left their house. She was living with Becky until she decided what to do next and was thinking of moving back to the US, but it would be difficult while Chris was awaiting his trial. She would also have to give one term's notice to Cherry Blossoms, so it was unlikely that she would be leaving before the end of the term.

Kelly and I walked past each other with brief acknowledgements once in a while, but generally, we kept away from each other. I was not the only one who kept away from Kelly. Most of the other mothers also kept away from her. Now that there was no reason to have Kelly on their side, they ignored her, not wanting to be associated with her. It really showed her who her true friends were. And there weren't that many left. Becky was proving loyal, but I could tell that she was relishing her new position as Queen Bee of Cherry Blossoms, and that for once, Kelly needed her rather than vice versa. Kelly had fallen from a much higher position than I would ever know, and that would always hurt more.

I hadn't seen David lately, but Becky seemed so much happier that I assumed that things were working out in their favour. Becky was where she wanted to be as head of the PTA at one of the most prestigious nurseries in the world. It suited her fine. And with Kelly gone, she revealed a softer, nicer, more genuine side of herself, as if the pressure that had built up around the Lion Cubs class had been Kelly's creation. Without Kelly at the helm, the class seemed more peaceful, less pressurised and less competitive. A few new children had started, replacing Anastasia, Chloe and Arabella, and their mothers seemed nice and genuine. It was funny how one person had the power to transform the whole dynamic of a class.

I had plans to meet Annabelle for coffee the following week, and it turned out that we had a lot more in common than we knew. In the end, I realised that I should have been more patient and stayed true to myself, rather than trying to adapt myself to fit in with the rest of them. Somehow, along the way, I had lost myself. Mary had shown me her support, and in a few weeks Chloe and Laetitia were coming back to London from Paris for a visit.

I realised that I shouldn't take anything personally. Mostly, it was all about them and their busy, complicated lives. Kelly was the obvious example of someone always looking to climb the social and economic ladder to keep up with other super-rich people. But there was also Mary, who was working day and night to support her family, and Laetitia, who had to take on her family business, which took away her choices rather than giving her any. Then there was Irina, always followed by her bodyguards, and whose freedom was the most at risk, to the point where she moved countries to protect her family. I realised that I had much more freedom than any of them, whether concrete freedoms or personal, mental ones of not comparing myself to others constantly, or not trying to reach an unattainable perfection, like Kelly had done.

For many of these women, their lives shone like a four-carat, brilliant-cut, D-colour, internally flawless diamond. Their lives looked so inviting, like a pool on a hot summer's day, like an illusion, but with this sparkling, shimmering and enticing image came the pettiness, the backstabbing and the stress of keeping up this image of perfection. Now that I understood them more, it was easier to see through them, and to see that they had their insecurities, just like I did.

As we walked through the forest, the sun shone through the leaves above us and created shadows under our feet. I was wearing an old pair of jeans with frayed edges, a new top I had bought from one of the French boutiques on Great Western Road, and hiking boots I had bought in Canada that winter. I was still not a fashionista by any means, but I was learning to appreciate that sometimes, wearing a nice top or dress could make me feel good.

Holland Park was not as green or as vast as the parks in Canada, but it was special. It wasn't better or worse. Just different. Just like my life here: not better or worse, but different.

'This park is really beautiful, isn't it?' I said to Michael. When the sun shone, London was transformed from a dull, grey city to a vibrant, powerful, dynamic, beautiful one. It had taken me some time to realise this.

'Did I just hear you compliment London for the first time?' Michael looked at me with mock wonder.

'I'm learning to like certain bits,' I said, smiling. I stopped walking, stepped back and looked at him with our hands still interlocked. He was still as handsome as the day we married. 'And it is better with you by my side.'

'So, is this your cryptic way of telling me that you want to stay in London?'

'Yes. I never imagined that I would be raising my children in a city. I always thought I would give my children a large house, a big garden, big open spaces. That I would let them play with worms and chase squirrels and chipmunks. That they would get so much dirt under their fingernails, it would be impossible to clean them. That we would go camping together, like I did when I was growing up. So it has really taken time for me to get used to living here. I think I've been battling it the whole time.'

'Sounds like it's not only the Alpha Mums that you've been battling with.'

'I know. In the end, they're just people – richer and thinner, but with problems like everyone else.'

'Can I get it in writing that you are willing and happy to stay in London? I don't want you turning around in two months telling me that you want to move again!'

'Don't worry. I think this time I'm committing to London. Look at Kaya.' We both turned to Kaya and looked at her. 'It may not be exactly what I had in mind, but this is good enough.'

Kaya was crouching down, with dirt on her knees and her hands, picking up flowers and smelling them. She was beaming, with a smile as large as an ocean. Despite all the drama with the mothers, Kaya had remained oblivious and had been growing and developing more than I could have ever hoped for. Cherry Blossoms had that magic touch, and had turned her from a taciturn and quiet child into a confident, happy one who was eager to learn and who looked forward to nursery every day.

I felt happier and stronger than I had in a long time. Settled. Serene. I knew there would be challenges ahead, from pushy mothers to Kaya's disappointments, to fights with Michael, but I knew that we were stronger as a family than we had been before. I knew myself better and felt confident to take any of it on. The blog had given me an inner confidence that hadn't been there before.

'I love you, Michael,' I whispered into his ear.

'And I love you, Sophie-Bee.' He kissed me on my nose.

At that moment, Kaya came running towards us, with mud and dirt splattered all over her jeans and boots, and hugged us tightly. The scepticism that had kept me company for the past six months was leaving me little by little, and a new optimism seemed to take its place. I felt at peace for just a moment, knowing that this was where I was meant to be for now, even with its highs and lows. My blog may have been a way for me to weather a storm, but it was also opening new doors to real friendships. And with the excitement of new love, of new beginnings and new friendships, I believed that my future in London was starting all over again.

Acknowledgements

I want to thank my family for their unfailing support of this project, my Faber Class, who are talented and brilliant writers – you are all amazing! – and our tutor Shelley Weiner, who helped me believe in myself. This novel wouldn't exist without all of you. My editors: Angela Clarke, who was the first to put a seed in my mind that perhaps I had a tiny bit of talent, and Donna Hillyer, who pushed this novel to be the best it could be.

About the Author

Isabella Davidson is the author of the popular blog *Notting Hill Yummy Mummy*, which chronicles the entertaining lives of west London residents. Through the blog, she has written features for *The Times*, *The Saturday Times Magazine*, *Corner* magazine, and has been interviewed by *Financial Times*, *Harper's Bazaar*, *The Spectator*, *The Times* and many more.

She started *The Beta Mum* during the six-month Faber Academy novel writing course. Prior to starting her writing career, she worked for a Nobel Prize-winning humanitarian organisation and as a doctor for the National Health Service. She grew up on four different continents before settling down in London fifteen years ago. She currently lives in west London with her husband and their two small children.